FOR LOVE OF SELF

BOOK 2 OF THE BLESSED BE SERIES

ROBIN REARDON

IAM Books
www.robinreardon.com

FOR LOVE OF SELF
Book 2 of the BLESSED BE series

Copyright © 2023 by Robin Reardon

Cover and formatting by Sweet 'N Spicy Designs
Front cover photograph adapted by Alex Calder
Back cover photograph by Michael Walsh

Scriptural references in *For Love Of Self* come directly from the *World English Bible*, 2022, available in electronic format through eBooksLib.com and through electronic book retailers. The following information about the *World English Bible* comes from eBible.org: "The *World English Bible* (WEB) is a public domain (no copyright) modern English translation of the *Holy Bible*, based on the American Standard Version of the *Holy Bible* first published in 1901, the *Biblia Hebraica Stutgartenza Old Testament,* and the *Greek Majority Text New Testament.*"

ISBN: 978-1-7340569-6-9

Praise for the works of Robin Reardon

"Reardon's prose is gorgeous. She always surprises with her originality and her emotional writing. I anxiously await whatever she writes."
— Amos Lassen Reviews: Best Books of 2020

"Spencer's story is an introspective, heartfelt portrait of a young man at a crossroads in his life, and this novel is yet another compelling example from this author's impressive body of work. It leaves the reader breathlessly anticipating the next book in the series."
— Christopher Verleger, EdgeMedia Network (*For Love Of God*)

"Thanks for bringing alive the gay faith experience at such a dramatic time and place!"
— Kittredge Cherry: Founder/publisher, Q Spirit (*For Love of God*)

"I don't give five stars lightly, saving them only for books that I feel are out of the ball park. I adore everything about this series."
— Cheryl Headford, Love Bytes Reviews (the *Trailblazer* series)

"Robin Reardon invites the reader on a trip that will lead her characters to embrace hard truths about themselves and those they love but also reveal a vast store of courage they never knew they had."
— Sammy, Diverse Reader

"Ceasing to give, we cease to have.
Such is the law of life."

*Richard Chenevix Trent (1774–1860), Anglican archbishop
and poet*

"Anoint our eyes to see, within the common,
the divine." .

Edwin Markham (1852-1940), Poet Laureate of Oregon

CONTENTS

Note that while reading all three of the *Blessed Be* books in order will take you on Spencer Hill's journey with him—his first love, his successes and failures, and the maturity he gains along the way—each book can be read and enjoyed individually.

FOREWORD

By Jane Wicker, Unitarian Universalist Lay Minister

Robin Reardon's second book in her *Blessed Be* trilogy, *For Love of Self*, is a beautiful, engaging, thoughtful, and revelatory exploration of what life is like as a Unitarian Universalist minister, in all its facets and complexity.

As a long-time UU, I so appreciate Robin's portrayal of our religion. We are a strong, caring group, with an incredible commitment to social justice and to building bridges between communities. All of this is reflected in these pages. Robin's expert characterization of her main character's daily life, relationships, joys, and struggles with his work as a minister resonates with my experience.

There are seven UU Principles, which are central to our belief.

1st Principle: The inherent worth and dignity of every person
2nd Principle: Justice, equity, and compassion in human relations
3rd Principle: Acceptance of one another and encouragement to spiritual growth in our congregations
4th Principle: A free and responsible search for truth and meaning
5th Principle: The right of conscience and the use of the democratic process within our congregations and in society at large
6th Principle: The goal of world community with peace, liberty, and justice for all
7th Principle: Respect for the interdependent web of all existence of which we are a part

In *For Love Of Self,* the protagonist (The Reverend Spencer Hill) frequently celebrates the lighter side of UU. As he says, "self-ridicule is a hallmark of a sense of humor," and we UUs are very good at laughing at ourselves. At the same time, however, we take these seven principles to heart and use them to guide us in all aspects of our lives.

For a Unitarian Universalist, with or without a belief in God, faith is imbued with love, which guides how we worship, how we treat each other, and how we relate to the world. For example, the Unitarian Universalist Association sponsored the public advocacy campaign called Side With Love (https://sidewithlove.org), which seeks to harness love's power to stop oppression. It promotes action in many ways that echo the UU mission, including environmental issues and support of LGBTQ+ rights.

One aspect of UU presented in *For Love Of Self* concerns the lay ministry. As a lay minister myself, I act as an extension of the minister's care. Lay ministers are spiritual friends, accompanying members of UU congregations through life's challenges and transitions.

We embrace equity. We celebrate diversity. It's true that we have our difficult and divisive moments, but what we hold as a touchstone is the light we find in each other and in our faith community.

Unitarian Universalists support each other in so many ways. But we also challenge each other. And the most important challenge is quoted on the Side With Love website:

"What is love calling you to do?"

Jane Wicker
Arlington, MA
May 2023

CHAPTER 1

"Weren't you nervous?" Ruth's voice over the phone carried a teasing tone.

"No more than you'd expect," I lied. Whatever the expectation, I'd been more terrified than that.

In fact, I was still shaking inside, just a little, after having delivered my very first sermon yesterday to the congregation of my brand new church—new to me, at least: Unitarian Universalist of Assisi, Vermont.

Ruth wasn't done. "I'll bet they loved you, Spencer. I've heard you preach. That deep voice? That skillful pacing and meaningful inflection? All that stuff you learned from my own brother? I bet you wow-ed them."

I chuckled. "They were very generous. Very forgiving." I smiled, though she couldn't see that. "I think I'm going to like it here."

"Donnie says hi, by the way, and congratulations."

My breath caught, just for an instant. "How is he?"

Ruth paused long enough for me to know that whatever she said next would downplay any negativity in Donald's progress out of the cult that had claimed him three years ago.

"He's, you know…. It isn't easy. But he's determined, and so am I."

It had been an uphill battle, and Ruth Rainey had proven herself to be a soldier of the finest mettle. She had moved to Manhattan just before my second year at General Theological Seminary, and she'd stayed with me for several months while she'd set about rescuing her twin brother from the clutches of the Risen Christ group (I can't bring myself to call them a church). It had taken the private detective less than a week to find Donald. It had taken nearly two years, and the help of a deprogrammer, to extricate him.

It still hurt. I had come damn close to loving him and, I think, to him loving me. He had been my first romantic relationship. He had shown me what sex between two men should be. And because of him, because of how well he had shared his acting experience with me, I had refined the delivery style that had turned my lackluster public speaking into what listeners at seminary had referred to as "nearly a performance."

This assignment, this parish, was not what I had envisioned for myself. While I'd hardly expected my first posting to be in my home town of New York City, I had hoped for something a little —make that a lot—more cosmopolitan than Assisi, Vermont. It was not quite a farming community, and it was not quite not a farming community. Certainly, at roughly 30 miles south of the Canadian border as the crow flies, it was remote. While I looked forward to glorious fall colors in a few weeks, I wouldn't say the same about anticipating the winter here. Ursula Stockton, my advisor at Union Theological Seminary where I'd fine-tuned my Master of Divinity for the UU Church, had done her best to convince me Assisi would be just what I needed.

"You've been a city boy all your life, Spencer. You need to

see another way of life, to value it, to understand and value the people who live it." She'd given me a wry glance. "And a lesson in humility never hurt any good pastor."

Despite my misgivings, the Assisi congregation had been as welcoming as I'd led Ruth to believe. My predecessor, Minister Emerita Reverend Vanessa Doyle, had retired earlier than she had hoped. Two bouts of cancer had sapped her stamina to the point where, at the age of sixty-eight, she felt she was no longer able to serve the congregation the way it deserved. She had moved out of the small house associated with the church and into a smaller cottage.

My interview with UU of Assisi had fallen on what Vanessa referred to as one of her bad days, so I'd met only with the business manager and with the membership director, who doubled as the music director.

But it was Vanessa who greeted me at the house next door to the church, the day I arrived in Assisi to stay. As I approached in the second-hand Jeep I had bought, I didn't see her at first. What I saw was a massive, white creature, a dog close to the size of a bear, the bushy fur of its long tail brushing the grass. Vanessa, who turned out to be only a few inches shorter than my six-foot-two, looked nowhere near that tall next to the dog. Perhaps in solidarity with the dog, Vanessa's short hair was as close to white as mine was to black.

"Spencer Hill," I said as we shook hands.

"Vanessa Doyle," she responded. "Welcome. Welcome to Assisi." She smiled broadly. "Pretend Klondike isn't here. He'll give you space that way, and you can make friends later if you want to. May I help you with your things?"

Klondike. A good name, I thought, for that dog. I handed her a couple of small bags while I hefted two larger ones, leaving in the car the boxes containing the remainder of the worldly goods I hadn't put into storage. A moving van would follow later this afternoon with the furniture I expected to need here.

The house was red brick, like the church, with four rooms and a half-bath downstairs, and two bedrooms and a bath on the second floor. The wooden staircase was old but in good repair despite the complaining creaks I heard as I ascended.

Downstairs, in the small kitchen, was a breakfast nook, its window overlooking a large back yard. Just outside the window, obscuring half of it, was a huge maple tree, its leaves already turning from green to an interesting freckled pattern that included reds and yellows. On the nook's built-in table was a smorgasbord of food.

"The folks didn't want to overwhelm you with a welcoming committee the minute you arrived." Vanessa's smile seemed fond as she spoke of her congregation. "But they couldn't stop themselves from feeding you."

The white bear sidled up to her, his head tilted just enough to look at her face.

"Klondike, this is not for you." She ruffled the fur on his head.

I asked, "If I give him a peace offering, will he respect me in the morning?"

Vanessa laughed. "If you'd like to give him a slice of that turkey, you could set it on the floor where I'm pointing. It's where his dish used to be. But don't pet him. Keep him at a distance for now."

Klondike scarfed up that turkey slice in one gulp.

"Is he dangerous?"

"No, though his breed can be aggressively protective. But I want him to understand that he can't push you around. Watch this." She moved to another corner of the room, called to the dog, and clapped her hands. "Up!"

Klondike stood on his hind legs, his front paws on Vanessa's shoulders. In that position, he was at least as tall as she was. She bumped her forehead gently against his. "Down. Sit."

The dog obviously saw Vanessa as his leader. And she was

right; I was not ready to get close to a dog nearly as tall as I was. He was gorgeous, though, with merry black eyes and what resembled black lipstick around his mouth. There was a golden-brown patch on each ear. His white coat was thick and long, dense enough for winters up here.

I asked, "What kind of dog is he?"

"Great Pyrenees. A willful breed. But well-managed, the GP is a wonderful companion, if you have lots of space." She tilted her head at me. "Do you hike?"

"Not yet. But looking at the scenery as I drove, I was thinking I should probably have a go."

"I can tell you a lot about nearby trails. And GPs are great dogs to hike with, if you decide to be friends."

"I'll keep that in mind."

That had been a Friday. It had taken me a long time to fall asleep that first night. My townhouse in New York, left to me by my parents, had seemed quiet. It was in the exclusive Gramercy Park area, its rooms large and very comfortably furnished. But the night after my interview here, when I'd stayed overnight in a nearby bed and breakfast, had given me a taste of what quiet really was. And now that I was here to stay, the quiet felt almost oppressive.

"That's counterintuitive," I said aloud into the silent bedroom. "Quiet ought to feel like space extending all around me, not like something closing in on me."

But it didn't feel like space. Rather, it did close in on me. I think I got up three or four times, not because I needed to use the bathroom, but because it was only by turning on a light and moving through space that I could convince myself I wasn't encased in cotton batting.

~

Saturday was a busy day. I did my best to remember the names of everyone who gathered in the church function hall to welcome me, their new minister. Vanessa, bless her, stayed close and introduced me, and in quiet moments she prompted me to recall the names of people I would see most often. There was Violet Verette, membership director, also the music director, married to Alvin, both apparently in their sixties. The volunteer business manager was a widower, also sixty-ish, named John Thompson who, as Vanessa whispered to me, was not likely to remain single for long. A woman named Deena Cunningham volunteered as secretary two days a week, Monday and Friday.

There were four lay ministers of various ages, I guessed between the ages of thirty and fifty. I remembered the youngest one better than the others, partly because of his age and partly because I liked his name: Marshall Savage. Also, he was every bit as tall as I was. Marshall was the only man of the four. He didn't say much to me, but another lay minister, Loraine Fuller, possibly forty-five, seemed determined to make sure I knew who she was and how involved she intended to be in what she called "your new ministry." She seemed a little forward but not actually obnoxious.

At one point I looked around the room, assessing the demographics. I kept my voice low as I asked Vanessa, "Is the age of these folks representative of the congregation as a whole?"

She released a long breath. "I'm afraid so. Violet and I have done what we could to encourage younger members." She turned to look around the room, and she pointed to Marshall Savage. "You might want to talk with Marshall. He teaches high school, and he might have some influence with the younger set. I've been meaning to do that myself, but...."

It was the first time she had said or done anything to indicate how much of a toll her diminishing health had taken. I assured her, "I'll do that. Thanks."

～

Vanessa invited me to have dinner in her cottage. "You might rather have a bit of alone time," she opened, "but if you're up for homemade chicken pot pie, Klondike and I would love for you to join us."

I laughed aloud. "Sorry," I said. "It's just that I had an image of Klondike seated in a chair opposite you at the dinner table."

"Oh, no," she assured me. "He's not even allowed scraps while I'm eating. If he gets goodies after his dog food, it's also after I've had my own meal."

"I'll consider myself cautioned. No feeding the dog from the table." I almost winked as I added, "Klondike and I will both behave ourselves."

～

Vanessa was an excellent cook. The delectable dinner was followed by an equally delicious apple crisp served with decaf coffee. During the meal she gave me tidbits of information about some of the parishioners and, most usefully, about the lay ministers.

"They know what's expected of them," she told me, "though one or two wouldn't mind being in more of a leadership role."

"Should I infer that there's a bit of work to get them all to paint between the lines?"

"Especially Loraine Fuller. She's a very effective lay minister. Loves to help people, very good at being supportive for people who are having difficulties in their lives. Everyone appreciates that part of her role." Vanessa hesitated.

"I get the feeling there's more to it." I knew there must be, based on Loraine's behavior at the welcome party.

"Loraine is a lesbian and quite 'out' about it, which in itself is not a problem for this community. We're fairly progressive. But she can be a little intent on calling attention to that part of her life, I think in an effort to enhance acceptance. And it's just not necessary here. When she found out you're gay, she was extremely enthusiastic. Though she did say, 'Too bad he's not a woman.'"

I smiled. "So I should expect her to approach me with ideas about making the parish more gay-friendly?"

"Yes. Think of it like that, and you'll do well with her. She's actually a great asset to the congregation, and I'm sure you'll get along fine."

"Anything helpful you can tell me about Marshall Savage?"

She raised one eyebrow slightly. "So you've sussed him out?"

"I beg your pardon?"

She shook her head quickly once or twice. "Ignore me. Why do you mention him, specifically?"

"I didn't have a chance to speak with him, really. You said he teaches high school?"

"English. Yes."

"How long has he been a lay minister?"

"Just under a year."

"You've said Loraine is quite effective. Would you say the same of Marshall?"

Vanessa seemed to search inside her head. "He's soft-spoken, and he's the sort of person who hesitates to take the lead on things. My sense is that people who want to express how they're feeling without necessarily having someone suggest actions or directions they might take would prefer him to, say, Loraine, who often does offer advice, though she shouldn't. That's not supposed to be part of the role, of course."

"I wonder what prompted him to become a lay minister. I would have thought that role would be more appealing to someone like Loraine."

Vanessa seemed to hesitate again. "Once you know more about his history, you'll likely understand what makes him want to help people."

I could tell I wasn't going to get any more specifics right now. My offer to help with clean-up was refused, so I finished my coffee and excused myself. "Think I'll head back, then. I want to give tomorrow's sermon another run-through."

And I did. I'd been over it and over it, and it was hardly the first sermon I'd ever delivered; my time at seminary had provided me with ample practice. But this was different. This was my new ministry, emphasis on "my." I didn't expect to bowl anyone over, but I did want to make at least a passable first impression.

A minister's first sermon, traditionally, should let the congregation know who the new leader is, not just personally but also ecclesiastically. My congregation would want to know how I see the UU approach to God, or to the Universe, or to whatever spiritual guidance might exist. And I would need to describe my own spirituality in a way that aligned with the seven UU principles and with the church's commitment to inclusion and diversity.

As members of the UU Church, we are encouraged to follow our own hearts in terms of what God is, and whether there even is such an entity we should call God. I had much to learn, though, about the makeup of my congregation, despite the information I'd been given. How many of them came from Christian backgrounds, as I had? How many from Judaism? Buddhism? There could be many traditions represented here, including atheism. But I couldn't expect them to announce their starting places. It was my job to open the lines of communication—not to give

9

them a metaphorical blank page and tell them to write, but to write on a page myself and let them respond to it. I had to talk about what the word God meant, and didn't mean, to me.

Does an entity some call God exist? I'd learned first-hand how easy it is to transfer to God the perception most people once had of their parents, who might have seemed strong and protective and who seemed to know everything. Even into my early twenties, I had hung onto a subconscious confusion between God the Father and the man who had sired me, a confusion probably exacerbated by my father's deserted vocation as a Catholic priest. I'd had to learn to separate serving God from pleasing my earthly father. It had helped when, during my year at Union, I had begun to use the pronoun "it" rather than "He" when referring to—well, to whatever God is. This would not be antithetical to the UU tradition, though I expected there would be some members of my congregation to whom it might be jarring.

So did my faith include a belief in God? This is a question my congregation would want to know. Coming from a very Christian tradition, and moreover having been certain at one point that I was destined for the Episcopal priesthood, it was a question I was still contemplating as I reviewed my first address to the Unitarian Universalist Church of Assisi, Vermont.

CHAPTER 2

Vanessa met me at the church at eight-thirty, two hours ahead of the Sunday service. I'd been given a thorough tour before, but I appreciated the refresher she gave me, especially considering my anxious state. We also went over the order of the service, including the point at which she would introduce me to the congregation.

Her steady voice and confident demeanor went some distance toward calming my jitters, though I was glad that she would open the service, and that I would be seated off to the side until it was time for the sermon.

It was a cool day in early September, the blue sky decorated with little white fluffs that do nothing to interfere with what warmth the sun still offers at summer's end. Donald had a word for it: apricity, meaning the feel of warm sun coming through cool air. Donald had been full of eccentric words and phrases I'd never heard of.

Correction: Maybe Donald still *is* full of those things. It's not like he's dead.

As people gathered in the sanctuary, Violet Verette sat at the upright piano off to the side of the altar and played music that I recognized as one of the pieces from Book 1 of Claude Debussy's piano preludes, "La fille aux cheveux de lin," also known as "The Girl with the Flaxen Hair." It's a fairly well-known piece, sweet and gentle and not even three minutes long. I had played it at some point in my years of piano study. A trained pianist myself, I could have done a better job, but that wasn't my role, and I appreciated the effort. I did notice that the piano as a little out of tune, and its tone generally was not great in this space. Perhaps it wouldn't have been great anywhere else, either. The church's budget was not large.

Violet was just rounding in on the final notes when something stabbed at my chest. Debussy's Book 1 collection also contained another piece I had worked on: "La Danse de Puck." Puck's Dance.

I stopped breathing.

Puck. I had known a Puck. I had loved being in the company of a Puck. I had loved Puck's humor, his face, his laugh, his mouth, his cock, his....

My breath restarted with a sharp spasm of my chest.

Doing my best to attend as Vanessa addressed what had been her congregation, the images in my mind were of a different place. New York City. A different time. Nineteen eighty-three, three years ago. In my mind's eye, I saw Donald in the role of Puck, as I'd seen him act for the first time, in *A Midsummer Night's Dream*. His playful carnality had caused me to become uncomfortable in my slacks. And I saw Donald, his face intense and then amused and then intense again as he described how much the work of an actor has in common with that of a minister. I saw him laugh with abandon at the delight a small child took in his banter. And I saw his fingers as they caressed my nakedness, teasing tender flesh until I lay helpless, both wanting and not wanting to progress to the passion that would meld our bodies together in the agonizing ecstasy of a union that seemed both physical and spiritual.

Puck. Donald would always be Puck to me.

I closed my eyes briefly, took a few deep breaths, and turned my mind back to where I was, here, now.

For the first hymn of the service, Vanessa had chosen "Morning Has Broken," a favorite old chestnut, and something that might serve to make people at least a little comfortable with the change in ministers. After all, Vanessa had led them for a long time.

The order of the UU service included a time for people to express whatever joys or sorrows they had recently experienced. I had come to love this time, for it provided me with opportunities to gauge the spiritual perspective of the parishioners. Five different people spoke, and I paid close attention as they asked for spiritual support from the membership. One child spoke, a little girl maybe ten years old whose dog was sick. I guessed that her request—that we all send healing thoughts to the ailing Troy—had been suggested to her by her parents, though of course I couldn't be sure. I made a mental note to find her after the service.

Following the offertory was a short talk by one of the lay ministers. Of course it was Loraine Fuller this Sunday, to welcome the new, gay minister. She acquitted herself well, I thought, with only one reference to sexual orientation. I decided she showed a keen introspection.

And then it was time for the sermon. Vanessa took the pulpit for what would probably be her last time.

"In the short time I have known Spencer Hill," she opened, "I've formed a definite opinion of him." She turned and gave me a grin, and there was a quiet chuckle from the congregation. "Despite his few years, he has come through fires that many face but that few survive with the same spiritual determination of this young man. I believe his mind is keen, his heart is open, and his love is sincere. I do not believe we could have found a better new minister."

I felt a shiver go through me as she concluded, "So, to all of you, I give The Reverend Spencer Hill."

At the pulpit, I smiled broadly at what I now considered my people, taking in their applause—something that surprised me a little, coming as I did from the Episcopal tradition, which does not encourage applause during a service—and when it died down I took a moment to breathe, noticing with pleasure that the small church was nearly full. My gaze fell on many individuals I had met the previous afternoon.

Using what I knew to be a typical method of address in the UU tradition, I said, "Thank you, Reverend Vanessa. I will do my best to live up to that generous description."

I gave everyone a chance to take me in visually as I glanced around the sanctuary with as benevolent an expression as I could. This was an act, and yet it was real. The fact that reality is enhanced by a good performance is one of the dichotomies of this life I had chosen. I'd been told many times that my deep, strong voice was an asset to my calling. I brought it to bear as I began my first sermon.

"Many philosophers see the concept of God as something that, as children, we once considered our parents to be. For all we could tell, we knew little or nothing, and they knew everything. They knew about things we had no concept of and performed actions that seemed almost magical to us.

"As we grow older, we're faced with a choice. As we realize that our parents are people and not gods, do we lose faith in trust and love? Do we lose our hope for beneficence and protection from a source much wiser and more powerful than we've learned mere people can be? Or, unwilling or unable to relinquish those things, do we transfer our expectations to an unknowable being —omniscient, omnipotent, perfect in all things—who loves us and takes care of us, even as it demands loyalty and laud?

"The very question 'Does God exist' implies that we can talk about God the way we discuss cows, or trees, or ice cream. We can no more prove that God exists than we can prove it doesn't. Most traditions centered on God consider it to be the uncaused cause. It causes existence. So, to say that God exists is to confuse the source of existence with the things it caused to exist.

"Do I believe in God? No. And yes. No, because I can't bring myself to pray to God the way I might appeal to a parent. 'Please help my team win this game.' 'Please give me a pony for my birthday.' Is even the plea to ask God to save my spouse or my child from death caused by accident or disease the same as asking for life to be arranged in a way favorable to me?

"If I am in a traffic accident where everyone dies but me, do I believe that God has intervened on my personal behalf? Did God reach out a hand and save me, alone? And if I believe that, must I also believe God allowed—even intended—for everyone else to die? How can I explain that to the loved ones they leave behind? Do I say, 'God's plan was that your beloved should die and I should not?' Can I say that even to myself?

"And yet, do I feel gratitude that I was spared? Yes. Do I feel God's presence in my life? Yes. But I don't see it as a plan. I don't see it as a succession of decisions made by a being apart from me, or apart from life itself.

"I perceive God as a unifying spirit, or force, the goal of which is to bring us together through love. All kinds of love. Love of a parent. Love of a child. Love of a romantic partner. Love of a friend. Love of a pet. All these kinds of love comprise the love I want to feel when I consider what God is. When we relate to each other with love, we can feel God connecting us with one another. Each aspect of the love I feel is like a window through which divine love comes into my life. And my goal, as a physical being on this beautiful, mysterious, ever-changing and ever-constant earth, is to have as many windows as possible. And please, God, may they all be open."

Just in time, I remembered to announce the affirmation. Nothing I said about it would be new to these people, and yet they would benefit from hearing it, as I would benefit from saying it.

"And now, as we recite the affirmation, our promise to each other, let the joining of hands represent our connection with one another, and let our speech help us to carry our love out into the world."

The UU affirmation is a lovely thing. It speaks of love, of truth, of service, of knowledge, and of fellowship. It expresses the intention that all souls grow together and in harmony with the divine. As was customary, I led the congregation in its recitation.

I had chosen the closing hymn, "Gather Us In," from the UU hymnal, *Hymns for the Celebration of Life*. The text speaks of the various sources of faith, the various ways different people might perceive it, and the conviction that despite these differences, we are all one, all souls together. Apparently, this was not a hymn familiar to everyone here. Just as Ruth had once told me about UU congregations, the first couple of lines sounded thin as many people took the time to read through the text to make sure they agreed with it before joining in. It was a challenge to chuckle and sing at the same time, but I managed it.

Shaking hands with everyone as they left the church, I could tell there were people who weren't entirely convinced that this new guy was what they'd hoped for, but I believe there were many more who were either pleased or were happy to give me a chance. Loraine, of course, was full of praise, despite the fact that I hadn't referred to sexual orientation at all.

"That was a wonderful sermon, Reverend," she said, holding my hand in both of hers. "Very thought-provoking."

Okay, I'll take that, I thought, so I smiled and thanked her.

After the last person shook my hand and moved on, Abby Chisholm, mother of the little girl with the sick dog, approached me. Her voice low, she said, "Reverend, would you speak to Cheryl about her dog? We don't think he'll live, and we can't seem to convince her to accept the situation."

"Of course. Should we do that as soon as the crowd leaves?"

She hesitated and then nodded.

I found the Chisholms, Abby and Walter and Cheryl, under a large tree in the church's side yard.

"Do you mind if I remove this robe?" I asked them. "It's a little warm under here." They agreed, and I lifted the voluminous, dark red thing over my head. I wore a lightweight suit under it, so I was still in a kind of uniform.

Cheryl sat on the ground, and I sat beside her, knees bent, arms around them, my head tilted sideways in her direction but my eyes on the ground. I wanted her to feel supported, not confronted.

"I'm sending healing thoughts to Troy right now," I told her, my voice low but steady. I didn't want my words or my voice to bring the little girl to tears. "And I'm sending thoughts of comfort to you."

Her eyes were on her small hands where she pulled gently on grass blades. She nodded and sniffled once.

"Can you tell me what's wrong with him?"

She shook her head. "No one will tell me."

I glanced up at her parents, a sense of confusion making me scowl slightly. They shrugged their shoulders as if to say they didn't want to tell her the truth but were sorry they had to avoid it. I had to assume Troy was not long for this world.

"How does he act?"

17

Her sweet face crumpled and she looked up at me. "He won't eat. He won't come to me when I call him. He won't smile."

"Is it all right if I give you a hug Cheryl?"

"CC."

"I'm sorry?"

"Cheryl Chisholm. CC."

"Is it all right if I give you a hug, CC?"

She nodded and leaned toward me. She cried quietly, her little body shaking slightly in my arms. After maybe a minute she pulled away. "Gramma says everything happens for a reason." Her eyes shot pain into mine. "What's the reason?"

Oh, boy. I hated that expression. But how to respond about it to a child? I had to tread lightly. "I think your gramma is counting on a belief that there is someone who has a plan for everything that happens, and that the plan might have some bad things in it but will turn out all right in the end."

I glanced up at the Chisholms to gauge where they stood on what I considered a flawed outlook. Walter closed his eyes briefly and gave his head a few quick shakes.

CC repeated, "So what's the reason?"

"I see it a little differently," I told her. "It seems to me that there is a reason something happens, like if you work hard on your school work you'll get a good grade. But I don't think you get good grades because it's in someone's plan for that to happen."

I waited to see if she was following me. I wasn't sure, but I continued.

"So if Troy is sick, something happened to make him sick. I don't think anyone had a plan to make him sick."

She went back to the grass blades.

"What does Troy look like?"

CC perked up a little. "He's mostly white with a few big brown spots."

"Short hair or fluffy?"

"Short. But he likes it when I brush him."

"What's his favorite treat?"

Her face lifted to mine. "He loves ham! It's his absolute favorite. When we have sliced ham from the store, there's always a few slices for him."

"Do you have any other pets?"

She shook her head and pulled a few more grass blades.

"Have you met Klondike?"

"Troy's afraid of Klondike."

I leaned toward her a little. "I'm kind of afraid of Klondike, myself."

CC giggled.

I wasn't sure what else I could say that wouldn't make the girl sadder, and I was willing to go only so far in contradicting her grandmother. Abby had seemed to think I could help CC face the reality of Troy's imminent demise, perhaps even talk about dogs going to heaven. But that felt wrong.

So I told her, "CC, will you call me tomorrow and every day to tell me how Troy is doing? That will help me send just the right kind of thoughts. Will you do that?"

She nodded. Mrs. Chisholm held out her hand, and CC rose. As I stood I got the sense there was someone behind me, and I turned. Vanessa.

She smiled. "Forgive me for eavesdropping. It wasn't out of doubt about you. I wanted the Chisholms to know I supported you. And them."

I tilted my head and smiled. "I appreciate that."

"And I don't know what else you might have said to CC. Her folks haven't told her that Troy's cancer," and her voice showed the slightest strain at the mention of her own disease, "is quite bad. I doubt he'll make it through the week."

I picked up my discarded robe and walked with Vanessa back toward the church. She stopped at the open double doors. "By the way Spencer, you did a great job providing CC with an alternative viewpoint without criticizing her grandmother."

"Thanks." Was I glowing? I couldn't tell. Somehow, this praise meant more than if Vanessa had complimented my sermon.

CHAPTER 3

Vanessa had been right about Troy. Despite a call Monday afternoon from CC telling me the dog was doing a little better, the call I got early on Tuesday evening was from Abby Chisholm.

"We've just called the vet," she told me, her voice catching on stifled sobs. "He'll be here in half an hour. Can you come?"

It took me a few minutes to appreciate that here, in this community, the veterinarian would go to the dog for this act of mercy, not the other way around.

By the time I arrived at the Chisholms', someone else from the church was already there. It was Marshall Savage. He sat on the floor of the living room, CC beside him, Troy's head in CC's lap. Marshall looked up as I entered and, I swear, blushed nearly crimson. His dark red hair topped the typical red-head complexion, and what would have been a light flush on me was almost a flame on his pale, lightly freckled face. It was a sweet face— vulnerable, even, though that might have been partly because of what he knew was about to happen.

Abby, standing beside me, spoke in hushed tones. "Thank

you for coming, Reverend. I didn't know CC had already called Marshall."

"That's no problem."

Looking a little embarrassed, she said, "My husband told me it was silly to involve the minister in the death of a dog, but...."

I laid a hand lightly on her forearm. "This is as much about CC and your family as it is about the dog. Love is love, and CC is in pain."

As I lowered myself to the floor, facing CC and Marshall, I smiled inwardly. In a small parish such as this one, it was entirely possible and even appropriate for the minister to involve himself in the death of a family pet. If I'd been in a large city? I couldn't imagine a direct, personal connection with a child and her family for a reason such as this. I made a note to thank my Union advisor for sending me here.

CC leaned against Marshall's shoulder as she slowly stroked Troy's back. It was obvious his breathing was shallow and quick, between short periods where it seemed he wasn't breathing at all. None of the three of us moved when the veterinarian, Dr. Lombardi, arrived, until I made way for him so he could be close to Troy.

He readied the tools of his profession and then spoke to CC.

"I'm going to give him some medicine now, CC. He'll barely feel it. It's just to make him relax and to ease his pain. All right?"

She nodded, and I watched as Troy's legs released some of their tension.

"Now, CC," Dr. Lombardi said, "if you haven't already said goodbye, you should do it now."

I could tell CC was struggling not to weep. A few tears coursed their way down her cheeks as she bent over Troy and kissed his head. Her voice squeaked, making it almost impossible to tell that she said, "I love you, Troy."

"One more injection, CC, and he will ease painlessly into a sleep. He won't wake up."

CC nodded and a sob escaped her.

My own eyes watered as Troy's body went completely limp. And then I heard Marshall say, "Oh!"

His face, wet with tears, was nearly shining with a kind of beauty I don't think I'd ever witnessed.

"What is it?" I asked.

Marshall seemed to be speaking to someone who wasn't in the room. "Oh, yes. How—" His voice caught, but his face shone. "How perfect. Yes." He closed his eyes as we all waited. Then he bowed his head and, almost inaudibly, said, "Thank you."

When he raised his face, still shining from some source I couldn't identify, he looked at me. "I don't know how this will sound to you, but something just happened. Something undeniable."

I gave him an uncertain nod, and he looked at CC.

Marshall took a deep, shaky breath before he spoke. "Troy is not alone. Another dog, named Angus, was here." Marshall's voice was shakier than his breath had been, but he kept talking. "Angus was a wonderful dog. Loved his people dearly. He died protecting my father from a grizzly bear."

No one spoke while Marshall took a moment to collect himself. Then, "Angus was a very old soul. Troy was a sweet soul, fairly new to life. Just now, Angus came for Troy. He filled the room with his love for Troy, and he carried him away. Oh, so tenderly. He carried Troy away."

Marshall smiled at CC as copious tears flowed down his cheeks.

Dr. Lombardi lifted Troy's lifeless body and carried it outside, while CC and Marshall held onto each other and sobbed. They were still locked in an embrace when the vet came back in.

To Abby, he said, "Would you like to have Troy cremated or buried?"

CC lifted her head from Marshall's shoulder. "I want to spread his ashes all over the back yard. He loved playing there."

～

I stayed long enough to be sure there was nothing I could do to bring comfort to the Chisholms, but it seemed the comfort Angus had given them was beyond anything I had to offer. How pale, and how trite anything I might have said Sunday about dogs going to heaven would seem now, after what Marshall had said. I sat on the Chisholms' front steps and waited for Marshall.

"Reverend," he said quietly as he passed me—an acknowledgement, nothing more.

"Marshall?" I called as I rose to my feet. "Could we talk a minute?"

He stopped but didn't turn. "I know what you're going to say."

Beside him now, I said, "Do you? That's funny, because I don't. What am I going to say?"

He heaved a sigh heavy with exasperation. In a voice that wasn't quite his, he said, "Spirituality is one thing, Marshall. Magical thinking is something else entirely." He turned, his face now defiant.

I wanted to chuckle, but I didn't want him to think I wasn't taking him seriously. "That doesn't sound like me. Who else would say that to you?"

He crossed his arms over his chest protectively. "I think you know."

The only name I could come up with was Loraine. "And I think I can't know. But what I do know is that what you said in there was excruciatingly beautiful. And I don't think you would have invented the loving presence of your dog. I believe you truly felt it."

Skepticism? Is that what I saw on his face then?

"In fact," I went on, "although I couldn't say precisely what I felt, I did feel something. Whether it was Angus coming to carry Troy away, or it was the love you felt for Angus once and for CC now, doesn't matter as far as I can see. Love is love."

I wanted to say more. I wanted to speak from a sudden rush of emotion I couldn't name, a warm and uplifting wave of something I felt coming from this man. But there were no words.

He blushed, less violently than before. "Thank you." I watched as he walked to a little blue car, his slender form not quite rigid but not quite limber, as though he felt the need to steel himself against something invisible to me. If he had turned toward me at any point, I would have waved. But he didn't. The little car's tail lights disappeared over the crest of a hill. But whatever had nearly overcome me, that unnamable wave of emotion, remained with me.

I walked to my own car, and as my fingers touched the door handle, I froze in place. In my head, I heard Vanessa's voice: "So you've sussed him out?"

She'd said that to me Saturday evening, during dinner. I hadn't known what she'd meant, and when I'd expressed confusion she had dismissed the statement and gone on to something else.

Sussed him out. What could that mean, except that Marshall was gay? Vanessa had thought I'd guessed as much, but when she saw I hadn't, she was unwilling to reveal what she knew. Commendable; she wouldn't "out" him.

If I was right about Marshall, that might explain the flushed face when he saw me; he might believe I knew. But—wait. Why would that embarrass him? Because embarrassment certainly is what it looked like.

Was he attracted to me? Was that it? It was no secret, I was sure, that I was gay. I'd revealed that during my interview, and I'd made it clear I didn't care who knew. But did he know? And would that matter? When we're attracted to someone, that isn't based on sexual orientation. So did he know I was gay?

I shook my head and opened my car door. This internal discussion was pointless.

∾

Wednesday I had lunch with Loraine Fuller, the first of the meetings I planned with each of the lay ministers. If I had worried she might want to intrude upon my role as minister, my concerns were assuaged. As Vanessa had indicated, Loraine had an agenda, but it wasn't taking over my job.

We sat across from each other at a small table in the town's only diner, plates of hamburgers and fries before us. Her dark brown hair was cut fairly short—not in a masculine style, but it looked easy to care for. She wore what appeared to be a cotton shirt under a knitted vest the same dark blue as the strips on the shirt. Her build was solid but not heavy, not tall and not short.

"I'm in earnest about this, Reverend."

"You can call me Spencer if you like."

She pointed a fry at me. "I'm in earnest about this, Spencer."

It was a challenge for me to focus on her next words. Her use of a french fry as a pointer sent my mind careening back to the first meal I'd had with Puck. With Donald. He'd wanted to make a point about the religious subtext he saw in the play *Sleuth*, and he'd used french fries in the same way.

"...and I'd be happy to work on the program. I've collected a lot of relevant material, both scriptural and historical."

It took me a second to integrate what my ears had heard but my mind had slipped away from, but I recovered well enough. She wanted me to hold an open meeting about the topic of sexual orientation. I had to be very careful with my response. I also wondered if Loraine had suggested this to Vanessa and had not met with encouragement.

"Your enthusiasm is impressive," I told her, and I meant it. "Do you have reason to believe it would be well attended? Do you have a sense of how many people in the congregation would participate?"

She made a face I interpreted as *That's not the point*. "Certainly all the gay and bi people in town, not just those in our congregation would attend. My goal would be for straight people to come, too, to learn more about what it means to be gay. Reverend, nothing like this has ever been done here."

I nodded, doing my best to look thoughtful. "Although out people like you would likely be there, in my experience when someone is gay and not completely comfortable being seen that way, they would avoid a gathering such as the one you're suggesting."

"Well... they shouldn't."

"Tell you what. Why don't you put together a rough draft of what you think this would look like. I have to be honest with you, though. I'm reluctant to push forward with any kind of special interest so early in my tenure here. We can revisit the idea at some point in the future."

She scowled. "I have to say I'm disappointed. I thought you'd be keener on moving our cause forward."

Our cause.... I couldn't tell her outright that it wasn't my cause.

"As regards your cause," I said, trying not to stress *your*, "what do you see as your objective? What's the end game?"

"What do you mean? Isn't that obvious?"

"I'm trying to understand what you think success looks like." I saw her puzzled expression and tried again. "This program you're suggesting wouldn't be an end in itself. I believe you see it as a step, moving forward in a specific direction. For example, is there something about the way our community perceives you as a lesbian that you feel needs adjustment or correction?"

"It's not just our community. But, yes, I often feel as though people see me as different from straight people."

"You are different." I held a hand up to stop any objection. "I think what you're looking for is the kind of acceptance in which you aren't made to *feel* different because of your orientation."

"Respect. I want respect."

"Can we agree on the goal of respectful acceptance?"

She squinted, not at me but at something inside her mind. "Okay. Sure."

"And I think that's what everyone wants for themself, really. But gay people are often made to feel as though they aren't getting it. And they're not wrong. I hear you about that, believe me. But here's the thing." I hunched forward a little. "We are making progress. It can feel very slow, and we see setbacks all the time. We see bigotry winning in some ways and with some people. But you mentioned history a minute ago. History shows us that changes in society happen slowly, and usually only after enough people within that society see the change as a good thing."

I wasn't finished, but she interrupted. "I want to help them along."

"I understand that. So do I. We just need to be sure we're helping and not pushing. No one likes to be pushed. Kindness begets kindness. Love begets love. And when someone makes an adjustment that they think is their own idea, that change is real, and the changed person brings others along with them."

She sat back hard against the booth behind her. "What are you saying? That we just have to twiddle our thumbs and wait?"

I shook my head. "Far from it. What you do in your role as lay minister is hardly inactive. When people who know you're gay see you reaching out to help someone in trouble, they're more likely to seek you out when they need help. When they do that, they don't care that you're gay. And Vanessa tells me you have an abundance of exactly that kind of love. I mean, the kind of love people need from a lay minister. The love they need from everyone, of course, but you've generously put yourself in a position where you expect to help people. And the more you're seen as helping others, the less and less important your sexual orientation becomes. That is how we win. That is how we gain respectful acceptance."

Loraine's brow furrowed in a way that made her appear distressed. Sad, even. "But that will take forever."

I smiled. "It seems to me you've made a lot of headway here already. Vanessa spoke highly of you, and what I heard last Sunday tells me you're insightful and open-hearted. Surely, she and I are not the only people who've noticed that. And in fact, I'm in awe of your courage."

She watched my face for several seconds. Then, "So we're on the same page?"

I nodded. "I'm reading all the words on it, taking them all in, looking for direction from what they say and also from what they don't say. That can take longer."

I picked up the bill for lunch, and Loraine surprised me by giving me a quick hug as we parted outside the diner.

Thursday morning I met with John Thompson, the business manager. I wouldn't say that I wished I hadn't, but I will say it wasn't a fun meeting.

John was pleasant enough, but it was during this meeting that something I'd learned in seminary about a minister's role came home, as they say, to roost. John went over with me all those chores that had been Vanessa's, chores for which John handled finances but for which the execution was all mine.

There was making sure the church building or function hall was heated in winter in time for services, for bake sales, for the boy scout meetings, for the Knameless Knitters, who got

together as a group and who knitted, crocheted, and anony-
mously donated warm clothing for people of reduced means who
lived in and around Assisi, and for various and sundry gatherings
that might take place in the church or function hall. There was
contacting workers as needed to repair anything that might go
amiss, from heating to plumbing to building repairs.

By the end of this meeting the list of chores seemed so long
that I wondered when I'd have time to actually minister. I sent up
a silent prayer of gratitude for Deena Cunningham, who would
do most of the work of putting a printed program together for
Sunday services.

CHAPTER 4

My meetings with the next two lay ministers, one on Wednesday evening and the other Thursday lunch, went smoothly and were decidedly less intense than my meeting with Loraine had been. Andrea Beale and Jenny Pratt were both very caring, sensitive people. Andrea, in her mid-forties, was married to a man named Jacob. Jenny was single and probably around thirty-five.

I met with Deena later Thursday afternoon and learned that she would help me collect information about special requests from the congregation during services—people who were sick, or had just had a baby, that sort of thing. She would type up the program and have copies produced. And she was very clear that I needed to tell her my sermon's theme by nine o'clock Friday morning.

I had called Marshall Savage's number a few times, never reaching him. I left messages on his answering machine but got no return call. Friday, I decided to visit the high school.

Not knowing quite how I was going to approach Marshall here, I started in the principal's office and got permission to observe his tenth grade English class, the last period of the school day. Following directions to the classroom, I pondered how easy it was to get permission to do something because of being a minister. Of course, it helped that the office administrator was in my parish.

There were two doors into the classroom, one that led to the front and the other to the back, which was the one I eased quietly open. All I wanted was to listen. But I didn't hear Marshall's voice. Instead, I heard the voices of what must have been three students, coming from the front of the class. Not being able to see the students, I had to create the scene in my mind. At first I heard only one voice, apparently a boy, chanting in a sing-song rhythm as he intoned some of the verses of the witches' scene from Shakespeare's *Macbeth*. He was part of the way through the poem.

"Fillet of a fenny snake,

In the cauldron boil and bake."

He continued with "Eye of newt and toe of frog," as one girl's laughter rose above the chanting.

"What's a fenny snake, anyway?" she said, apparently to no one in particular.

Seemingly undaunted by the interruption, the boy chanted through to the lines,

"Lizard's leg and owlet's wing.

For a charm of powerful trouble,

Like a hell-broth boil and bubble."

Then three voices, two girls' and a boy's, finished that section of the poem:

"Double, double toil and trouble;

Fire burn and cauldron bubble."

And then I heard Marshall's voice. "Okay, okay, I get it. The whole thing sounds made up. And guess what? It is. But it's also very real. Darla," Marshall addressed one student, "a fenny snake can be considered to be either a snake from the fens regions of eastern England, or it can be interpreted as a magical creature. Shakespeare includes both real and imagined creatures in this poem, so it could be either." I heard him exhale through his nose. "The three of you can sit down. In a minute, we'll try again with a different set of witches."

There were giggles from the class, and above the sounds of three students returning to their seats, he talked about the poem.

"The witches in this scene are not just witches. They represent the presence of pure evil in the world, and their purpose in the play is to inveigle or charm their way into Macbeth's mind, to plant the seeds of his undoing. In fact, their intent is to feed this poisonous brew to the unsuspecting Macbeth. It's easy to recite this poem in a silly way."

Marshall repeated the lines I'd just heard the students chant, giving the couplets an even greater sing-song effect than the three teens had. I heard laughter from the class.

"You won't see this kind of verse anywhere else in Shakespeare's works," Marshall told them. "The device he's employing here is intended to set the witches' voices distinctly apart from that of the humans in the story. These verses, done right, will have a kind of mesmerizing effect on the audience. Almost hypnotic. And once the trance is in place, the evil that the witches represent can get you to do its bidding."

There was a pause, I assumed to let what Marshall had just said sink in to distracted teenage brains. Then, "Jonathan? You're First Witch. Eva? Second. Jimmy? Third. You're up." He waited through the sounds of the three students moving to the front. "Start at the beginning of the scene. See if you can convince everyone here that they must do whatever you want them to."

His voice a harsh whisper, Marshall read the stage direction: "Scene One. A cavern. In the middle, a boiling cauldron." After a short pause: "Thunder. Enter the three Witches."

This time, the students read their lines with a quiet intensity that raised the hairs on the back of my neck. I wasn't sure whether I was more impressed with Marshall's stage direction, with the way the students interpreted that, or with the fact that Marshall was not limiting his role assignments to girls.

I'd heard enough to get a sense of Marshall, and I didn't want to interfere with his class. I went outside, back into the pale sunshine of the September afternoon, and sat on a bench to wait for school to be over, about twenty minutes from now. I tried to focus my thoughts on the students, on the seasonally cooling rays of the sun, on the spots of color on distant hills, even on the ants at my feet—anything to keep from making the connection my mind wanted to make.

Donald.

I hadn't seen the man in three years. Why couldn't I get him out of my head? I'd had a few relationships since then, but they didn't haunt me.

Donald had been an actor when I'd met him. Maybe he'd be an actor again, now that he was out of that cult. And, all right, Marshall wasn't one of the actors in the scenes I'd just over-heard, but the direction he gave his students told me he knew a little something about the craft. And I had to put all that aside. I had to be open to who he was as a person, and to who he was as a lay minister in the parish that was now my responsibility.

The sound of the school bell signaling the end of classes for the day brought me to attention. Unsure of how quickly Marshall would leave, and equally unsure of whether there was another door he might exit through, I moved to where I could see his car. I didn't have long to wait.

Walking beside him was a female student, perhaps someone from his last class. She talked excitedly, nearly skipping along, and I wondered if she had a crush on her teacher.

I walked toward the car, my pace leisurely. Marshall gazed forward, keeping his replies to the girl minimal, until they reached his car. As he turned to bid her farewell, he saw me and froze. The girl turned to watch me as well, and I decided to take advantage of this opportunity.

I smiled. "Mr. Savage. Glad I caught you." I turned my smile toward the girl and held my right hand out. "Hello. I'm Reverend Hill, from the Unitarian Universalist church here in Assisi." She gave me her hand but said nothing. "And who might you be?"

"Darla."

So she was one of the actors from that class. "Glad to meet you, Darla. Your last name?"

"Willis. And we're Catholic."

"I'm sure you're enjoying Mr. Savage's class. And I'm not trying to evangelize you, though of course you'd be welcome." I looked at Marshall. "I was hoping for a moment of your time."

Marshall dismissed Darla with a nod, saying, "See you next week, Darla. Good work today."

She walked away, throwing a couple of glances over her shoulder at us.

Marshall positioned a canvas bag in front of him, arms pressing it against his body as though he wanted to create a barrier between us.

I kept my tone as even as possible. "I wasn't sure whether you'd received my voicemails, and I was at this end of town, so I thought I might run into you."

"Oh yes?" His voice implied skepticism.

"I've met with the other three lay ministers, and I wanted to set up a time when you and I could talk about your work in the parish. I was impressed at the way you were with CC, by the way." I was tempted to say more, but I wanted Marshall to talk.

"Is that necessary?"

"Sorry? Is what necessary?"

"Do we need to meet?"

Puzzled by his reluctance, I asked, "Is there some reason you'd rather not?"

He let out a breath through his nose and gazed into the distance as though searching for words. Again, although tempted to speak, I waited.

Finally, "Very well. Is now good?"

"It is. Shall we go someplace and have coffee?"

He opened his car door, tossed the bag into the back seat, and locked the car. "Let's walk instead." Without waiting for assent from me, he turned and headed toward a row of trees across the parking lot. I followed, still puzzled by his attitude.

The trees lined a dirt path, tangled bushes and tall, brown grasses on the other side of it. Marshall walked quickly, and I was glad of my long legs.

"What do you want to know?" His voice held an edge—more irritated than angry, but I didn't like it. I stopped walking and waited for him to do the same. He turned toward me, perhaps seven feet away, impatience on his face.

"First, I'd love to know why you seem so reluctant to talk to me."

He half shrugged, lifted his arms out to his sides and dropped them, and shook his head like he didn't know what I was talking about.

"Marshall, I left two messages for you. You ignored them. Now we have a chance to talk, and you act as though it's an imposition. Why?"

"Maybe I don't want to have to account for myself."

I moved forward, closing half the distance between us. "Okay, well, for one thing, that's not what I'm asking you to do. Not right now. And for another, we all have to account to someone or something. None of us exists in a vacuum. As a lay minister, you do—at least to some extent—need to account for yourself to the leader of your congregation. That would be me." Then it hit me. "Is that it? You object to me?"

He closed his eyes briefly, and his shoulders appeared to slump. "Not exactly."

There was nothing I could do with that. I ignored it and said, "Let's just walk—no, let's *stroll* along this path and talk about life, the universe, and everything."

I saw a spark of recognition on Marshall's face. "Forty-two?"

I laughed. Referring to *The Hitchhiker's Guide to the Galaxy* by Douglas Adams, I said, "Yes. That's the answer. But that's the easy part, right?"

He smiled. He actually smiled, and it changed his whole face. He looked like a sweet young boy. "The hard part is knowing what the question is. And it isn't just what's six times seven." He tilted his head slightly, and with a tease in his voice asked, "Do you have your towel?"

"And my babel fish."

I moved forward, setting an easy walking pace, and Marshall fell in with me. He said, "Just don't recite any Vogon poetry to me."

"Promise."

We talked very little about the church, and not much more about his role as a lay minister. And in truth, for the time being I didn't need to know much more than how he had seemed to me at the Chisholms' on Tuesday evening. At some point I wanted to explore ideas about involving some of our younger church members, but this wasn't the day for that. But we talked and talked, and we walked for much longer than I'd expected to. What really got things going was when I asked about Angus.

"I grew up in Montana," he opened. "My dad was a forest ranger. Mom taught school. Third and fourth grades, together in the same classroom. Small community." He chuckled humorlessly before going on.

"I got Angus when I was seven. He was a mutt, the kind of dog that's adorable as a puppy and unidentifiable once he's grown. His fur was longer than Troy's, dark with light brown highlights, if you can picture that."

"I can. Sounds like maybe he had some German shepherd?"

"Maybe. He was about that size. We used to walk together in the woods. I cherished those times, alone with him. And then Dad decided we should take him fishing with us." He hesitated, and then added, "At first I didn't want to. But it turned out okay. In fact, those were about the only good times with my dad."

"Why do you say that?"

"He didn't abuse me, or anything. But—I guess I was just never masculine enough for him."

I was tempted to say something about my own orientation in the hopes that it would make Marshall feel he could say whatever he wanted to, but I couldn't think of a good way to do that without appearing to make an assumption.

About five paces later, he said, "You know I'm gay, right?" "I do now. You know I'm gay, right?"

"Yeah. Anyway, when I came out to my parents, I was fifteen. They, uh, they did not take it well. Dad said something about how he thought he was raising a man. They sent me to this camp."

Camp. I shuddered internally. "Religious?"

"Assembly of God."

I did shudder then, involuntarily, and hoped he didn't see. My knowledge about that denomination was limited, but I knew that it was very strict. Life must be lived without sin, or serious atonement was necessary. The resurrection was considered to be physical, and the return of Jesus would be physical as well; he would appear in person. They didn't shun medicine, but they believed in divine healing. And, certainly, one of the sins that must be avoided at all costs would be that of homosexuality.

All I said was, "Oh, my."

"Yeah. The camp was horrible. I won't go into it."

He seemed to need some breathing space, so I waited for him to speak again.

"Anyway, Angus was really my dog. But I couldn't take him to the camp. And like I told CC...." He paused here, and his voice sounded strained when he continued. "My dad took Angus hiking with him while I was still in that prison, and they ran into a brown bear."

Another pause, and into it I said, "Didn't you tell CC it was a grizzly?"

Marshall's voice took on a peculiar tone. "Well, slap my mouth and shame on me."

"What?"

"Sorry. I reverted to childhood for a second there. You're right, and my father the forest ranger would be horrified. The general brown bear species is Ursus arctos. The grizzly, Ursus arctos horribilis, is a subspecies. So it's a kind of brown bear. Grizzlies are somewhat smaller than the true brown, which lives on the coast and eats lots of fat-rich salmon. In the forest, grizzlies have a more limited diet. And they tend to have lighter-colored fur. They also tend to have a less pleasant character, probably because their food sources are more scarce. But," and here Marshall took a deep breath, "I advise you to stay away from all of them."

Nervous all of a sudden, I looked around for bears, hoping Marshall wouldn't notice. "Good advice. Are there any around here?"

"No. In Vermont, it's the black bear you need to avoid."

I waited for Marshall to return to the story about Angus, but he didn't. Perhaps he felt I knew enough already, based on what he'd told CC. Over the sounds of our shoes crunching on the dirt as we walked, I filled in the gaps mentally. Gap, really. While Marshall had been experiencing the hell of a conversion therapy camp, his beloved dog died attempting to protect the man who'd sent Marshall away. I gathered that the man had survived.

Marshall stopped walking rather suddenly. He seemed to have pulled into himself somehow. "I need to go back now." There was a pleading look on his face.

"I think I'll walk a little farther," I told him. "See you Sunday."

Marshall turned and walked back the way we'd come, head down, his pace so fast I would have been hard-pressed to keep up with him.

I watched him for about a minute, thinking about what he'd told me, realizing that he hadn't asked anything about me. No problem, I thought; that wasn't why I'd sought him out. And maybe he would have, if something hadn't overcome him.

I didn't really want to walk any farther along this path, but I went on for another five minutes or so, in case Marshall looked back. And on my return walk to the school, I couldn't help chuckling over the fact that what had allowed Marshall to relax a little and talk to me was a shared enjoyment of that superficially silly, absurdly witty, secretly deep, and almost troubling series of books by Douglas Adams.

One scene that had created a special place for itself in my brain was in the second book of the series, *The Restaurant At The End Of The Universe*. Arthur Dent (essentially the protagonist) is about to order a meal. He decides he wants steak. So the staff wheels out a cart with a live cow on it, a cow that can speak. It asks Arthur which part of itself he would most enjoy, praising the various characteristics of different cuts. Arthur is horrified. I can't recall now whether it was the cow, or Arthur's companion Ford Prefect, or someone else who said something along the lines of, "So you want meat from a cow only if it doesn't want you to eat it?"

CHAPTER 5

Saturday I went for a hike. Well, that is, a walk in the woods. Talking with Vanessa on the phone Friday evening to ask about trails, she suggested that I start with a walking trail rather than with something she referred to as hiking, which I gathered involved scaling heights on trails that could be at least a little dangerous for someone who didn't know what they were doing. I definitely did not know what I was doing. So Vanessa directed me to a five-mile loop through the woods to the east of town.

"When you get to a pond, McGowan Pond, the trail goes all the way around and then feeds back onto itself. You come back the way you went in."

Sounded simple enough. Then she added, "If you think you'd like to do something more adventurous in the future, you should get yourself some decent boots. You can walk the pond trail in sneakers, but they wouldn't do for a real hike. And you'll need…. Never mind. If you decide to do more rugged trails, let me know and I'll help you figure out what you'll need."

I set out Saturday just after noon, having reached a kind of writing block on my sermon for Sunday. It was entirely possible that doing something I'd never done, being in nature, clearing my mind, would help clear the block. Deena had been very stern with me Friday, because I couldn't give her a sermon theme, and she abhorred typing simply, "Sermon by The Reverend Spencer Hill." I promised to do better, knowing there would probably be more scoldings from Deena in future.

The trail, as Vanessa had promised, was easy, mostly flat, and very lovely. Fairly narrow, it led north through the woods, with rocks and tree roots making me glance down frequently to avoid tripping. The air was chilly, but through the leaves that remained on the trees the sun felt warm. I stopped many times so I could raise my eyes to the clear blue sky, and the brilliance of the leaves—deep orange, brilliant red, luminescent yellow—fairly lifted me off the ground. My breathing felt deep and nourishing, and my mind felt open to whatever I encountered.

Except bears. I didn't want to encounter any bears.

I heard water before I saw the pond. Beside the trail, a sparking brook, or stream—no more than a foot across—bubbled its way over pebbles and colorful fallen leaves, flowing away from where the pond would likely be. I stood watching the water, nearly invisible in its clarity, letting it carry away any and all thoughts that might be bouncing around in my brain.

I no longer saw God, thought of God, or communicated with God the way I had when I was in the Episcopal Church. These days, rather than seeing God as something apart from me, I saw myself as a part of God. This change in perspective also changed the way I communicated with God. I used words seldom, now. I relied more on the kind of feeling that comes from loving connection—a connection that linked not only people with God, but all of creation with God. So, in a way, that bubbling stream was communication. I was connected to it in ways not limited to physicality. The stream and I were both part of Creation.

Maybe five minutes went by. Maybe it was fifteen. It didn't matter. When I moved forward again, in the direction the stream was coming from, my steps were small and light, even tender. I approached the pond slowly, quietly, in almost a dream-like state, stunned by sparking light and by sun on the water, coming to me through the trees. And then I stopped suddenly.

I caught sight of a figure moving through the trees, maybe two hundred feet to my right, approaching the pond from the east. It was a young man.

He was naked.

I positioned myself off to the side of the trail, stepping as quietly as possible behind a wide pine tree. It wasn't that I wanted to spy on this man. For a reason I couldn't have described, I didn't want him to see me. I didn't want to call attention to myself. I didn't yet know whether an encounter would enhance or diminish this soul-fulfilling feeling that had come over me on the trail.

Oh hell. Of course I wanted to watch him.

He approached a small opening at the pond's edge, his left side toward me, and began what looked like a slow dance. Arms straight up, fingers and eyes to the sky, he began to sway. As his lithe body moved from side to side, his arms seemed to flow rather than bend in achingly graceful arcs. Slowly at first, he bent his body left, then right, then left, eyes closed, his face nearly glowing in a kind of rapture.

With a movement that was somehow both graceful and abrupt, he bent sideways and down in an arc and swept the ground with his fingers, straightened again, fingers sweeping the sky, and back down in the other direction in a repeat of a motion worthy of a trained ballet dancer. He repeated these body arcs a few times and then stood still, arms extended toward the water, fingers held gently apart as if embracing something or someone.

Nearly a statue, he stood like that for several seconds, giving me a chance to take in the full effect of his beauty. He was slender, not skinny, and when he moved there was just enough muscle definition to be masculine. His skin looked tanned, but I saw no tan lines. His auburn hair hung in slight waves down his back and below his waist, stopping just above where the inward curve in the small of his back curled out again in the painfully sweet sweep of his ass.

My breathing quickened, no longer that deep, nourishing flow, and then he moved again. First one arm and then the other pulled in toward his chest and out to the sides, and he began to twirl and fling his arms. He lowered his ass almost to the ground and up, head forward and then back, until I could no longer follow his motions. It was almost like watching a whirling dervish. As his body flung itself one way and another, I could see his erection, stiff and dark, the shaft firmly rooted and emerging from a rich nest of dark curls, the moist tip extending energetically from the envelope of skin that no one had cut from him.

Suddenly he stood straight, then bent back slightly, arms stiff and tense, fists clenched hard. His mouth opened wide, his throat tensed and his Adams apple rose, but no sound came forth. From his penis came a milky stream that arched slightly away from him. His penis pulsated once or twice, and then he collapsed onto the ground, knees on the dirt, elbows near his knees, head on his hands. I watched as his chest heaved, taking in deep, lungs-full of the sweet air.

Oh, how I wished I could bring myself to do as he'd done! How I wanted to strip as naked as he had, to fling my body with abandon, exposing all of myself to what was purely natural. And, to be honest, how I wanted to mix the creamy milk of my own manhood with the arc of his. The urge to free my own penis was almost irresistible. I closed my eyes and clung tightly to the pine tree, sap helping to hold my fingers to the bark and away from myself.

By the time I had recovered enough to relax a little, to open my eyes again, this wood sprite, this dryad, this… this Puck had begun dressing. I hadn't seen where he had left his clothes, but there he was in what seemed to be a long, dark brown, leather skirt. Ragged slits in the leather, at irregular intervals, started at the hem and went up to the middle of his thighs. There was a wide band of leather, which he fastened around his hips, far enough below his navel to reveal the beginnings of the inguinal ligament, that line that starts near the hip bones and leads diagonally down toward the genitals. He wrapped a thin, leather thong around the center of this band and fixed it into a metal ring so that a single, long, thread of leather dangled down the front of the skirt.

As he started to walk away, he wrapped another string of leather around his hair behind him, creating a ponytail that swayed and brushed his back as he moved, silently, but not seeming to make any effort to be quiet, through the trees, going back the way he had come.

I don't know how long I sat at the base of that pine tree, arms around my knees, mindlessly watching ants in their busy preparations for the change of season, listening to the scurrying of wood mice and other tiny creatures as they gathered food to store away against the coming of winter. Bouncing around in my head, unanswered, was the question: "Who *was* that?" I'd encountered no one remotely like him here, and yet there was something so primal, so unpretentiously natural about him that he seemed more at home here than anyone I *had* encountered. More at home than I would ever be. Anywhere.

By the time I stood, the sun was low in the sky and my muscles ached with the chill. I decided to save the part of the trail that went around the pond for another day, and I headed back, my steps slow and a little heavy. Or perhaps it was just that my thoughts were coming thick and fast.

At first they were productive. They gave me a theme for my sermon, about how different perspectives, different ways of being, different ways of reacting to the same vista and following different muses came together to weave the intricate tapestry that was Creation, with each thread following its own path but weaving together with the others to make a whole that is perfect in its imperfection.

So that was good.

But then there was the ache. The pain, even, of wanting. The dryad had awakened in me something I hadn't felt since Donald and I had been together. It was something that had been missing from the relationships I'd had, from the men I had known, since I'd lost Donald.

Fucking was marvelous. Having sex with someone you care for was fantastic. But even as I had enjoyed those interim (which is how I viewed them) couplings and relationships, I'd known there was a whole dimension missing. The dryad, in his utter abandon and magnificent disregard for propriety, had seemed invulnerable to shame. As much as I had allowed myself to believe I had left behind me the shame that scripture had led me to think was my due as a gay man, I knew there remained vestiges of it, dragging at my feet, ready to climb up my legs and wrap themselves around my groin and my heart if given the tiniest opening.

But aside from the shame, aside from the physical pleasure of sex, was the feeling I'd had when I'd been with Donald. If Creation was a tapestry, then he and I had been two separate threads who'd found each other in the warp and the woof, and we had woven our threads around each other in beautiful unity. And it had come to a screeching halt when the thread that was Donald had bumped into something, a slub of wool perhaps, that had sent him in a different direction, a direction I couldn't follow, a direction I knew would make the beauty of his thread fade, drain it of color, render it leaden.

Ruth had essentially rescued her brother. I hadn't spoken with him since he'd been swallowed by the cult, but I was in touch with Ruth fairly often. The way she spoke of Donald gave me an image of a man, once vibrant and mercurial, now lack-luster and maybe even sluggish. I didn't want to see him. The alteration he had undergone, the clash between how I'd known him and how I thought of him now, would have been jarring enough to be painful. And I felt it would be a pain that would transfer to him when he saw my reaction to what he had become.

CHAPTER 6

My sermon the next day was inspired. From what I could tell of the congregation's reaction, anyone who'd had doubts last week was at least almost ready to let go of them. I saw Vanessa wiping away tears, and she wasn't alone. Abby and Walter Chisholm hugged me afterward, though CC hung onto Marshall.

Loraine, bless her heart, praised the subject from her own perspective. "What a beautiful way to get people to see how we," by which I knew she meant homosexuals, "are woven into the world with everyone else." I smiled. Hadn't I just described the beauty of Creation's tapestry as including all perspectives? So, hers was in there, too.

It was late in the afternoon before I could retire to the quiet of my little house, where I was still finding white dog hair in places. My answering machine was blinking, and one of the messages was from Ruth.

"Spencer? I waited until I thought services would be over, but I suppose you're in great demand in your new congregation, so I missed you. Anyway, please call back before ten tonight, if you can. I have news! It's about me, not Donald. He's doing fine, though. Okay? Talk later. Hugs!"

I was due to have dinner with Andrea and Jacob Beale and their teenage son Duncan, but I didn't need to be there until six. So I called Ruth.

"Ready for your news, Ruth," I told her. "It sounded like it might be good."

"Well, I think so." Her voice seemed to hide an excitement she was trying to hang onto by not letting all of it out at once. "I'm engaged."

A warm delight started somewhere in my chest and spread up to my eyes, which watered slightly. "Oh, Ruth. That's wonderful! Do I know him?"

"You do. Nelson Carroll."

"Really? Donald's deprogrammer? I really like him." And I did. I'd met him during my second year at seminary, and his approach to Donald—gentle, persistent, loving—had impressed me. Moreover, it had worked, at least as well as it probably could have.

"I thought so. And I'm so glad! Your opinion is very important to me."

"I feel the same about yours, Ruth. It seems to me that you two are very well suited. Is he joining the UU church?"

"Oh, that happened two years ago. That's where we'll be married. And—" The pause seemed awkward.

"What?"

"Oh, Spencer, I wish you could marry us, but we're close with Reverend Elaine."

Dr. Elaine Stein. I knew her well. When I'd decided to leave the Episcopal Church and become a UU minister, I'd talked with her many times. Her brilliant mind and her open heart had helped make my decision easy.

"Oh, Ruth, of course she must do it. I'm not the least bit slighted. But I do insist on an invitation."

She laughed, an excited, musical note in it. "Of course you have to be there."

"Do you have a date yet?"

"We do. It's in two weeks. There didn't seem to be any point in putting things off."

Two weeks. I wasn't sanguine about getting away from my new parish that quickly.

Ruth must have sensed my hesitation. "Don't worry. It's on October first, a Thursday, so I'll bet you won't have a problem getting away. There won't be very many people there, but Nelson and I would love it if you could join Reverend Elaine at the altar and bless the marriage."

"Absolutely. I'll let people here know right away."

After we ended the call, it occurred to me that while I was in New York, I'd like to go to my storage unit and bring a few more things back with me.

And then it occurred to me that Donald would be at the ceremony.

Duncan Beale hadn't attended my welcome party or either of the services since I'd arrived, so I hadn't met him. Given how small Assisi was, I was fairly sure he'd be in Marshall's English class, but I knew nothing else about him. Within a few minutes of my arrival at the Beales', however, I began to suspect that hospitality was not the only motivation for inviting me.

If my fifteen-year-old self had met Duncan, I'm not sure either of us would have recognized the other as belonging to the same species. His hair was the first thing I noticed: dyed black, about four or five inches long all over and extending away from his scalp in all directions, no doubt with the help of the major portion of a can of hair spray. His eyes were rimmed with black, and from one pierced earlobe hung a silver chain with a tiny human skull, also silver. Around his neck he had wound a long, black leather strand several times, and threaded onto one of the loops in the front was a small, silver item made to resemble the skeleton of a human hand. He wore a light grey sweatshirt with the Hard Rock Cafe logo in black on the front. The arms of the sweatshirt looked not so much cut off as gnawed, a few inches below the shoulder. Under that he wore the ubiquitous jeans, scuffed and torn in places.

As for me, I now wore my very dark brown hair longer than I had in the past. It flowed smoothly from a part over my left eye, just long enough to cover half of my ears, long enough in back to reach a shirt collar. I had on a dark brown turtleneck knitted into a ribbed pattern, and darker brown slacks—pretty standard for the late nineteen-eighties. So while I don't think most people at that time would have seen my appearance as square, or rigid, no doubt Duncan thought even worse thoughts.

I held my hand toward him, not knowing whether he'd bite it. He ignored it and threw himself onto one end of a beige couch.

"Don't mind Duncan," Andrea told me. "He's sulking because we've told him he has to sit at the table like a human being for dinner tonight."

Duncan's interpretation was different. "Usually they just throw road kill over the fence into my pen." His voice broke a few times, and I remembered how embarrassing that could be.

Uncharitably, I thought a fenced pen might be a better way to handle him while I was here.

But Duncan did as he was told by his father, whose stern tone brooked no argument. Duncan made his displeasure known through his hunched posture and lack of conversation. At one point I attempted to engage him.

"Are you in Mr. Savage's English class, Duncan?"

He looked at me without raising his head, his startling blue eyes peering at me from under his dark eyebrows. "Who wants to know?"

Andrea was not pleased with his response. "Duncan!"

51

I didn't take my eyes from his, though I did my best to appear casual. "I believe he has you working on Macbeth. Have you had a chance to read any of the parts in class?"

Duncan made a scoffing sound by way of answer.

Jacob was not amused. "Duncan, answer the man. It's a simple enough question."

Duncan's eyes flitted from me to his father to me again. "Once. It was lame." Now his eyes dropped to his plate.

I wasn't letting go that easily. "Lame? Do you mean the play? The part he gave you? Or your delivery?"

Duncan sat up enough to let his back hit the back of his chair. "What's the diff, man? Why should I have to study that sh—that stuff, anyway?"

"Seems to me you're making a study of it already. Shakespeare wrote a few very colorful characters into his works. You appear to have a flair for the dramatic, yourself."

Over Andrea's smothered laugh, Duncan said, "What's that supposed to mean?"

I shrugged as though it mattered not at all to me. "I think you put a lot of thought into your look. You've made an effort to be different from most people around you. That hairdo, for instance—"

"It ain't no 'hairdo.'"

"What is it, then?"

"Style, man. Something you obviously don't have."

I motioned with my hand when Jacob looked like he was about to intervene. I wanted to see where Duncan would take me, how he would react to my response.

"Style is a generic term. As long as someone's stylistic choices are deliberate and congruous, they can be said to be a style. Now, I grant you that my style and yours are not the same. But while your style might reasonably be said to require a lot more time and attention, my choices are within the definition of style. My look is as deliberate as yours."

Silence. So I added, "What do you think your style says to people who see you?"

Very slightly, Duncan extended the middle finger of his right hand in my direction. I don't know whether his parents saw that gesture, but I laughed. "I see. I suppose that works some of the time."

I turned to Andrea and complimented her part in that day's service, essentially dismissing Duncan. It was a bit of a risk, but I didn't see another way to deal with the surly youth. I wasn't about to criticize him. If possible I wanted him to think. And I wanted him to know he hadn't put me off. If he wanted to offend or otherwise intimidate the new pastor, he was going to have to try a lot harder than that.

I must have had some effect. Because as I approached my Jeep after thanking the Beales and saying goodnight, I saw that Duncan was leaning against the driver's side door.

"You don't scare me," he told me.

"I'm glad. I didn't intend to." He didn't move, so I chuckled. "You don't scare me, either."

"No?"

"Duncan, I grew up in New York City. I've seen people who look a lot scarier than you. I've been in the wild and crazy crowd outside the Eighth Street Playhouse, waiting for the midnight showing of *The Rocky Horror Picture Show*. If you don't know what that is...." I shrugged as though he ought to, even though I suspected he probably didn't. "Now, I wouldn't call your look tame, but I also wouldn't call it scary."

I extended my key toward the door lock, unlocked the door, and pulled it slightly to move Duncan away a little. I grinned at him. "I can't wait to see what you wear for Halloween."

~

Monday morning I called Vanessa and asked if I could invite her and Klondike for afternoon tea. She was delighted. I was both nervous and happy, not only to have company, but also to make her feel welcome in what used to be her home.

While Ruth had lived with me, her first months in the city, she had taught me to cook. At least, she'd taught me more than I'd known at that point, which wasn't much. Now I knew enough to keep myself fed with a reasonable amount of variety. So when Vanessa arrived, the house still smelled of freshly-baked peanut butter cookies. I had even bought dog biscuits for Klondike.

"Peanut butter? How wonderful! One of my favorite cookies," she said as she entered the kitchen.

We sat at the breakfast nook while Klondike, off in a corner and having wolfed down his biscuits, chewed happily on a toy Vanessa had brought with her. The maple tree outside, now almost devoid of colorful leaves, let in soft afternoon sunlight.

"How very Norman Rockwell!" Vanessa laughed. "It seems as if you've made yourself at home here."

"I have. Yes. I imagine you were quite happy here."

She nodded as she swallowed a mouthful of cookie. "I also love where I am, though, so I hope you don't feel as though you've usurped my space."

"Thanks. Glad to know that."

We chatted about a few parish-related things, and then I moved on to the topic that had made me want to talk with Vanessa.

"That was a lovely walk you sent me on. I spent quite a bit of time there in contemplation."

"Isn't it gorgeous? Especially this time of year. Are you ready for something a little more adventurous?"

"I might be."

We talked for a while about what that would mean, what gear I'd need as a beginner and where to get it, and what nearby trails

I might start with. Then I turned the conversation back to my pond walk.

"While I was there, someone else approached the water. He didn't see me, as far as I could tell. It wasn't anyone I've seen here in Assisi so far."

"Oh? Can you describe him?"

"I'll do my best. First, he must have undressed out of my sight, because when he approached the edge of the pond, he was naked. Maybe in his mid-twenties? Long auburn hair." I stopped. Vanessa was nodding.

"Sky clad."

"I beg your pardon? Is that his name?"

She laughed. "No. It means he was naked. I think that must have been Adam Cooper. He belongs to a community calling themselves Forest Dwellers. They have a kind of compound east of here, which they refer to as The Forest."

"Forest Dwellers," I echoed. "That might explain the clothing he put on before he left. There was a lot of brown, a kind of—I don't know, almost a skirt, really, and strips of leather."

Vanessa nodded again. "Yes, that would have been someone of The Forest. And, as I said, probably Adam."

"Interesting. How is it you come to know them?"

She shrugged. "I've tried to interest a few of them in our church, if only in terms of opening interesting discussions, maybe even an occasional exchange of attendance. They know we're open to Pagans, and I'm very interested in their practices. But it seems they prefer to worship in their own way."

"So they're Pagans? Does anyone at church identify as Pagan?"

"I don't know whether you've met Roberta and Shane MacPherson. They're in their nineties now. They moved into town about eight years ago. Living out there in the community got to be too much for them. They come most Sundays, but they also attend some ceremonies in The Forest."

"I don't recall meeting them."

"They've been in church for both your sermons, but they pretty much keep to themselves. I'm sure they wouldn't mind if you reached out to them, though. They're quite friendly and welcoming."

"I think I'll do that. I'd like to know more about the Forest Dwellers." I also wanted to know more about Adam, but that wasn't something I was willing to say aloud.

"One thing you should know. If you have occasion to write the words Pagan or Paganism, be sure to capitalize them. To these folks, it's a religion with as much integrity as any other, even though there's no real organization, nothing institutionalized. I kind of agree with them. I mean, we capitalize organized religions. Judaism, Christianity, Islam, Buddhism, etc. You get the picture."

"I do. And I'm happy to offer them that respect."

I told Vanessa about my intended foray into Manhattan for Ruth's wedding.

"Oh," she said, "silly me. I meant to let you know that if you need to be away on a weekend, I'm ready and willing to step into the breach. I'd just need enough notice to brush up on one of the sermons I have ready in case of need."

"That's very generous of you. For this trip, I'm hoping to be back no later than Saturday."

"Just announce it this coming Sunday, and add that I'm available during your absence." She thanked me for tea, headed for the door, and turned just before stepping out. "One more thing, Spencer. I strongly advise you not to go to The Forest on your own."

"On my own?"

"Without an invitation. If you can even get one."

"Oh? Why not?"

"They're.... Let's just say they value their privacy."

"You mean, like being sky clad?"

Her smile was enigmatic. "Among other things." And she was gone.

I felt like the Adam in Eden being told I could have any thing but one, which of course made me focus on that one thing. I needed —wanted, at least—to procure an invitation to The Forest. Perhaps the MacPhersons could help me with that.

So Tuesday I looked up their telephone number, but when I called, no one answered, and no answering machine picked up. I decided to drive by their house.

Their address was barely within town limits. The mailbox, at the intersection of the main road and a long, curved, dirt drive-way, had the letters "MacP" on it. A rough-hewn log cabin stood well back from the road in a small clearing, various kinds of trees everywhere else. There was a sheltered spot for a car on the side of the cabin, but there was no vehicle that I could see. It seemed unlikely that an elderly couple would be able to get around this rural community without a car, and although it was possible that one of them might be at home, I decided to wait until I could contact them by phone rather than just appear on their doorstep.

After another couple of stops to visit a few parishioners, I went home and called Vanessa.

"I drove past the MacPherson's today. Looks like no one is there."

"Oh, no. They won't be there until, probably, Thursday."

"Vacation?"

"They'll be at The Forest for Mabon celebrations."

It was not a term I'd ever heard before. "For what, now?"

"Mabon. The harvest celebration. Honestly, Spencer, I don't know a lot about it. I think the library might help, if you want to know more."

I was getting the sense that I really did need to know more about the people in The Forest. Even Vanessa, who claimed not to know much, knew that the MacPhersons would be at a Pagan celebration I'd never heard of.

My next outing was the town library. It was not a large library; after all, Assisi was not a large town. I recognized the librarian, a woman apparently in her sixties, short and slender and bird-like in a charming way. "Hello, Mrs. Holland."

"Reverend! How nice to see you here."

"Thanks. Thought I'd kill two birds with one stone, as it were. If you have time to give me a short tour, I'd love that. And I also have a research project."

She laughed and waved her arm around slowly. "It won't take long."

On my tour, I noticed there were only two other people there, in the periodicals section. I recognized one elderly man, but I didn't interrupt him. When Mrs. Holland spoke, it was in what she called her "library voice."

Tour completed, Mrs. Holland asked, "What's your research project? May I help?"

"I'd like that, yes. I have two, actually. One is to find out more about the history of Assisi. The other concerns a Pagan harvest celebration called Mabon."

She walked me back first to the history section and pulled out one book very quickly. "This is the most inclusive. There are a few other books with references to Assisi, but I'd start here."

We moved to the social sciences section and, after a moment or two of thought, she pulled out two books. "You can check all these books out or read them here. I think they'll be very useful."

Back at the front desk, we went about the process of setting me up with a library card.

"Mrs. Holland, is there a reason why these two books aren't shelved in a section on religion?"

She looked up from her administrative task. "We follow the Dewey Decimal system."

"I believe there's a category for religious works, no?"

"Well, yes."

"Isn't there a subsection for Paganism?"

Her lips seemed to purse slightly. "As I've mentioned, this is a small library. These two books cover several unusual religious practices, but they're not particularly about religion, per se."

I think it was at this point that I noticed a hand-written sign, white paper with thick, black lettering, that read, "It's been three days since a librarian has bitten someone."

Mrs. Holland's expression changed, and she looked thoughtful for a few seconds. "Wait here."

She returned with another book. "In here you'll find some information about the religions history of Vermont. I don't know if that will help you in your project, but I daresay you'll find it interesting."

CHAPTER 7

The library books I'd taken out were eye-opening. Maybe even eye-popping. Apparently the area had quite the history around religious practices.

It seems that at one time Vermont was a hotbed of religious movements. Joseph Smith, who would eventually found the Mormon tradition, was born in Vermont, though his father moved the family to New York State before Smith was visited by… well, by whatever visited him.

In the mid-nineteenth century a man named John Humphrey Noyes started something called Perfectionism, or Bible Communism, where followers shared everything—including each other, evidently, and all men were married to all women, and vice versa. His group in Putney got into trouble when he declared that Jesus had returned to earth and was part of his community, and he and his staunchest followers moved to New York State.

I can't imagine what it was about Vermont that it spawned not only these two movements but also a few others, and it's a little mystifying how both Smith and Noyes ended up about a hundred miles apart in New York.

But the part of this history that interested me the most was that when the Perfectionist community undertook the exodus to New York State, a splinter group traveled north instead, eventually running across a seemingly unrelated community and settling down with them. The group the Perfectionists merged with had been formed almost by accident in the late seventeenth century. It was composed mostly of women from all over New England who had been tried and acquitted of witchcraft. It seems being acquitted was not enough to remove the stain on these women's reputations, and persecution of various kinds persisted.

At first the community outside of what is now Assisi consisted of about five women and two sympathetic men. They had gone as far away from populated areas as they could, short of crossing into Canada, to get away from anyone who knew them. But word seems to have spread, because over time other women and some men who had either been accused of witchcraft, or who knew they were about to be accused, found their way north. At about the same time as the Civil War, the renegade Perfectionists—not the ones who said Jesus was one of their group—joined up with the descendants of the original refugees.

I had to speculate that members of this merged community were the predecessors of the group now known as Forest Dwellers. My library books about Vermont talked only about English settlers who seem to have followed or founded some flavor of Christianity. So the Forest Dwellers remained a mystery to me.

Meanwhile, the two books Mrs. Holland had selected for Paganism information were equally mysterious. From what I could tell, the lack of organization and hierarchy in Pagan traditions meant that—well, that almost anything goes, even beyond the latitude within the UU tradition.

Some Pagans tended to hold to one of many sets of ancient tribal beliefs and practices, while others were much more free-form. Some Pagans belonged to groups or communities, while others more or less practiced on their own. I couldn't quite tell whether the term Pagan would include witches, or if Wicca was considered a separate belief system from Paganism. And then there were those who adhered to Druidism.

It made my head spin. Coming from the fairly regimented tradition of the Episcopal Church (which has its roots in Catholicism), and despite having migrated over to the much more open and varied tradition of Unitarian Universalism, the apparently wide-open landscape of Paganism confounded me. I decided to put off my visit to the MacPhersons until after Ruth's wedding.

Whenever I'd asked Ruth how Donald was doing, her responses had always left me with the impression that there were things she didn't want to say. I met one of those reasons at her wedding.

Although I was looking forward to the event, to seeing Ruth and Nelson and talking with Elaine Stein, knowing that Donald was sure to be there ate uncomfortably around the edges of my anticipation. It wasn't that I didn't want to see him. It was that I didn't know who he was now. And, of course, it was also that I still had pretty strong feelings about who he had been.

I chose a hotel on Madison Avenue not far from Ruth's church. I still had the wealth I'd inherited from my parents, which had increased after I'd sold the Gramercy Park townhouse where I'd grown up. So although my hotel was not the most luxurious I could have chosen, it was very nice; I still enjoyed the creature comforts money could buy.

Ruth had said it would be a small ceremony, and in fact there was nothing like a rehearsal dinner. So Wednesday evening I had dinner with Ruth and Nelson. She had invited me to their apartment, but I figured they had enough to do getting everything ready, so I countered with an invitation to dine at my hotel's restaurant at my expense, and they accepted.

I'd forgotten how attractive Nelson was. His Nordic coloring, from the light blond hair to the icy blue eyes to the broad shoulders, had always appealed powerfully to me. If he'd been gay, I would have been in trouble. And I couldn't help wondering whether his looks had helped him to work his way into Donald's life, which might have made extricating Donald from the cult's clutches a little easier.

"Tell me about your congregation," Nelson said after we'd placed our dinner orders. "What kind of people are in it?"

I chuckled. "Not very many, as it happens. Assisi is a small, rural community. There's a Catholic church, and one other that identifies rather vaguely as Protestant. But we have a fun mix of folks. Including," I added with a somewhat evasive grin, "some people who've moved into town from a nearby community of Pagans."

Ruth seemed fascinated. "Really? What are they like?"

I described the walk on which I'd seen the sky clad Adam Cooper, minus my personal response to his beauty. And I provided an abridged version of the history that, I believed, led to the current incarnation of the Forest Dwellers.

Ruth wanted to know, "Have you met any of them yet?"

"I have plans to visit a couple who moved into town, who sometimes come to the UU church now. They're still affiliated with the Forest Dwellers, from what I can tell."

I turned the conversation to Ruth and Nelson, asking about their life and their plans for the future. I heard more than I asked for about their honeymoon, which would be to the Virgin Islands. Then, during a lull between dinner and coffee, I could tell there was something Nelson wanted to talk about, and it seemed to be something Ruth would rather not. He prevailed.

"Spencer, you know Donald will be at the ceremony, correct?" I nodded, hoping I seemed less interested than I was. He went on, "I think it's only fair to warn you that he's bringing somcone."

There was a heavy pause. I prodded, "What does that mean, 'someone?'"

Ruth laid a gentle hand on Nelson's forearm, but if that was intended to silence him, it failed.

"He has a boyfriend. Bruce Cobb."

All eyes were on me. I nodded again, doing my best to appear unconcerned. Our waiter stopped by with coffee. I added more sugar than I'd intended and had to will my hand not to tremble as I stirred as carefully as possible to avoid spilling the over-sweet stuff. I started to lift the cup to my face, but I was sure my emotion would cause the thing to shake.

I sat back and tried to appear casual. "Is he good for Donald, do you think?"

Ruth's sideways glance toward Nelson told me all I needed to know about her opinion. No.

Nelson said, "He's anti-religion, which might be good in the short term."

The short term.

At the start of my relationship with Donald, he had seemed ambivalent at best about religion in general. His father had been a stern minister in the extremely severe Lutheran Synod, a denomination whose claim to fame was belief in the inherent sinfulness of mankind, our only hope of salvation being strict and unrelenting adherence to scripture as they interpreted it. Donald's father had rejected him for being gay. But Donald had also told me that although he would have chosen a different denomination, he had often wondered whether the ministry called to him. He had told me he didn't pray, but he'd also said he missed religion.

In our very first interactions, Donald, the actor, had tutored me, the budding priest, in the ways that theatre—and plays themselves—connected directly with the ministry I was headed for.

"So Bruce is an atheist?" I asked.

Nelson nodded. "Devoutly, if that's possible."

"And does Donald now identify as an atheist?"

Ruth's voice was edged with scorn. "So he says."

I felt stable enough to take a sip of coffee. "I'll be interested to meet this fellow tomorrow."

It rained. It rained hard. I've heard rain on the wedding day is supposed to be good luck for the marriage, but I would have wished for the gorgeous October weather I knew New York City is capable of conferring upon its man-made environment.

I was at the church a good ninety minutes ahead of the two o'clock ceremony, hoping to have a chance to talk with Elaine. But there had been a funeral that morning, and she was still at the gravesite when I got to the church, arriving back only twenty minutes or so ahead of Ruth's ceremony and needing some time to dry out.

"Spencer, I'm so glad you could come. It means the world to Ruth."

"As long as I'm not stepping on your toes." I chuckled, knowing that was far from what was happening.

Hurriedly, we reviewed the ceremony and my part in it. "I haven't prepared anything," I told Elaine, "except a few words of blessing."

"Perfect. I'll bring you forward right before pronouncing."

A warm glow spread through me. Ruth would be pronounced a wife, and Nelson her husband. Some things in the world were very right.

The service was pretty standard UU fare, with no promises of honoring or obeying. In accordance with the UU respect for each person's beliefs and values, Ruth and Nelson each spoke of their own commitment for each other and for their union. Elaine spoke of the sanctity of love.

Waiting for my turn to speak, I admired the subtle tastefulness of Ruth's dress, a pale cream sheath, cocktail-length, beneath a sheer lace of the same color that draped softly around her shoulders and arms. On her head, over the short, auburn hair, was a cream pillbox hat adorned with lavender netting. Her bouquet was purple lavender and creamy roses.I allowed my eyes to wander over the congregation. I was going for surreptitious, but I probably failed. As I spotted Donald, it was all I could do to control my facial muscles, given the lurch from that large muscle in my chest, known as my heart. Even in that quick glance, I could see that Donald seemed stiff and on guard, and his face looked drawn and a little pinched. He watched Ruth and Nelson.

The only eyes I noticed trained on me belonged to a large man with very black hair who sat beside Donald. Bruce Cobb, no doubt. The stare of his dark eyes from beneath heavy brows nearly scorched me. I smiled slightly and looked away.

My speech was short and sweet.

"There are some marriages that seem especially blessed by the characteristics that lead to an almost ethereal beauty," I opened, painfully aware that I was pitching my deep voice in a way that I hoped would leave an impression upon Bruce. "I believe this is one of them. Ruth is like a sister to me, and both she and Nelson seem to enable each other to blossom into the best of what they can be, individually and together. So although I offer my own heart-felt blessing, I suspect it will be mere icing on the cake for this union. Ruth, Nelson, go forth in love."

There was a reception in the church's function hall, which someone had festooned with colorful bunting and other decorations. There was champagne and sparkling water, and a long table featured various kinds of finger food. A cake waiting in the corner tempted people to hover near it from time to time. Another table held wrapped gifts.

There were probably fifty people in the room. From several feet away, I saw Donald approach Ruth and give her a long hug. Bruce shook Nelson's hand.

I girded my proverbial loins and headed in Donald's direction, Bruce's eyes on me the whole way.

Donald saw me when I was a few feet from him. I smiled. "It's been a while."

I watched that familiar face as the beginnings of a smile formed, and my heart fairly melted. I thought the smile would blossom into something letting me know he was glad to see me. But it didn't.

He said, "You've come a long way."

Did he mean in my vocation? Or did he mean from northern Vermont? I couldn't tell.

A deep, throaty voice said, "Bruce Cobb. Donald's lover."

So much for subtlety there. I turned to the fellow, who was a few inches shorter than I was but heavily muscled, and held my hand out. "Spencer Hill. Glad to meet you."

Ruth seemed nervous. "Spencer, can I steal you for a minute?"

"I'm at your disposal."

In truth, I was glad for the reprieve, but I was annoyed with Ruth. She had not prepared me for this. Or, not well enough. With her reticence in the past year to speak in any detail about Donald, and her omission of the presence of Bruce Cobb, she had hidden from me that his life had been usurped by this over-bearing and dark influence.

Ruth ushered me over to the gift table. "I'm pretending to ask your opinion about what these boxes contain." She pointed to a few gifts and smiled a smile I didn't believe.

"Why?"

"I just don't think there's anything to be gained from an interaction between you and Bruce."

She reached toward another gift, palm open as though inviting it to reveal its contents.

"Why do you say that? Are you afraid of what I might do?"

"Bruce is a man of few words. By that I mean he relies on a limited number of them. And many of them are unpleasant. I'm afraid that if he says to you anything like he's said in my hearing, your response will knock his knees out from under him and he'll react in a very disruptive way." As part of her act, she laughed as though she had said something very funny. "He's probably watching you right now."

I gave her a sly grin. "Look, I can control myself. In case you didn't know, I'm now a fully-fledged minister, expertly trained in the art of diplomacy."

"Exactly what I'm afraid of."

"Never fear, dear almost-sister. I will do nothing to disrupt your celebration."

And I didn't, though I was sorely tempted at one point. I went toward the drinks station, not noticing through the small cluster of people that Donald and Bruce stood nearby. This cluster moved away just as Bruce leaned toward Donald.

Speaking as quietly as his growling voice would allow, Bruce said, "I don't like that *Reverend* Hill. I don't like self-made men who worship their creator."

I didn't know whether to be more offended at the insult, more tempted to correct the fallacy that I was self-made, or more stunned at what was almost a witty statement from this... *be kind, Spencer...* this hulk of a man. I decided on the third option. And I laughed. And as I did, I recognized the quote. It's attributed to John Bright, an English statesman famous for his speeches. He is also credited with the expression "flog a dead horse."

Donald, who knew my laugh well, turned and saw me. His face told me he was horrified, but that he didn't know what to do. As Bruce turned, he appeared flustered at first, but that moved quickly to something like belligerence.

"Yes," I said. "I heard what you said. Misappropriated, and profoundly mistaken."

I moved away as quickly as I could without seeming to retreat.

For the rest of the time I stayed at the reception, I tried in vain to let my joy for Ruth blot out the darkness I felt toward Bruce and the concern I felt for Donald. At one point, while listening politely to a guest ramble on about something I've since forgotten, I sent a silent prayer to the Universe. Despite my insistence to my own congregation that I didn't use prayer to ask for things, in my mind I whispered, *Please bring that relationship to an end. Please bring Donald to his senses. He doesn't have to turn to me, but please turn him away from Bruce.*

Lying in my luxurious hotel bed Friday morning, I contemplated my plan to go to where I'd stored things from my parents' townhouse when I'd sold it—that is, everything I'd cared about keeping. I intended to decide whether I wanted to bring any of it back with me. Of all of it, the only thing I truly missed was my piano. If I had it moved north, it would take up nearly half of the living room in my new home. But I had a feeling that once I saw it, I would be unable to resist.

The hotel's dining room was quiet and peaceful, with white linens, silver flatware, and crystal set on the tables, ready for breakfasting guests. Autumn sunshine through large windows brightened both what it touched and what it didn't quite reach, and I thought, *Where were you yesterday for Ruth's wedding?*

My order of eggs Benedict and a mimosa had just been

placed before me when someone appeared behind the chair opposite me.

Donald.

"May I sit?" he asked.

Stunned into silence, I gave have a slight nod, my food forgotten.

"I wanted to apologize for yesterday," he said.

I had forgotten how long his eyelashes were. I had almost forgotten about that startling ring of brown around the hazel color of his eyes. His light brown hair, once long enough to be styled in various ways for the different acting roles he had, was now cropped quite short.

I managed, "You did nothing wrong."

"On Bruce's behalf, then."

"Accepted."

His errand accomplished, he made a move that might have indicated he was about to leave.

"How have you been?" I asked, for want of any better ideas. I willed myself to avoid mentioning the Risen Christ cult, his entrapment in it, or his escape—an escape into the arms of someone I found objectionable.

He shrugged, and on his face I saw resignation. I saw capitulation. I saw him giving up on—on what? On himself?

Instead of answering my question, he said, "You've changed."

So have you. But I didn't say that aloud. "In good ways, I hope."

"You look younger. Makes me wonder if there's a portrait of you in an attic someplace, aging." There was that smile. The one I had wanted yesterday. "And yet you seem so much more sure of yourself. Less rigid. So much—I don't know, maybe more free."

I gave him my fondest smile. "I began to breathe sometime in my third year at General, and at Union, preparing for a vocation in the UU church, my lungs expanded fully." We watched each other's eyes for a moment, and then I added, "I'm happier than I've ever been."

His smile, which he'd held onto, began to sag. Did he not want me to be happy?

Quickly I added, "You started me on that path."

I wanted that smile to brighten again, but before that could happen Donald's eyes widened and locked onto something behind me, and Bruce Cobb walked around the table. He ignored me. To Donald he said, "Time to go."

I wanted Donald to tell Bruce to leave. I wanted him to tell him to go to hell. But he stood, and my throat tightened to see how submissively he behaved.

I stood. "He's only just arrived. We were having a conversation."

To me, Bruce said, "It's over." He took Donald's arm.

"Donald?" My tone was somewhere between insistent and pleading, but Donald said nothing.

Bruce wheeled toward me. "You know your problem? All you people who are so very good because you're afraid of hell? You're just bad people on a leash."

Icy cold, pitched to slice, my voice said, "Whose words are you misquoting this time?" He glared at me. I added, "And you might think it's invisible, but I see the leash you're holding right now."

My barb had landed. Bruce knew I meant the leash he had on Donald. But the barb landed on Donald too, which made me wish I'd kept silent. Donald's eyes filled with tears, and he jerked his arm away from Bruce and turned to walk toward the door.

My fists clenched so hard that my nails nearly bit into my palms as I watched Bruce follow Donald outside. On the sidewalk, they moved past the closed window nearest me, going fast. Donald's head was down, his jaws tight, as Bruce gesticulated and spoke in a voice almost loud enough for me to understand the words. I did my best to take some solace from Donald's posture. Maybe he would rebel. Maybe he would put up a fight and tear away the cords Bruce was using to control him.

And then it occurred to me to wonder how Bruce even knew where Donald was. Surely, Donald would not have told him he was coming to find me. Ruth probably told Donald where I was staying, but would she have told Bruce? I doubted it. Would Donald have told him? I doubted that, too. That left one conclusion: Bruce had followed Donald.

Low in my belly, something churned. As it began to rise, I recognized it as bilious rage, a feeling I couldn't remember having since I was a child suffering at the hands of bullies. And there was something else, something that terrified me because of what it represented.

Hatred.

I will not hate, I chided myself. *I will not allow it to take hold.* Hatred, as I saw it, was a source of isolation, of separation. And the source of hatred was fear.

I sat down again, picking at what would have been a delicious meal if I'd been able to enjoy it.

"Something wrong with your meal, sir?"

My waiter had snuck up on me. Or that's what it felt like.

"No. It's fine. It's my appetite that's at fault. Give me a little more time to work on that, eh?"

He smiled and left.

What was I afraid of? It couldn't be of losing Donald. That ship had sailed. No; it was of Donald losing himself.

Puck, the mercurial. Puck, the playful. Puck, the adventurous. Puck, the tease.

Puck was either dead or dormant. I prayed it was the latter.

CHAPTER 8

The worldly goods I had left in the city when I'd moved to Assisi took up three storage units. As I stood in one of them, the idea of going through anything and making decisions about what to retrieve felt overwhelming. I left that facility and went to the climate-controlled place where my piano now lived.

There it sat, swathed in layers of protective material. Silent. Asleep? Forlorn? Forlorn was how I felt, looking at the shrouded lump. Inside was an inanimate object to which I had brought life, an object that had helped me survive when survival had seemed almost out of reach. My fingers twitched, aching to feel again the silky-smooth keys, their black and white pattern appearing so regimented and yet capable of rendering the most sublime resonance.

I moved to a set of boxes set off to the side that held, I knew, more black and white patterns: black notes on black staff lines printed on white paper. This printing, for those who could read it and render it on piano keys, revealed something akin to magic. It took enormous power of will not to tear those boxes open, extricate the black baby grand piano from its wrappings, and make that magic happen.

My piano had been my best friend from childhood. How could I leave it here?

I couldn't. I wouldn't.

Before I left New York I made arrangements for the piano and the boxes of music to be moved.

The other thing I did was to leave something behind. That was Donald. I had to relegate him to a part of my past that would never be resurrected. As if to exorcise his spirit, I took in a deep breath, intending to feel a release as I exhaled. Instead, that release took the form of tears.

My sermon that Sunday was about letting go. I spoke of how to know when we're hanging onto something that wasn't really there, and how to trust that we won't disappear when we release our hold.

"Who's to say," I asked, "that what we think we want is what we're really looking for? Is it possible that we're striving for the specifics, the particulars of our goal, and that those specifics hide the reality of what would make us happy?"

Vanessa called on Monday morning to invite me for lunch. Over bean and mushroom soup and grilled cheese sandwiches, she asked about my trip to New York.

I told her how lovely the wedding was. I described my hotel in glowing terms. And I told her my piano should arrive in a few days.

"A baby grand," I said. "It will probably take up a large portion of the living room, but it feels just too sad to leave it in storage where it can't sing."

"How nice! I didn't know you played. Might I hear you sometime?"

"I'd like that."

We ate in silence for a minute or so, and then she asked, "What else happened?"

"I beg your pardon?"

"It seemed as though something about the trip inspired your sermon topic."

I waited too long for a denial, too long to say that I didn't really want to talk about it. Vanessa kept her gaze on me, gentle but persistent.

"Spencer, I'm not your confessor, of course. I've got no right to dig into your life. But is there anyone else here you can talk to about things that trouble you? I just want you to know I'm here."

"It's an old relationship," I said. "One that ended three years ago."

I told her about Donald, about how my feelings for him had shown me that I couldn't reconcile my nature with the Episcopal priesthood, how I had barely begun to allow myself to be open to life's possibilities when he almost literally slipped through my fingers and into the chasm of a religious cult.

"His sister, Ruth, and I became fast friends. She was determined to rescue him, and in fact the man she married was the deprogrammer she hired. But I had to move on. In fact, I hadn't seen him since that time."

"And he was at her wedding."

"His plus-one was a man who seems to have taken control of him. Bruce is an atheist and quite vocal about it. Donald is supposedly an atheist now, too, but that doesn't square with the man I knew. He seemed—" I searched for the right word. "He seemed cowed."

"How sad."

I sat back and rubbed my face. "I thought I was over him. Maybe if he'd been with someone who seemed good for him, I wouldn't feel as I do. But he used to be so much fun. He had a penchant for unusual vocabulary words." I chuckled. "I wasn't always convinced he wasn't making them up. He used to laugh a lot. Sometimes he seemed like a very precocious child."

I threw back my head and laughed. "One time he was on a bench in Central Park, studying the script of a play he was in. This young boy trotted away from the two women with him and ran to sit on the bench. Donald looked around and then said to the boy, 'Can you see me?'"

Vanessa laughed with me. "What did the boy do?"

"He laughed that tinkling laugh that kids have and shook his head. And Donald said, 'Rats. Guess I didn't take enough potion.'"

It was amusing, and sweet, but it wasn't funny enough for tears to come to my eyes. Even so, they were there. When I could speak again, I said, "When I met him, he was playing Puck in *A Midsummer Night's Dream*. As Ruth said, it was type casting. But he's not Puck anymore."

"Does he seem to want to be with this other person?"

I recalled how Donald had pulled away from Bruce in the hotel restaurant. "I don't think so. I don't see how he could. I think he just doesn't know how not to depend on him."

The MacPhersons were something short of delightful. Vanessa had contacted them while I was in New York, ostensibly just checking in as she might have done in her role as minister. Apparently she spoke to them of me, because when I phoned to see when I might visit, Mrs. MacPherson was not surprised.

I drove to their home Wednesday after my return from the city.

"Reverend Hill!" Mr. MacPherson greeted me, beaming a welcoming smile. "Do come in."

"Spencer, please."

"And you must call us Shane and Roberta."

Vanessa had told me the MacPhersons were in their nineties, but they seemed younger. Shane had only a few white wisps of hair, but Roberta's long hair, held away from her face by wooden clasps, had almost as much pepper as salt in it. Their faces were only a little wrinkled, and they both had dark, lively eyes. They seemed almost like merry wood sprites.

"I'm sorry I've missed you at services," I said as I took the chair I was offered. I wanted to ask if they'd enjoyed their Mabon ceremony, but I felt so ignorant about what it would have entailed that it seemed inappropriate.

"Oh, that's as much our fault as yours." Roberta waved a hand as she headed toward the kitchen. "I guess we wanted to get the measure of you."

Shane said, "You come from New York City, is that right? Must be quite a change for you, being here."

"It has been," I agreed, "but it's been a good change. I think the parish here is just about the right size for me. In a city parish, I'd be less likely to get to know everyone. And I'm really enjoying that here."

Shane told me about the house, about how he had designed it, and how it had been built with the help of several people. Roberta joined us again with an earthenware teapot and mugs to match, along with brownies on a plate of the same pattern. I used Shane's mention of "several people" to shift the conversation slightly.

"Reverend Vanessa tells me you moved here from The Forest. Were those the friends who helped with the construction?"

Roberta handed me a napkin. "Yes, indeed. They wanted to make sure we were well settled out here, away from the community."

"I hope you feel a part of the Assisi community now."

77

There was a pause, just long enough to register. They both smiled, but neither said anything.

Disconcerted, I reached for a brownie as Roberta poured steaming liquid into a mug for me.

I said, "I understand you've just celebrated Mabon." I pronounced it as Vanessa had, as though it were spelled *May*bon.

Shane nodded. "Just so you know, we say Mabon." He made it sound like *Mah*bon. "Yes. It was good to be back in the fold for the festivities."

He didn't elaborate, so I took a risk, even though it might serve to embarrass me further. "I think I might have seen someone from The Forest recently. I was walking in toward McGowan Pond when I saw a young man approach the water. I don't think he saw me, but—"

"Oh, he knew you were there," Roberta assured me. "That was Adam Cooper. Our grandson."

He knew I was there.... *And did he know I watched his orgasmic dance?* I felt an urge to protest that I hadn't been spying on him, or at least that it hadn't been my intention to do so, but there was no way to do that without sounding disingenuous. "Ah," was all I could manage, while my mind raced on to wonder how much of his display, if any, had been for my benefit.

I changed the subject, at least a little. "Do Forest Dweller children come to town for school?"Shane shook his head. "Not until they're twelve or so. There is an accredited grammar school there, though it's quite small, of course."

I made a note to ask Marshall how well he thought these children adjusted when they had to leave The Forest.

After a few more of my attempts to collect information about The Forest, all of which were met with polite but vague responses, I decided to take another risk and be direct.

"I hope this won't be offensive, but I'm very interested in the Forest Dweller practices, so I was wondering whether I could visit the community."

Both Roberta and Shane gazed rather blankly at me, not apparently offended, but seeming unsure how to respond.

So I asked, "Is there any way that could be arranged?"

"Why?" Shane's question was not sharp or huffy, but I felt as though it was intended to put me off.

"Well," I began rather lamely, "as someone in a ministerial vocation, and in a denomination that is open and accepting of all belief systems, I'm naturally interested in learning whatever I can about a spiritual approach that's new to me."

Clearly my explanation wasn't enough. Roberta tilted her head at me. Shane pursed his lips and then said, "We don't like feeling as though we're some kind of circus sideshow to be examined out of curiosity."

"Oh. Oh, believe me, I'm not thinking of it like that. No. I—"

Roberta, more gently than her husband, still denied me entry. "I'm sure you can understand that we're sensitive to being gawked at. If someone is genuinely interested in our approach to Paganism with the possibility of joining with us in a committed way, we would be open to that." She smiled. "I doubt that's you."

"Well, no, I suppose not. But I have to say I'd be delighted if some of the Forest Dwellers wanted to learn more about my church, even if they didn't intend to join the UU tradition. It's in that spirit—"

Shane interrupted me this time. "You aren't used to being gawked at. You aren't used to having your religion ridiculed. Unitarian Universalism isn't parodied by puerile mockery of your sacred principles."

"I'm so sorry," I nearly stammered. "I've offended you without meaning to. But I can assure you, the UU tradition is often ridiculed. In fact, we do a lot of that ridicule ourselves." I was tempted to add that self-ridicule is a hallmark of a sense of humor, and it appeared he had none.

"Like what?" Roberta wanted to know, which surprised me, seeing as how she and Shane attended the UU church, at least sporadically.

"Oh, gosh, there are so many…. Okay, here's one. We joke that we start prayers with the phrase, 'To Whom It May Concern.'"

Roberta chuckled. Shane did not.

"Here's another. We're so busy discussing what is or isn't true about God and heaven, that when we die and arrive in heaven we argue about whether we're really there. Or when we die, and we see a sign that says 'Heaven' on the left and a sign that says 'Discussion About Heaven' on the right, we go to the right. Or this one: A UU parishioner asked a visitor who came to a UU service how he liked it. He said he couldn't believe half the things the minister said. She told him, 'Great! Then you'll fit right in.'"

Roberta laughed, and Shane looked like he was trying not to smile. I kept going.

"Did you know we can walk on water? We just have to wait until winter."

Then I offered my final proof. "And we often repeat things others have said to ridicule us. Somerset Maugham wrote that UUs earnestly disbelieve in almost everything anyone else believes, and we have a lively sustaining faith in we don't quite know what."

Shane finally gave in and chuckled, so I added, "And surely you've witnessed how often people at church are slow to join in singing a hymn because they're reading the text to see if they disagree with it."

Shane held up a hand briefly. "All right, you've made your point. But I don't think a UU has ever been burned at the stake."

"I can't give you an example of that, but I can tell you that Unitarians have often been mistreated, tortured, and killed for holding to their beliefs."

"Who did that?" Roberta wanted to know.

It pained me to say it. "The same people who burned Pagans and witches. That is, mostly Christians."

Shane let out a long breath through his nose. "Still, we're sensitive to being ridiculed and worse. Perhaps over-sensitive."

I shook my head. "If one out of every five bald men I saw came up and punched me, pretty soon I'd start to avoid all bald men."

"Then you can understand why we're reluctant. Especially this time of year."

"Mabon?" I asked, pronouncing it as he had, this time.

"Samhain."

I struggled to connect what I heard—"Sowhen"—with anything I'd read in my library book. "I'm sorry. I don't know what that is."

"You probably think of it as Halloween."

Just in time I stopped myself before mispronouncing yet another Pagan holiday. "So, the costumes, the trick-or-treating...."

"Samhain is one of the four most important holidays of the Pagan calendar. It marks the end of one year and the beginning of the next. It represents the cycle of life. Your Christian All Saints Day, November first, is a deliberate conflict with Samhain. We see a veil between the living and the dead, and Samhain is when that veil is the thinnest. Souls from the past and souls from the present can meet once more. It's an interstice between what was and what will be."

I struggled for words and came up with "It sounds very important, indeed. But attending UU services, you must have picked up that as a group, we don't all consider ourselves Christian, so it isn't *our* All Saints Day."

"You welcome Christians."

"We welcome everyone." *Which*, I stopped myself from adding, *it seems you do not.* "In any event, of course if the community would prefer that I don't visit, I will not. Although I do wish I could communicate my intention in a way that you could accept."

The two MacPhersons glanced at each other. Shane said, "We will consider it."

I smiled. "That's all I ask at this time." And then I had a brainstorm. "You know, I've been trying to come up with a way to get more of our youth interested in spiritual things. Teenagers are conspicuously absent from church services. If I can't get them to come on Sundays, maybe I could come up with an alternative activity. And now I'm thinking that one idea might be for something that specifically involved teens from the general Assisi community and teens from The Forest."

More blank stares. So I added, "Of course, that's something to be considered down the road."

I stood, making it clear I was ready to leave. "I hope to see you both on Sunday. And," I tilted my head at Roberta, "I would love to take one of these delicious brownies with me."

"Give me a second," she said, and disappeared.

I walked slowly toward the door, Shane behind me. We shook hands as Roberta approached, a foil-wrapped bundle in her hands. It seemed she was awarding me the entire batch of brownies.

My drive back to town was made under a cloud of something like frustration. While I had to admit that my initial interest in The Forest was inspired by Adam Cooper's dance, I was now fully focused on increasing my own understanding of a belief system I knew nothing about. And I was also, quite sincerely, interested in doing something with teens. And the idea of bringing kids together from the town and The Forest was even more inspiring to me than Adam Cooper.

I tried to remember what Vanessa had said about the Forest Dwellers in general (not to go there without permission) and the MacPhersons in particular (she'd used the terms friendly and welcoming). *They prefer to keep to themselves,* she'd said, and that would seem to apply to all of them.

In the Old Testament book 1 Kings, the Queen of Sheba decides to test the wonderful things she's heard about Solomon, even to challenge him. She shows up on his doorstep, in full regalia and pageantry, only to be overcome by his generosity and wisdom, far beyond what his great reputation had prepared her for. She says, "The half was not told me."

While I wasn't expecting to challenge the MacPhersons, I did show up in ignorance—which I admitted to them. Their welcome had felt something less than whole-hearted, at least once they knew that I wanted an invitation to The Forest. So maybe the analogy with Sheba and Solomon was imperfect, but my thoughts echoed the words, "The half was not told me."

My thoughts were so focused on the mixed welcome I'd received that it wasn't until I walked into my house that I remembered: Adam had known I was there.

CHAPTER 9

Thursday morning. And I was even more excited than I'd expected. My piano would arrive this evening!

I had located a tuner who had promised to be here Friday morning. Rearranging the furniture in my living room to make room for the baby grand helped drain off some of my over-excited energy, but there was still a lot of it left. So I packed a lunch and headed for the wooded lane where Marshall and I had walked together.

At first it seemed the path went on forever, but by about eleven o'clock I reached a point where it began to take on height. The path grew rockier and narrow, my lungs began to strain for air, and it was necessary to pay more attention to my footing than to the glorious autumn colors all around me. I slowed my pace, but even so I could feel the muscles in my legs burn. It felt good; it felt like I was doing something good for my body. And certainly it was draining energy.

When I came upon a large expanse of exposed granite, I allowed myself to stop and take in the view of rolling hills that grew into larger ones and then larger ones still, in the distance.

The patchwork of colors nearly took away the breath I was already struggling for.

I sat on that granite shelf and ate my lunch. The sun had warmed the gritty surface, a satisfying contrast with the chilly air. I stayed for quite a while and considered what my Sunday sermon would cover. The uncertain welcome I'd received from the MacPhersons made it seem appropriate to stress the importance of welcoming the stranger, the "other," the people we might not understand at first but who were just as deserving of love, and (as we must assume until proven wrong) were just as capable of showing love. I hoped that the MacPhersons would be there, and that my words—earnestly yet gently delivered—would help them feel comfortable moving forward with my visit to The Forest.

By late afternoon I was about half-way back to the school, the gathering dusk leeching color from my surroundings, when I saw Marshall. Head down, hands clasped behind him, he reminded me of images I'd seen of the composer Beethoven, who was said to wander the woods contemplating—one presumes—music. I stood still, and he was almost upon me before he noticed me.

"Oh!" His face showed surprise and then, quickly, something like irritation.

"Good afternoon," I said. "Lovely day for a walk. I've been up to the granite ledge."

"My lookout." His voice was so quiet, he seemed to be addressing himself rather than me.

"Are you headed there now?"

He shook his head. "It'll be dark soon."

"Of course." Awkward. I tried again. "Good to bump into you. I've been meaning to ask you something, actually."

He watched my face for a good five seconds before saying, "Go ahead."

"I've learned a little about the Forest Dwellers. I understand their children attend a grammar school there, but that they come into town for school after that."

"And?"

And, I nearly said, *we're back to you resenting me for reasons I don't understand.* "I was wondering how well they fare. How well they adjust."

"There are some issues. Sometimes the other kids make them uncomfortable. They tend to hang together, which presents a single target for anyone who wants to throw figurative stones at them. But there aren't very many of them." He shrugged. "Academically, they do fine. I haven't seen many cases where their earlier schooling seems deficient in any important way."

"And socially? Aside from the bullying, I mean. Do you think very many of them end up leaving The Forest eventually, or do they usually return?"

"It's mixed, as far as I can tell. Why are you so interested?"

I told him essentially the same thing I'd said to the MacPhersons about my general interest in spiritual belief systems. "As far as I know, Roberta and Shane MacPherson are the only Forest Dwellers who've left The Forest and stayed in the area. They come to our church, as you know, and I feel much like Vanessa did, that a certain amount of exchange with the forest community would be beneficial for all."

"Yeah, well, good luck with that." He took a step forward as if to continue his walk, and I almost let him go. Almost.

"Marshall?"

I waited until he replied, "What is it?"

"Don't you think the teens from both communities would benefit from some activity outside of school, something that connected our church and their belief system?"

I couldn't tell whether the look on his face was sour because he didn't like my idea, or because he didn't like the idea of working on a project like that with me, or both. But it was sour.

"Okay, look, Marshall. I'm still getting the feeling you dislike me, or resent me, or have some other reason for—well, it seems as though you'd prefer to avoid me. What's going on?"

We were standing maybe three feet apart on the path, just close enough for me to tell his breathing was agitated. He closed his eyes briefly, and when he opened them he said, "You don't want to know." He began to move away.

"I do, though. I do want to know. We need to work together, and if there's something I'm doing that's bothering you I'd like to know so I can—"

"All *right!*" I saw his fists clench and unclench. "But remember that I tried not to tell you."

"Noted."

"I'm attracted to you."

So I was right. "I see." *Think, Spencer; how should you handle this?* "Very well. I'll do my best to keep our exchanges limited to what will help you fulfill your lay minister role." I nodded again, and as if dismissed, Marshall walked away from me. Quickly.

I saw my idea of teen activities grow pale to the point of disappearing. If I couldn't get an introduction to The Forest, and I didn't have someone like Marshall to connect me with teens who didn't come to services, what hope was there for my project?

It might have been harder to get that conversation with Marshall out of my mind if it hadn't been for my piano's arrival. The movers were as careful as they could be, and I hoped it wasn't just because I was watching them now, at this end of the trip. I tipped them well and watched as their truck drove off through the nearly-dark early evening.

As soon as they left, I stood silently looking at the swathed lump, a feeling rising in my chest as though I was about to be reunited with a long-lost lover. Tenderly, I removed the soft cara-pace that I, myself, had created to protect the piano before it had been moved out of the townhouse, the only home that it and I had ever known before now. At the first sight of the polished black finish, I felt a warm rush that started in my heart and went all through me. I sat on the padded leather bench and ran my hands horizontally, slowly, along the black panel, waiting for just the right moment, just the right feeling to lift it up and reveal the black and white keys that were also keys to all the emotions I had felt as I had learned, practiced, and worked until, finally, I'd made magic.

Gingerly, as though I might hurt something, I pressed a white key, and then another, and then I played a chord with one hand that extended an octave and a third, a stretch not difficult for me, but one that would be a challenge for many pianists. I smiled as I might have at a child attempting something they'd almost mastered, because yes, the piano tuner would have work to do. I wouldn't play anything now; I wouldn't do anything that might embarrass the instrument, as though it knew it wasn't at its best.

A movement outside caught my eye, something at the window. I looked just in time to see a very dark head dodge out of sight. Curious, I went to the front door and opened it to see Duncan Beale heading for a bicycle lying on the grass.

"What's your hurry, Duncan?"

He lifted his shoulders, dropped them, and said, "Saw the moving van. Thought maybe you'd come to your senses."

"You thought I might be leaving town?" I smiled. "You'll have to try harder if you want to get rid of me." He didn't move. "Wanna come see what the moving van was here for?" I leaned on the door frame, arms crossed comfortably across my chest, and tilted my head sideways by way of invitation.

Duncan shrugged again and dropped the bike. I stepped aside as he came through the doorway, noticing that he now had a slender silver circlet through a piercing near the end of his left eyebrow. He made straight for the piano and stood beside the bench, staring silently at the keyboard as I watched from my position. With a tenderness I wouldn't have expected from him, he reached out a finger and pressed a key so slowly that it made no sound.

"Is it broken?"

I shook my head and moved to the bench. I sat down and held my hands over the keys. "The piano tuner will be here tomorrow, so this won't sound great yet."

Silently, I apologized to the piano for exposing its temporary imperfection. I let my fingers fall onto the keys that revealed the gentle opening melodies of Chopin's "Barcarolle in F sharp major," which had been my favorite piece since I'd learned it.

While I played, Duncan stood still, watching my hands as though hypnotized. I released the final chord, noticing that this small room did not allow the sweet reverberations I was used to, in the large music room at home with its high ceilings and floor-to-ceiling windows.

I sat quietly, hands in my lap, eyes on the keyboard, as Duncan stood silently beside me, for maybe fifteen seconds. Then I looked at him. "Would you like to play?"

He took a step back. "I can't do that."

"Would you like to?"

His eyes flicked to my face, an odd mixture of hope and resignation in them.

"I wouldn't be any good."

I smiled. "Not at first, no. I wasn't either, when I started. No one is. Well, almost no one." I nearly pushed away the idea that came to me then, not sure I wanted to entangle my life with this rebellious young man's, but—hell, it might be good for both of us. And who would have thought Duncan Beale would be so fascinated by this kind of music? I almost *had* to nurture that. "I could show you how."

He looked as though he didn't know whether he wanted to step farther away or closer. Finally he said, "Sure."

I had Duncan sit on the bench and just finger the keys, regardless of what happened musically, while I opened boxes until I located my earliest primer music books. I placed one on the piano.

"First thing is to learn where middle C is. It will be a solid place you can always find, kind of an anchor for everything else on the keyboard."

We worked together for about forty-five minutes, much longer than I had expected to be able to hold Duncan's attention in this way. He was no genius, no Mozart, but I knew aptitude can grow as interest does.

Suddenly he jumped up. "Fuck. I'm late for dinner. I'll catch hell."

"If you like I can call and let them know you're on your way."

"Yeah. Thanks."

"Duncan?" He paused at the door. "Would you like to do this again?"

"Yeah. Sure." And he was gone.

When Andrea answered the phone, I didn't say anything about piano lessons. She seemed surprised that Duncan would have approached my house at all, moving van notwithstanding.

I wasn't quite sure how I was going to arrange for something regular with Duncan, but that would have to wait. I wanted him to tell his parents about it when he was ready.

∾

My euphoria over the piano's arrival had abated, replaced by the pleasant anticipation of bringing Duncan into my world of music. I threw a hasty dinner together, thinking I'd spend the evening going through the boxes of music both for me and for Duncan. But once I started my meal, my thoughts turned to Marshall.

It occurred to me for the first time that my response to his confession had contained nothing of reciprocity. That is, I said nothing about any feelings I might have for him. Perhaps, I pondered, nothing occurred to me because other than the short time we'd spent bonding over *Hitchhiker*, his attitude toward me had put me off. Now that I knew why, did I need to reassess?

I pictured Marshall. Tall, slender, boyish face. With me, he seemed withdrawn, even retreating into himself in a way. But the way he'd connected with CC about her dog, and the way he managed teaching Shakespeare to teenagers, told me there was real depth to him.

When I compared him to other men who had attracted me, there wasn't much in common. Donald had been mercurial, lively, playful. There was Ralph, who was a little broody but who was an open book and had the most generous spirit. Amos, a tall-drink-of-water with sandy hair and a quirky sense of humor had regaled me with tales of his travels and the languages he'd partially learned as he'd moved with his ambassador mother around the globe. I still remember Amos occasionally stopping mid-sentence, a slightly confused look on his face, asking, "What language was that last word in?" I could never quite tell whether he was pulling my leg.

And here was Marshall. Of course, it might not do for me to have a romantic relationship with a lay minister in my congregation anyway, though I couldn't really think of a reason why not. It certainly wasn't a case of love (or lust) at first sight for me, and although something like that might have happened for him, he'd had more of a chance to know who I was as a person than I knew of him.

Perhaps I should change that. But could I do it without leading him on, into a relationship that might never be more than one-sided?

Forget it, Spencer. You can call Ursula tomorrow and see what she has to say. Go unpack your music. My advisor at seminary had been a great sounding board for many questions.

Only as I lay in bed, soft darkness enveloping me, did it occur to me how many similarities Marshall had with Donald, despite their differences. Both came from restrictive, fundamentalist Christian religions. Both had had domineering fathers who had rejected their gay sons. As adults, both had been drawn, in different ways perhaps, back to religion.

Ursula was intrigued. "So one of your lay ministers has the hots for you?" Her tone was teasing, but it made me uncomfortable.

"He said he was attracted to me."

"Are you attracted to him?"

"I don't know much about him."

"Mmmm. Whereas he's seen you bare your soul from the pulpit a few times now."

"His soul seems kind of available, actually." I told her about the dog and about how he seemed almost in pain when talking to me. "He handles his teenage students very well, though."

"So you admire him."

"Well… yes, I suppose I do."

"Is he physically attractive?"

"Boyish. Vulnerable."

"Vulnerable isn't a physical attribute."

I gave that a moment's thought. "It seems to be, with him."

Ursula took her own moment to think. "If you want my

advice, Spencer, I see a few ways this could go badly. I'm sure you've thought of them."

"I could end up leading him on without anything developing on my side. Or we could become involved in a way that negatively influenced my relationship with the other lay ministers. Or we could become involved and then have a rocky time, and he'd feel like he had to leave the congregation, or at least his role as lay minister. Or I would have to leave."

"And is there a good possible outcome?"

"Only if we truly fall in love. Otherwise I can't really think of one."

"And at the moment, at least, that seems unlikely. So do you have your answer?"

I let out a long breath. "I suppose just what I told him. I'll do my best to keep our interactions limited to our respective roles in the congregation."

I hoped that would do it. I hoped no one would get hurt.

Friday around noon I had a call from Jenny Pratt.

"Reverend Spencer? Um, this is kind of last minute, and I'm kind of embarrassed, but—well, I need to ask if you can help me with something."

"I'm here for you, of course. How can I help?" I hoped my tone didn't reveal irritation; the piano tuner was busy in the other room, and I was looking forward to an afternoon of going through several pieces of music.

"I need to visit Jasper Moore. He doesn't want any of the other lay ministers. I've seen him before, and so has Andrea, and so has Marshall. He won't talk to Loraine. The thing is, I don't want to be alone with him."

I struggled to recall a parishioner named Jasper, but my mind was a blank. "Can you tell me why?"

I heard her sigh over the phone. "He keeps coming on to me."

"I see. Have you set up a time with him yet?"

"I told him I'd get back to him. He doesn't know it's because I wanted to talk to you first."

"Where are you meeting him?"

"Well…. I used to see him at the church, or at the diner, or someplace like that. But last time he insisted I go to his house. I was very uncomfortable there. And he wants to meet there today, too."

I ground my jaw. I didn't like this fellow, and I'd probably never met him. "What time works best for you?" We agreed on five forty-five, when Jasper and Jenny would both be done with work for the day. "I'll pick you up."

I called Vanessa.

"That's so odd," she said. "Jenny didn't mention any problems to me."

"What can you tell me about Jasper?"

"I don't know much. He almost never comes to services. Divorced, mid-fifties. If he's making life difficult for my lay ministers… I mean, *the* lay ministers…."

I chuckled. "I agree. He needs to be set straight, as it were. I'll see what I can do."

"Let me know if I can help."

I said I would, but I had a feeling Jasper needed to be read the riot act by a man.

I managed to spend a few hours alone with my piano before heading out to get Jenny, so I was in a very good mood by the time she hopped into my Jeep.

"I really appreciate this," she said.

"How long has this been a problem?"

"He used to call every few months. But lately it's been, like, every other week. He's never done anything really dreadful, but it seems he's getting bolder each time."

"Why does he call? Is he in spiritual trouble?"

She gave a kind of snort. "Not that I've been able to tell. Though he claims he's in crisis so someone will go see him. He doesn't make much money. He does some kind of office work for a logging company. Dispatcher, or something like that. Some bookkeeping."

"Divorced, yes?"

"Yes. Which is one thing he says troubles him." She gazed out of the side window. "Ha. It troubles him, all right." Then, "I'm sorry. That was unkind."

I chuckled. "I think you're allowed to vent a little. And, by the way, this should never have happened. You didn't tell Reverend Vanessa?"

"No. I didn't want to bother her before, with her health and all, and it's only lately that it's gotten really bad."

"Well I hope you'll let me know any time you have a problem concerning your work. Will you do that?"

"I will. Yes."

Jasper's home, a few miles outside of town, was a glorified trailer, which is to say it had started life as a trailer and had been enlarged rather piecemeal by adding a few rambling extensions. A black pickup truck that had seen better days was parked on the side. There were no trees close by, and there was no lawn that could be called a lawn. Trampled weeds led the way from the truck to what passed as a front door to the trailer.

I stepped in front of Jenny and knocked loudly, and the door opened to reveal a heavy-set man in jeans fastened below a large belly, red and black flannel shirt open over a once-white T-shirt that had obvious holes in it. The air reeked of cigar smoke, and I wondered why any of the lay ministers would put up with this.

"Who the hell are you?" he greeted me.

Vanessa had been right. He hadn't been to services since I'd arrived. "Good evening. I'm Reverend Spencer from the UU church you belong to. I'm here with Jenny Pratt, who tells me you're in need of a lay minister's help."

He gawked at me, then looked at Jenny, and I could almost smell the wood burning to indicate there was a thought process happening. He must have realized that if he sent us away, that would be the end of Jenny's visits. "Yeah. Come in."

The less said about the interior of Jasper's home, the better; if he had any money, it hadn't been spent on furniture for a very long time. Everything seemed grungy, and the two lamps, dim as they were, couldn't completely conceal the sad state of the rug.

I pulled two banged-up, wooden chairs from the kitchen table for Jenny and me; I didn't want to sit on anything upholstered, and I doubted she did, either.

"Jenny tells me you're having a tough time," I opened.

"She knows. She knows how lonely I get."

"Tell me a little about your life."

"Like what?"

"Who are your friends?"

"Got no friends."

"That's sad." And it was, but it wasn't surprising. "Who else do you know from church? I don't think I've seen you there."

"Don't go much. Too tired."

"I need to ask you a personal question. Is there something about your health that makes you too tired to venture into town on Sundays?"

"Feel sick all the time."

I looked at Jenny who made a face that told me it was the first she'd heard about that.

"What does your doctor say?"

"Got no doctor."

I paused, wondering what the best approach would be for this man, who really was a sad case but who didn't seem to be doing anything to help himself.

"If I come and get you this Sunday, will you come to services?"

"Like I told you. I'm too tired."

It was becoming clear to me that Jasper was not in any kind of spiritual crisis, or not one that Jenny could help with. If he really was in need, Jenny's help would not fill it. "What were you hoping to talk to Jenny about this evening?"

Jasper seemed irritated. "I always talk to Jenny. She makes me feel better."

"I'm glad. What do you talk about?"

He glared at me. "Look, I didn't ask for you. I asked for Jenny."

I nodded. "I understand that, Mr. Moore. But here's the thing. It isn't appropriate for Jenny to come out here alone to see you. And Jenny is a lay minister, not a doctor or a therapist. She's tried to help you, but it seems your problems are more than she's prepared to address. And from what you've told me, you're worse than ever. You used to meet her in public. Now you want her to come to you here. She's not going to do that again. And because she's tried so hard to help you, without you feeling any progress, from now on when you need to talk to someone from the church you talk to me."

"That ain't what I want!"

"I hear you. I do. And I'm telling you that Jenny is no longer available to you. If you have physical problems, you need to find a doctor. In fact, I happen to know that there are a couple of doctors in our congregation. And from now on, if you have spiritual needs, you come to me. Now," I leaned a little forward, "would you like to pray with us?"

"You do what you like."

I bowed my head, as did Jenny. "I offer the love that runs through us all to you, Jasper Moore. I pray that it will fill you and make it possible for you to reach out to me and to our congregation when you need spiritual support. I pray that you will find your way back to the church, and take part in the spirit of love and connection that you will find there. For now, may the spirit of life and love be with you."

I stood, and so did Jenny. "I very much hope to see you in church on Sunday. Let me know if you change your mind about having me come and get you." I pulled a card out of a pocket and set it on a side table.

Jenny and I started toward the door, but Jasper came up with another ploy.

"Jenny can come get me."

"If you need help getting to church, I will come and get you. Not Jenny. Good evening, Mr. Moore."

And we were out. The air, now much colder than earlier in the day, was a welcome relief from inside that room. I breathed deeply, and I heard Jenny do the same. Neither of us spoke until we were on the road and well away from Jasper Moore.

"Thank you. So much."

"You're welcome. And I meant what I said earlier. You should never have been put in a position like that. You should let me know immediately if anything remotely like this happens again."

We rode in silence for a few minutes. Then I said, "Jasper really is a sad case. If there's any way I can help him, I don't yet know what it is. I think I'll ask Andrea and Marshall about their experiences with him."

"Andrea will give you an carful. Marshall...." Her voice trailed off.

"What about Marshall?"

"Marshall gave Jasper an earful."

I laughed. "Did he? He seems so gentle."

"He has no patience for people like Jasper. He did meet with him twice, I think, and told me he thought Jasper was a lost cause."

"He might be right."

"Marshall doesn't have a lot of patience with people who won't help themselves. But if someone's in real need, he's a sweetheart."

"He seems very genuine." I wasn't sure what I meant by that, but I was hoping Jenny would say more about him.

"I don't think there's a dishonest or duplicitous bone in his body. Of course, he's had so much trouble in his young life."

"Here?"

"Oh, no. I think this place is a god-send to him. No, I'm talking about his background."

"He's told me a little." Not knowing how much Jenny knew, I didn't want to betray a confidence.

"About the conversion camp?"

"Yes. And I understand he had a dog that died while he was there."

"Angus." Jenny sighed. "He almost died, himself."

My ears pricked up. "What he told me sounded like a terrible experience."

"Thank God he didn't succeed. He must have been in so much pain to attempt suicide."

I was glad for the darkness. Doing my best to sound unsurprised, I said, "Yes. I imagine anyone who attempts suicide is in a good deal of pain."

We rode in silence for the rest of the trip, while I thought back to my own brush with suicidal thoughts. I hadn't come close to taking any action, but I had stared into the cold, grey waters of the Hudson River, feeling shut out of the only life I had imagined for myself. Alone, with no family left alive, no close friends, and my only good connections being wrenched away because of who I was—a gay man with a calling to the Episcopal priesthood—I'd felt as though I'd been cast out of heaven as surely as if I were Lucifer himself.

But there had been a silver lining for me. That day, I had realized that the only real hell is separation from God. I hadn't found my way back quickly or easily, but realizing what was wrong, with help from a wonderful therapist and from my feelings for Donald and his for me, I had found the light again.

CHAPTER 10

I was restless all night. The image of a young Marshall, forced into a place where he was told that God had made him something God couldn't love, then told that he—Marshall—must fix that.... I'd heard about these places. Perhaps I needed to learn more about them.

And while in that physical and spiritual hell, to have his beloved dog die while protecting the very man who had cast Marshall into that prison must have pushed him further into a very dark corner of hell, indeed.

Something Vanessa had told me came to mind. She'd implied that something in his history had made him want to help people. It seemed likely he would be especially drawn to help people in emotional distress.

As I'd expected, Jasper was not at that Sunday's service. Neither were the MacPhersons, so my sermon about being open and welcoming to others did not reach them. I hoped nothing about my visit had discouraged them from attending. And I noticed that Marshall avoided me. Perhaps he was not acting any differently from how he had on previous Sundays, but that day I noticed it.

There was one bright spot. Sitting with Andrea and Jacob Beale was young Duncan.

As Violet played a lovely Schubert piece during the service, I regretted not having had the piano tuner work on that piano as well. I made a plan to call him.

After the service there was the usual procession of people filing past me as I greeted them. Duncan held back a little behind his parents, but his eyes were on me, so I nodded at him. Then, after most people had left, Duncan appeared again, alone.

"When can we do the piano thing again?"

I swallowed the surprise and pleasure I felt. "Was that time on Thursday good for you? Perhaps a little earlier, so you aren't late for dinner?"

"Cool." And he was gone.

～

I headed for home, a very short walk from the church. As soon as I was in sight of my front door, I saw Marshall sitting there. I nearly froze in my tracks; I'd spent so much time recently thinking about him, and talking about him, that I felt almost anxious at the idea of a conversation. Trying to assess the expression on his face got me nowhere.

"Marshall?"

He stood. "Can I come in for a minute?"

I nodded and did my best to smile as I unlocked the door, something many people around here didn't need to do because they didn't lock their doors.

I shrugged. "Still a New Yorker in many ways, I guess."

Marshall halted just inside the front door. "Wow," he said, staring at the piano. "What a presence."

"Isn't it, though? I've had it all my life. It was in storage in the city, and when I went down for a friend's wedding I decided I needed to have it with me."

He cocked his head slightly. "Are you any good?"

I raised an eyebrow at him, moved to the bench, and opened the keyboard cover. It took only a few seconds for me to decide on a piece. Making no announcement, I began to play.

With his eyes closed, Marshall swayed very slightly, and a slow smile spread over his face as he listened. When I lifted my hands from the keys after the final note, he said, "I don't know which piece that was, but I think it was Debussy."

"Clair de Lune."

"You are good. Very good."

I felt bashful. It was an unfamiliar feeling. I knew I was good, and although I'd always done my best to be suitably humble about compliments, my response to this enigmatic man was different.

"Thanks." I stood. "Would you like some coffee? Tea? I have a coffee cake that my friend Ruth taught me to make."

"I'd like that. Tea, please."

I chattered nervously as I bustled about the kitchen, Marshall watching from his seat at the table. "I take my tea very seriously. Darjeeling okay with you? I always use loose leaf tea and a teapot with this special basket that allows for the best flow during steeping. And of course the water must be at a rolling boil, and I always heat the pot to be sure of the best steeping temperature."

I paused, teapot in one hand and basket in the other. "Please tell me to stop babbling."

Marshall actually laughed. I couldn't remember ever hearing that before. "Babble all you want."

But I was silent for at least thirty seconds. "Do you want to tell me why you're here, or wait until the tea's ready?"

"Now's good. I, uh, well, it's kind of a bad news/maybe-good news kind of conversation."

"Give me the bad first, please."

"I've decided to resign as a lay minister."

I paced myself, not sure how I wanted to respond. I poured boiling water into the warmed teapot, basket and tea in place, and set a timer for three minutes.

I asked, "Is there a reason you'd like to share?"

"Yes. Because I'd like to do something else."

"Is that the maybe-good news?"

"I hope so. Vanessa mentioned you'd like to get something going by way of reaching out to teens. In particular, you suggested including kids from The Forest. I'd like to help."

I leaned against the counter and regarded him. In fact, I saw him in a completely different light from any of our previous encounters. Before me sat the man who had skillfully engaged teenagers in the works of Shakespeare. If he could help rally the Assisi youth....

"That would be absolutely marvelous." I shook my head in admiration. "I know how well you manage your students when it comes to Shakespeare, so—"

"How do you know that?"

The tea timer went off, and the final steps of tea preparation gave me a second to think before facing him again. "I confess I heard you. It seemed asking you to return a phone call wasn't working. The day I met you and Darla in the school parking lot, I had gone to the school to find you. I listened for a few minutes in the hall outside your classroom. It was the witches' scene from *MacBeth*." I waited, but he said nothing right away. "I was very impressed."

"Wait. You did what?"

"I—well, I couldn't think of another way to find you outside of church."

"You could have waited at my car, which is what I thought

you had done. But you hung out in the hall and listened? Why didn't you tell me that? When we were walking?"

I bit my lower lip, embarrassed at having been caught out in what could easily be called an invasive thing to do. I had thought about that a lot since then. The only excuse I'd come up with for eavesdropping, as it were, was that I already felt drawn to him. But I wasn't ready to tell him that.

"I have no excuse for listening. I apologize for my boorish behavior. As for not mentioning it during our walk, all I can say is that you seemed so distant, so unapproachable, that creating an opening for that felt awkward."

At first I thought he looked irritated. But then he sighed. "Yeah. I can see that."

I set slices of coffee cake on the table and poured tea for each of us. As I sat down across from Marshall, I asked, "Do you have any specific ideas about where to start? With the teens, that is."

"I was thinking of using some short works about life as a teenager—short stories, essays, that sort of thing—as starter seeds, kind of, and then helping the kids write about their own experiences. I say 'write' but of course it could be anything. Drawing, a song, whatever, just something to give them a plat-form for their feelings and experiences. Then we'd share them, and they'd get to know each other better. If that works at all, I'll encourage them to think of themes around spiritual practices." He took a forkful of coffee cake. "Delicious. You made this?"

I shrugged. "Not my recipe."

"Still." He sipped his tea. "So what do you think?"

"In a word? Brilliant. I love it. And if you need to relinquish your lay minister role to do it, I completely understand."

"I also have to quit that because I don't think I'm especially suited to it."

"Oh? Why is that?"

One side of his mouth lifted in a kind of smirk. "Jenny tells me you went with her to tell Jasper Moore off. I'm glad you did that. And I'll bet you were much gentler than I was when I'd had enough of him. I was kind of rude. I'm afraid I told him what I thought of him. Not very ministerial of me, I'm afraid."

I laughed. "I admit I was sorely tempted to do the same."

"But you didn't. And that's the difference between us. I can be sweetness and light to people who at least seem to have sweetness and light within them. But someone like Jasper brings out the monster in me."

I scowled in confusion. "You have a monster in you?"

His gaze was level, assertive, just this side of threatening. "I do."

I held his eyes with mine. "I look forward to meeting him."

By the time Marshall left, I realized something very important. He had captured my imagination. And the next morning, I realized something else: Although there were still potential problems I could see, there was no obvious reason why a UU minister and the person in charge of a youth group couldn't be romantically involved.

The rest of the week was full of busy work for me. Not only was I determined to give Deena a theme before Friday, ahead of deadline, but also there were several prosaic issues to handle concerning the church building. First someone found two mice in the function hall, so I had to call someone to deal with that. Then the toilet in the hall clogged, and my… um… ministrations with a plunger were not sufficient to the task, so not only did I have to call a plumber, but also (as with the varmint expert) I had to let him in, describe the problem, and lock up again when the job was done.

And then there was the meeting with the remaining lay ministers to see whether they felt the need to recruit a replacement for Marshall. They decided that, for now, they'd go on with three and let me know if the responsibility was too much.

All these duties meant that I had no time to work with Marshall on the youth group idea. I just hoped he didn't need me.

As it turned out, he didn't. He stopped by late afternoon on Thursday, a folder in his hand, about in the middle of Duncan's piano lesson, much to that young man's consternation. He seemed embarrassed to have anyone other than me know of his interest, and despite Marshall's offer to leave, he disappeared as quickly as possible.

"I'm so sorry," Marshall said. "I had no idea. But I suppose I shouldn't just stop by and expect you to have time for me."

"Not to worry. I think he's hooked. He'll be back next week."

"Does he have a piano at home?"

I shook my head. "As far as I know, he hasn't told his parents about this. It's only the second time he's been here."

"Could he practice on the church piano?"

"Damn." I snapped my fingers. "I meant to call about getting that tuned. I suppose he could, although when the church is not otherwise in use, it will be cold in there."

"True. In fact, I hope it was all alright that I got to the function hall early on Tuesday to turn on the heat for the teens. It's been cold lately."

I sighed; another task I ought to be doing? "So you have a key?"

He nodded. "Vanessa had given me a key last year. Can't remember why, now. Anyway, I'd like to tell you about my progress with the youth group."

He'd been busy. We sat at the kitchen table as he explained that Darla had volunteered immediately ("As I'd expected," was

Marshall's comment), and she had convinced a couple of boys to join. One of them had invited another girl.

"No one from The Forest has joined yet. But I've just begun. I'll work on them once we get a real program going. Meanwhile, what we did this week was come up with a name that suits our mission."

I laughed. "You don't waste time! What's the name?"

"Teens for Truth." He said nothing more, whether waiting for my reaction out of apprehension or anticipation, I couldn't tell.

"I like it. What was the genesis?"

"They liked the idea of not always having to *write* about their lives—that is, they have other means of expression. But what they really liked was the idea that they can say pretty much whatever they want, they won't be graded on it, and we agreed no one in the group will be criticized for telling their truth. Although," here he gave me a knowing glance, "I will be sure they don't stray into troubled waters."

"When are you meeting?"

"Tuesdays, right after school."

Good, I thought; it wouldn't interfere with Duncan's piano lesson, if I could get him to join. "Do you have a sense of how large the group might get?"

"You know, I really don't think it should be very big. Maybe ten? We'll have to see. But it could get unwieldy quickly if it's much larger than that."

"Should I be at the meeting next week?"

I couldn't interpret his facial expression. "Um… actually, they don't want you there."

I felt myself recoil just slightly. "Why not?"

"I think they feel they won't be able to be as open if the minister is there. But I'm going to work on them. Maybe once they're more confident, you could attend a few sessions."

"I'll hope for that, then. At any rate, you've made a wonderful start. I'm impressed." We smiled at each other for a few seconds. "And if I'm honest, it's a bit of a relief to know I don't have to devote a lot of time to it, when you've got it so well in hand."

I told him about some of the things I'd had to deal with that week. He let me go on before giving me yet another worry.

"Has anyone told you there's a small leak in the roof near the steeple?"

I allowed myself to close my eyes very briefly before I sighed. "Not yet, no. Though I suppose you have."

He laughed. "I don't imagine the spiritual calling you felt included running a small business."

"Not exactly. Though I was warned."

There were another several seconds of silence, and I expected he would say something about getting home to make dinner. Instead, he said, "Do you sight-read? The piano, I mean?"

"I do, yes. Why?"

He set his hand on the folder, which he had put at one end of the table. "I hope you won't think it's presumptuous of me, even though it is. I've brought a piece of music."

"Something you want me to play?"

There was a moment of hesitation. Then, "Something I want to sing while you play."

I blinked, stupidly. "Really? What is it?"

"A piece by Fauré. 'Les Roses d'Ispahan.'"

"I love that piece."

"You've played it, then?"

I shook my head. "I've never accompanied anyone. But I'm willing to try."

At the piano, he handed me the score, arranged for tenor. I played through it a couple of times to familiarize myself with the piano score, which was deceptively simple, with some key changes and a few unusual syncopated rhythms. The piano part seemed to have its own melody, which would stand out against the rest of the score if I had more time to work on it.

I told Marshall, "I'll try not to stumble too many times. At any rate, I'll be able to keep going, so don't stop singing if you hear something not entirely expected."

He shook his head. "You play it very nicely, especially considering it's new to you."

"Thanks. So. Ready?" He nodded, and I played the opening bars.

The sweetness and the lyric quality of Marshall's voice took me so by surprise I almost stopped playing just so I could listen to it. The piano was alone on the last couple of bars, and I did my best to render the notes sweetly, a final cadence to match Marshall's voice quality.

When I looked up at him, I saw tears in his eyes. He wiped them quickly. "It's been so long," he said, "since I've known anyone who could do justice to music like this."

Tempted to quip about Violet Verette's playing, which was certainly adequate but not much beyond that, I bit my tongue. Instead, I told Marshall, "You have a lovely voice. So well suited to Fauré."

We smiled awkwardly at each other for a moment, and then I asked, "Do you have other pieces?"

He flushed, the rich pink color flaming from his freckled cheeks to his forehead and into his reddish hair. "Funny you should ask."

He had three other pieces of sheet music by Fauré: "Je Me Suis Embarque," "Automne," and "Le Secret." I played through each one first, but even so I was not satisfied with my accompaniment; Marshall's voice was so lovely that I felt he deserved better than I was giving him. After "Le Secret," I said, "If you'll leave these with me, I'd be glad to work on them so I could do a better job of accompanying you than I've done tonight."

Another flush of his face made me realize that I had just indicated I'd like to do this again. And maybe again.

"I'd love that, though I think you did better than my voice
teacher used to do."

"Ah, but your voice teacher was probably a vocal specialist. I
am a pianist. Though I do sing, as well. Baritone."

"Really? Because I have some duets...." He stopped
speaking suddenly. "I'm being very forward."

I felt a rush of something I hadn't felt in some time. "You
are. And I like it."

"I, um, I should go. I haven't done a thing about dinner yet."

I stood and collected the music scores, stacking them neatly.
Then I didn't move. Marshall didn't move. I decided to take a
risk.

"I was about to make a light dinner, myself. Quiche, and a
salad, with a bottle of sauvignon blanc. I even have a berry pie,
courtesy of Jenny Pratt, for dessert. Would you, um, would you
care to join me?"

Another flush, a gratifying one. "If you let me help."

I grinned. "How are you at grating cheese?"

"I can do that. I also make a mean pie crust."

"Oh, good, because that's not my forté."

During my first year at seminary, back in New York, when I was
testing myself to see if perhaps I wasn't really gay, I'd met a few
times with a woman, also a candidate at General Seminary.
Once, at her apartment, we'd prepared a meal together, and she'd
played a recording I had thoroughly enjoyed. The dinner had not
been a particular success, but I'd bought a copy of the album for
myself.

While I didn't need to test the proverbial waters again
regarding my sexual orientation, I decided to play that album

while Marshall and I worked in the kitchen. It was a test, perhaps, but one of a different nature.

He knew the music right away. "Jean-Pierre Rampal! I love this collection. It's light without being insignificant. Great for meal prep."

I opened the bottle of wine and poured us each a small glass. "Inspiration," I said, as we clinked glasses.

What was I thinking? Is this really a good idea?

I watched as Marshall set about his task, asking about the location of things like flour, and a pastry blender. He made a long-suffering face when I asked what that was.

He was adorable.

Yes. This really was a good idea.

CHAPTER 11

Our dinner conversation was light and fun, at first. I described some of my experiences in New York, such as my "virgin" viewing of *The Rocky Horror Picture Show*. Marshall described some of the tricks he'd taught Angus.

"One of my favorites was having him do a figure-eight, weaving in and around my legs."

"Was he a particularly smart dog?"

Marshall shrugged. "I always thought so. It took me no time to get him to run an obstacle course I set up in the back yard—jumps that I made of sticks and branches, and tunnels I made out of barrel hoops."

"Do you see much of Klondike?"

He smiled and leaned his head backward briefly. "I love that dog. What a monster! But he has a golden heart. I've taken him hiking with me." Something changed in Marshall's face, a sobering. "Vanessa has made me promise that if she dies before he does—and she thinks that's likely—that I'll take him."

I gave that some space and then decided to lighten things up again. "She tells me I should take up hiking. But I've never done that, beyond the trail near the school. I have no proper equipment."

Marshall gave me a tentative look from the corners of his eyes. "Would it be too forward of me to offer advice about that?"

I smiled. "Vanessa has offered the same, but I don't think she'd mind if you took on that responsibility."

~

Marshall stayed well into the evening. We never left the kitchen table, but we talked for hours.

I learned more details about his life in Montana. At one point he referred to the religions conversion camp he'd been sent to.

I told him, "I've been meaning to do some research into those places. I don't want to pry, but I hope you'll tell me anything you'd like to about your experience." He was quiet, so I added, "Obviously, you should say nothing at all if you don't want to."

His gaze was almost heavy in its steadiness. "I don't talk about it, really. I haven't talked about it in any detail since the counsellor my parents sent me to after I—" He closed his eyes so hard his lashes nearly disappeared. Then he stared at the table. "After I tried to kill myself."

"Oh, Marshall." I needed to appear as though I'd heard nothing about that. "I'm so sorry."

He took a deep breath and let it out slowly. "I learned so much at that camp." I heard irony in his tone. "For one thing, I learned that sex is a dreadful, filthy thing. And it's something you should do only with someone you love."

A harsh sound escaped me, but I said nothing.

"Also, God created us to be sinful, evil creatures, capable of the worst kind of atrociousness. And God loves us so much that he'll send us to eternal damnation and conscious agony if we don't do something to change how he created us."

I shook my head, lost for words.

"Of course, none of this was really news; I'd heard it, in one way or another, all my life. But at the camp they made it crystal clear that homosexuality was the worst sin of all. One way they did this was to take us, one at a time, to the lake that was part of the camp. Two counselors would hold us under the water until we were nearly drowned. Once I came up, gasping horribly for air, and I heard one of them tell me that if I died, at least I would sin no more."

"God in heaven."

"So very early one morning I left my cabin and went to the lake alone. I took one of the canoes that were left on the beach and paddled away from shore. I used the legs from a pair of pants to tie heavy stones to my ankles. And I rocked the canoe until it tipped."

My eyes watered. I couldn't breathe. I felt my chin tremble, so I covered my mouth with one hand.

Marshall took a few deep breaths before continuing. "Two of the counsellors had decided to take an early swim. One of them saw the boat capsize. It took both of them to bring me up, because of the stones."

Impulsively I reached a hand across the table. Marshall took it in one of his.

"I came to on the beach, coughing up lake water. I barely heard one of them say, 'Suicide is a sin, too, kid. Just not as bad.'"

I couldn't stand this. And I couldn't stop myself. I stood and went around the table. Marshall stood, and I held him while he cried as I did my best not to let him feel my own sobs.

When I could speak, all I could say was, "I'm so sorry. I'm so sorry."

As he was leaving, he asked me to treat what he'd told me confidentially. "I'm sure you would anyway, but I need to be clear. If the school found out, they might not want me teaching the kids."

"Of course."

"No one else knows, except Vanessa and Jenny. And the school doesn't know I'm gay."

"I'll say nothing to anyone."

If I hadn't been so full of grief, hatred for Marshall's tormentors would have found its way into my heart. It tried. Hatred tried very hard.

After Marshall left, sometime around midnight, I went to my desk and opened the notebook where I wrote my sermon notes. I turned the pages past the notes I'd made for the coming Sunday and started writing. The theme I would give Deena the next day would be an attempt to help my own heart, my own intentions, to turn them away from the evil I'd heard, the hatred I struggled against because of Marshall's suffering and the people who'd caused it.

Love, I wrote, *is not just an emotion. It's not just something we feel for each other, for our families, for our pets, for our homes, or for anything else. Love is the source of all, the very heart of creation. Love is awareness itself. It's the awareness of God, of the universe, of absolute being. And because of what Love is, it swallows up pain, and hatred, and evil. When we acknowledge the supremacy of Love, when we let it fill our hearts and allow it to be the standard of our lives, evil will be consumed. Devoured. Overcome until it becomes the nothing that it truly is. Love does not conquer evil. Love leaves no room for it.*

As if he felt he'd gone too far, Marshall seemed to avoid me Sunday and, really, for the rest of the week. He didn't need me for Teens for Truth, and I had to see about the leaking roof, among other things. I got a phone message from him Tuesday morning letting me know that Jenny Pratt was helping out with the teens, but that was it.

Wednesday afternoon, I had a very interesting visitor. I was in the parish office, discussing with John Thompson how we might fit roof repairs into the budget, when someone knocked on the door. It was closed against the chilly late October drizzle, but usually visitors just walked in. When I opened the door, a man I'd never seen stood there. He said nothing, so I did.

"Welcome. Please, come inside."

He nodded, removed his muddied boots, and walked past me into the office. I caught a whiff of slight body odor as he passed. His clothing was simple, designed for work. He wore no coat or jacket, just a heavy woolen vest over a flannel shirt. He was apparently in his fifties, with a full head of shoulder-length salt-and-pepper hair on his head, and a beard to match, both glistening where the mist had settled.

I gestured toward a wooden bench along one wall, a padded cushion on it that a parishioner had made. Her brother had made the bench.

My visitor shook his head. "I'll stand."

"Very well. Then so will I." I held out my hand, and he shook it briefly. "I'm Spencer Hill, the minister here. What can I do for you?"

"Erik Stillman. Pleased to meet you, reverend. I'm one of the elders from The Forest. I understand you've been asking about us."

"Oh! Oh, yes. That's right. Did the MacPhersons tell you about my interest?"

He nodded. "What is it you want?"

"What I'd really like is for us, your community and mine, to

117

get to know each other better." He looked somewhat dubious, so I plunged ahead. "This isn't about religion. It's more about—well, community, I suppose. I believe there are some Forest Dweller children who attend the Assisi high school, and from what I've heard they don't feel especially welcome. I think that would change if we all knew each other better. And I suspect that people of The Forest know more about Assisi residents than we know about you."

I waited to see if he'd express any reaction—distrust, aversion, curiosity, anything. He didn't.

"You have a holiday coming up, if I'm not mistaken. Samhain." I pronounced it very carefully as Shane MacPherson had done. If Erik Stillman was surprised or impressed, he gave no indication. "Mr. MacPherson has explained to me how the celebration we call Halloween seems to treat the holiday very lightly."

"More like a travesty."

I nodded. "I hear you. And while I don't think we'll be able to get the town to abstain from something they see as great fun, I also don't believe there's any intention to mock Samhain. I suspect people here don't even know what it's about. So, just as an example of what I'm hoping for, a deeper understanding of the spiritual importance of Samhain might give Halloween a much richer meaning."

"You don't need to visit us to do that."

"You're right. And while I understand that a visit by anyone out of superficial curiosity would be offensive, I'm hoping that a visit by me, and maybe one or two others from our church, would open a door. We would certainly not be there to gawk, or to gather fodder for ridicule. We would be there out of sincere desire for understanding."

I told myself to stop talking. I might have said too much already. Mr. Stillman regarded me intently, as though trying to read my mind. I felt uncomfortable, but I stood my ground. I'd meant everything I'd said.

"You have an unusual aura," he said, finally.

See? I wanted to say. *See? This is the kind of thing I want to know about.* But I stood silent, waiting, with what I hoped was an open expression on my face.

"It's a mix. I see a lot of green. But then—" he scowled, though whether in confusion or irritation I couldn't tell. "But then there's white." He leaned back a little on his heels. "Yes. Definitely. But it's not as clear as I'd like."

"Is that bad?"

He seemed to be weighing a decision about how much to tell me. "It makes sense that someone in your role who is sincere about it would have some white, though by no means is it a given. But when it's less than clear, it can mean you're fooling yourself to some extent."

"Fooling myself?"

He shrugged. "In this case, it could mean your motives for approaching my community might not be entirely pure, and maybe you don't even know that."

I rubbed the back of my neck and wondered why these people were so resistant. Also, considering motives and their relative purity, I was trying to push away the thought of seeing Adam Cooper again.

"I don't think I can promise you that any of my motives about anything are entirely pure. That's something that might be said of anyone. But we do the best we can. I do the best I can. And even slightly muddled motivation can yield a good result."

I think that took him by surprise, but he said nothing.

"Look, Mr. Stillman, if this is a problem for you and your people, I will respect your privacy. I won't pursue the idea of establishing a connection." He remained silent. So I decided to put him on the spot. "Is that what you want?"

"We're not isolated because we want to be isolated. We're

aloof because we're cautious. Because we've been burned. Some, literally."

"Burned? Not recently, surely."

"No." His voice told me there was more to this question, something hidden, but I didn't know how to get at it.

"Is aloof how you want to remain?" I would get an answer from him, damn it.

He watched my face for a good thirty seconds. Then, "Let's see what you understand of Yule. Your Christian traditions adopted ours."

I shook my head, confused. "First, I'm not really Christian, myself, though I do come from that tradition, and we do have some Christians in our congregation. But understanding Yule, for example, is one thing I was hoping to learn from you."

"Learn what you can on your own. We begin Yule celebrations the evening of December twenty. It's a Sunday. I'll be at your service that morning. Depending on what I hear, I might or I might not invite you to our feast as we welcome Yule."

I wanted to protest. I wanted to tell him it wasn't my job, and it wasn't fair to my congregation, on the Sunday before Christmas, to turn my sermon into a lesson on Paganism. I watched him put his boots back on. But before I could put words together in a way that could assuage his concerns and clarify my position, he nodded and left. John and I stared for several seconds at the door he'd shut behind him.

John broke the silence first. "Of all the nerve."

I sat heavily on my chair. Elbows on the desk before me, I rubbed my hands over my face and massaged my hairline. Then I chuckled. "At least I got him to come to a service."

"That's not our role. We don't proselytize."

"No. And I wouldn't try to convert him. But I do want him—all of them—to see us as following a spiritual practice that welcomes everyone."

"Why do you want to know more about them?"

"Because I also want them to know more about us."

John shook his head. "Okay, well, for now let's get back to these numbers."

~

A week later, I saw Adam Cooper.

I had been visiting a parishioner whose unwed daughter had just died of an ectopic pregnancy, when I saw them. No longer dressed in leather wrappings but now wearing standard, warm-looking clothing, he was with two other people about his age—another man and a woman. His long hair was tied back with a leather thong, as before. They were moving slowly in my direction, seeming to scour the verges of the road as they went.

It was an area outside of town, a narrow lane bordered by leafless trees and few houses. Adam carried a burlap sack and a short pole with a loop on the end. His male companion was pulling a cart with several small cages on it, and inside one cage was a cat, screaming in protest. Another cage held a cat as well, this one more terrified than angry. Both cats were black.

I had to know what was going on. I pulled my Jeep to the side of the road, killed the engine, and got out. I waited until they were close and then called out to them.

"Good afternoon." They stopped walking, looked at me, and nodded but didn't speak. "I'm really curious. What is it you're doing with the cats?"

Adam spoke. His voice was almost as deep as mine. "Samhain approaches. The villagers will capture and torture black cats. We're keeping them safe. At least a week."

I was stunned almost to silence. Almost. "What did you say? They do what?"

He stood perhaps fifteen feet from me, but I saw his shoulders lift and fall, and he released a breath heavy with exasperation. "You don't know? They don't do that in the city? Or perhaps you just didn't know about it."

"Who would do that?"

The woman spoke. "Teenagers, mostly. From the town. We won't be able to find all the cats, so you'll probably see a corpse or two in a few days, bloody and dismembered."

"I—I had no idea." There was silence for several seconds, at least from the humans. One of the cats was growling menacingly. "I'm forgetting my manners. I'm—"

"We know who you are." Adam's look was inscrutable. Teasing? Challenging? I couldn't be sure.

"And I know who you are," I told him, holding his gaze despite a strong sense of discomfiture. "And your companions?"

"Annika Finley," the woman said with a fling of her long, blond hair, maintaining her distance.

"Jeremy Thaler." Jeremy seemed less forward, less assertive than either of the others.

I looked at the cats. "Are these feral, or are they someone's cats?"

Adam put a hand on his hip. "Doesn't matter. If they're letting them outside this time of year…."

"Samhain?" I asked.

The silence was laden with disdain. "Halloween. No one who celebrates Samhain would do harm."

I'd had about enough antagonism from these Forest Dwellers. "*Any* harm?"

Adam took a couple of steps toward me, the pole at his side, but he held it as though it could become a weapon at any moment. He was not as tall as I was, but there was something statuesque about him.

"We slaughter humanely." His voice carried disdain. "We treat animals and plants with respect. We honor them and acknowledge their sacrifice. Life requires death. Everything depends on how that happens."

Annika spoke up. "An it harm none, do as ye will."

I glanced at her, confused. The wording seemed antiquated. "Whatever you want?"

She glared at me. "The first part is that it harms no one. That comes *before* your actions. And you don't know that until you see someone else's point of view."

Jeremy spoke up. "So much better than your Christian 'Golden Rule.'"

I could almost see the air quotes above his head. I did my best to keep my tone from sounding defiant. "Okay, let's set a baseline, here. I don't call myself Christian. But what's wrong with that rule?"

Adam's voice was part defiance, part threat. "Who made you the judge of what's right and wrong? Why would you assume everyone else wants the same things you want? You aren't the center of the universe."

Nonplussed probably comes closest to how I felt at that moment. "Is that what you think of Christians?"

"It's what they think of themselves." He turned to his friends. "Let's go."

As I watched them move off, past my Jeep and looking again into the woods on either side of the road, a new significance came to me of the scene by the pond, the first time I'd seen Adam. Then, I'd thought of it as an unabashed unity with nature. Then I'd learned that he'd known I was there. And now?

Now it was a "Fuck you!"

CHAPTER 12

I wouldn't say that the black cat encounter meant I was "over" Adam. There had never really been anything to get over. What changed was the place he occupied in my head.

There had been a few moments, I'll confess, as I'd pictured that beautiful man standing naked and perfect in the autumn woods, when I'd felt a rush of lust. And although his beauty was still there in my mind, the perfection was gone. The scene was now tainted with the stain of intention, of a sly awareness, no longer free and uninhibited. Any innocence had died.

Although the idea of his perfection had initially inspired me to want to know more about his community, the loss of it did nothing to diminish my interest. If anything, I was now more determined.

The reason he and his friends had been on the road, though, haunted me. I had never been one of those boys who tear the wings from insects. My father had once told me, "Boys kill frogs for sport. But the frogs don't die in sport. They die in earnest." He'd said he was quoting an ancient Greek, whose name I've forgotten. I wondered, and I still wonder, what it is that would make someone, anyone, young or old, deliberately cause harm—

unnecessary harm, at that—to anything. It was a phenomenon that clearly went back as far as humanity.

~

The concept of juxtaposition inspired my sermon for the coming Sunday. It came to me on the walk I took to clear my mind, after I got home from my encounter with Adam.

In Paradise, Adam and Eve had no concept of anything bad. Which meant they had no concept of anything good. Which meant that the threat, from Yahweh, that if they ate a certain fruit they would die was meaningless to them; not knowing death, the consequence was empty. So when Eve repeated to Serpent (who certainly did know what "die" meant) how she'd been warned, he said, "You won't die. But you'll know good from evil." In other words, her innocence would die; henceforth, she would know duality. She would be pure, simple, uncomplicated, no longer.

Adam Cooper had proven not to be the innocent I had imagined. His actions had motive, agenda, even scorn within them.

The other juxtaposition was between Pagan and non-Pagan, or (in my case) Pagan and UU. Sunday would be All Saints Day on the Christian liturgical calendar, the day after Halloween, too late for me to use my pulpit to discourage the mistreatment of animals or anything else. But it was not too late for me to contrast Halloween and the Pagan holiday that gave had given to it. And it was not too late to ask my parishioners what they thought of the difference between the Golden Rule and the... whatever it was Annika had said. A kind of credo, a statement of belief? I supposed it could be called a Pagan credo.

At one point on my walk I found myself very near Vanessa's house. Daylight was not gone but was fading, and through her windows I saw lights. The idea of a cup of tea and perhaps a cookie or two was tempting, and I'd been meaning to ask her if she knew Erik Stillman. So I rang the bell beside her front door, ready to apologize for dropping by uninvited.

"Oh, Spencer. Good. I've wanted to talk to you about something. Come in."

I followed Vanessa to her kitchen, Klondike's nails clicking lightly on the floor behind me. Watching Vanessa move, it seemed to me she wasn't standing as tall as I'd seen her before, and I wondered if her health might be worsening.

She did, in fact, offer me tea and sugar cookies. If she wasn't feeling well, she didn't reveal it. Instead, she wanted to talk about someone else's welfare.

She didn't mince words. "Marshall tells me he's resigned as lay minister and is having some success with the youth group you and I had hoped would happen. How involved have you been with that?"

I kicked myself mentally; I'd been so focused on mundane things, church-related notwithstanding, that I'd neglected to tell Vanessa about either of these changes. I wondered, briefly, who had told her.

"I apologize for not mentioning this to you myself. I did talk to the other lay ministers, and they wanted to wait to see if a replacement was necessary. As far as the teen group, I haven't been involved much at all. Marshall and I talked about it, of course, but then he jumped right in, and it seems the teens would rather I stay out of it. Jenny is helping him. I'll give it some time, and then maybe attend a session or two." I took a bite of cookie and waited to see if she'd tell me if there was a reason for her question.

She held her teacup in both hands, elbows on the table, and regarded me for a moment. Then, "And how are you and Marshall getting along?"

As gently as I could, I said, "Why do you ask?"

"He's in love with you. And he's convinced that if there was ever a chance for something to develop, his—well, his confession, as he sees it, about what happened at that horrible camp has destroyed it."

I blinked stupidly, my mind either blank or so full of conflicting thoughts it might as well have been empty.

"Has it?" she prodded.

"Why would he think that?"

"Spencer, don't be thick. It's been, what, two weeks since he told you? And you haven't contacted him directly even once. Now, you can tell me this is none of my business, but I care very much about that young man. You don't have to answer, but I'm going to ask: How do you feel about him? Because however that is, I think you should let him know."

Two weeks? Had it been that long? "I—I don't know what to say. I've been really busy with a lot of things." If I hadn't felt pangs of guilt, I would have asked why she and Marshall had been discussing me.

"Which is not an answer. How do you feel about him?"

I felt one side of my mouth lift in a wry grin. "You're right. I could tell you it's none of your business. But actually, I'm glad you've brought this to my attention. The time got away from me."

Her sigh was thick with impatience. "And?"

I closed my eyes briefly, telling myself that she and Marshall must be close for her to know how he felt about me. And, I recalled, she was one of the only other people who knew about his attempted suicide.

"I'm still trying to work out how I feel about him. I think that's all I'm ready to tell you. But I hear what you're saying. At the very least, I will reach out to him."

She seemed to relax a little. "That's all I ask. Just don't leave him hanging, please."

"I won't. And now, there's something I'd like to ask you about. Have you ever met Erik Stillman?"

She nodded. "I have. One of the elders in The Forest. He's an interesting character. Did he come to you?"

"He did." I told her about the conversation I'd had with him.

She laughed. "So you have to prove you're interested and not just curious before he'll reciprocate. Will you do it?"

"I think so. Still considering what it would mean, though." I told her what my idea was for the coming Sunday service.

"So he has got you thinking. I shall look forward to that sermon."

I'll admit, Vanessa's chastisement stung. But it served its purpose, and although I chafed at her intrusion into my private life, I had to admit she was right that I should have been in touch with Marshall. I spent that evening thinking long and hard about my feelings regarding him. He had always seemed enigmatic to me, and when I collected the bits and pieces I knew about him, that adjective fit better and better.

The scene with CC and Troy was still very clear in my mind. The way he had worked with the reluctant teens to render Shakespeare was impressive. The more I knew about his background and his home life, the more vulnerable he seemed, though the way he'd taken charge of the new teen group belied fragility. Then there was his singing voice, which was both rich and sweet at once, the native musicality evident. And he made excellent pie crust.

Renaissance man was the term that came to my mind: intelligent; artistic; having a wide range of interests and expertise. He might miss the mark in the areas of sophistication and athleticism, but the term clicked into place as soon as I thought of it.

And then there was the way he felt about me, and the way he had handled those feelings. He'd been brave enough to tell me he was attracted to me, and then he'd backed off to give me space, to give me time to consider what he'd said, or to decide to avoid the whole issue if that's what I wanted to do.

I pictured his face, that boyish, open expression, guileless. His innocence had been ripped from him, but that had not spoiled him. I had sensed no bitterness, no seething anger at what had been done to him when he'd had no say in what happened.

The more I thought about him, the less I wanted to avoid anything. In fact, the more I wanted to find out whether, as Vanessa had put it, anything might develop.

As every time in the past when I'd called Marshall, I had to leave a voice message; did the man ever pick up his phone? But he called back soon after.

"Hello Spencer. What can I do for you?"

"I, uh, I was hoping we could make some time for more music. I must confess I haven't found time to work on your pieces yet, but it's at the top of my list now. Are you interested?"

It was a few seconds before he spoke. "That sounds good."

"Come to dinner Friday? If you can come around five, we can make some music and then do another dinner. Spaghetti this time?"

After another few seconds, I heard, "I'll bring the meatballs and the sauce."

We hung up, and I told myself, *Be careful, Spencer.* Marshall was so sensitive, and so creative, that it would be too easy, and too destructive to lead him on. But I also didn't want him to think he'd ruined anything. He hadn't. He definitely hadn't.

Duncan had shown up last Thursday, despite his misplaced embarrassment at having Marshall see him playing the piano. He came again that week.

At one point I asked if he'd heard about Teens for Truth.

"Yeah. Sounds lame."

I did my best to sound uninterested, as though it didn't matter at all. "Why do you think that?"

"Truth? They're not going to do that."

"I think they might. But if you aren't interested, fine." I would ask him in another few weeks, when I could say something more specific about the group.

When Marshall arrived Friday afternoon, he set a black carrying case on a table near the piano and grinned at me. "To be revealed anon."

In the kitchen, he lifted a large plastic tub from a tote bag and removed the cover.

"It's a family recipe," he said as he set the container of sauce on my counter. "Came to my mom from her grandmother."

I opened the lid and sniffed. "Wow. I almost want to eat first. But after a meal and wine, we might not make as much good music." I grinned at him, and only when I saw the expression on his face—anticipation rather than amusement—did it occur to me how my comment might have sounded.

"I, um, I brought more music." He handed me a folder. In it were two music scores and a few photocopied pages. On top was Mendelssohn's "Sonntagsmorgen," a duet for two voices. Beneath that was another duet, Humperdinck's "When at Night I Go to Sleep" from his opera, *Hansel and Gretel*. Each had piano accompaniment. The photocopied pieces were very different from these two. The scores were spare, evidently medieval in origin, and with no composer indicated I assumed they were from that most prolific of composers, Anonymous.

"You've got my attention," I told him. "I'm glad we decided on music first, because I'd die of curiosity if I had to wait to find out what strange and wonderful things you've brought."

I settled onto the piano bench and lifted the keyboard cover. "Let me play through the Mendelssohn a couple of times."

As I played, Marshall stood close beside the bench, leaning in to turn pages as needed. It surprised me that having him so close made me a little breathless, and I blame that for the few notes I missed the second time through.

"I have another copy," he told me, reaching for the folder, "so I'll use that one. But I know the piece well enough that I can still turn pages."

I almost told him not to bother, that I was good at turning pages, but the rush I felt when he was close to me was too tempting.

"I've sung German before," I said, "but I don't know the language. Walk me through the text?" Marshall's German sounded convincing to my ears, but we both laughed at some of my attempts. "I'll probably just do some nonsense syllables for much of the piece."

Marshall stood beside me, his score in his hands, and I played the opening notes. His voice part began two measures ahead of mine, and once again I was struck by the clarity, the sweetness of his voice. He glanced up at me as I sang my opening notes, but I was reading my score and couldn't guess at his expression.

We made it through with only a few keyboard fumbles and several of my wrong vocal notes. After the final cadence the room feel silent.

"Spencer." I looked at him. "Is there anything you can't do?"

I laughed. "Well…. Finance makes my hair hurt. And I can't draw to save my soul."

"Your voice…."

"Come to that, *your* voice…."

He bit his lower lip briefly. "Am I wrong, or do we sound pretty damn good together?"

I gave him a soft smile. "You're not wrong."

We went through the Mendelssohn a few times until I could at least play all the notes, even if I was still singing "la la la" too often for my satisfaction.

"The next one will be easier," he told me.

"Is it in English?"

He laughed. "Yes. And it's best done quite slowly."

The Humperdinck was exactly the right kind of song for Marshall's voice, though I'm not sure I did my part justice. "I think my voice is not ideal for this one."

"It does have a lot of substance."

"On to the others, then?"

He handed me one of the medieval pieces, and as I looked it over he opened the case he'd brought. At first I thought it was a violin, but I quickly realized it wasn't quite the right size or shape. And the bow was strung differently as well.

He readied the instrument for playing. "Can I have an A?"

I played the standard 440 A on the keyboard, watched as he tuned the four strings, and then said, "Okay, Marshall, I give up. What is that?"

"A vielle. It's medieval. They were made in slightly different shapes and sizes. Some had five strings."

"But yours looks modern."

He nodded. "It's about fifty years old." He played a short tune and lowered the instrument to his side. "When I was at the University of Vermont, my major was education, but I minored in music. One of the professors introduced me to medieval music, and when he died—still a young man, around forty—he left me this in his will. I could never afford one on my own."

I couldn't help wondering about the nature of the relationship. Maybe Marshall would tell me someday. "It has a rather strident sound."

"A lot of medieval music is like that."

I looked at the music he'd given me. "And what, pray tell, is the language on this one?"

He laughed. "It's medieval French. Shall I walk through the pronunciation with you?"

"Please. And I'm glad there's no piano part for this one, or there'd be no hope."

When I'd struggled hard enough, Marshall played a few notes to set the key. "Ready?"

I'd thought I was, but although it was easy enough to read the music, the pace was fast and the language strange to me. There were three parts, and Marshall played one on the vielle. Our two vocal lines wove in and around each other, both in the same range. We sang it through three times, each time a little better.

"What do you think?" he asked.

"I'm not sure. I've never heard anything quite like it."

"The other one is shorter and easier." He handed me a single sheet with the title "Sumer Is Icumen In."

I laughed and shook my head. "Another medieval language?"

"This is old English, actually." He went through the pronunciations and I imitated him as best I could. The piece was a round, and there was no instrumentation. It was great fun, once I got the hang of the wording. We sang through it a number of times, more energetically with each repetition. When we finally stopped singing, we both gave way to joyful laughter.

"That was amazing!" I told him. "Was it that professor who gave you all this ancient stuff?"

"It was."

We grinned at each other for a few seconds. I let out a long breath. "Dinner?"

"Dinner."

CHAPTER 13

We chatted about innocuous things as we went about our respective tasks to prepare dinner—what trails Marshall liked for hiking, how much longer in the season one could be in the woods without skis or snowshoes—as light jazz played in the background. He asked for an enameled pot for the sauce, but I didn't have one. He shrugged and used the pot I handed him. I got the spaghetti water going and put a salad together, and I decanted a fairly expensive bottle of Chianti Classico I'd brought with me from New York. I said nothing about it, waiting to see if Marshal knew enough about wine to appreciate it.

At one point, each focused on his own task, we collided. We laughed a little awkwardly, but we didn't move very far apart. He was tall enough that I could look almost directly into his blue eyes. So I did. And those eyes looked back at mine. His mouth, slightly open, pulled mine toward it, and we kissed.

It was light, at first, a little tentative, but he opened his mouth to me and I responded with a sudden passion that surprised me. I held his face in my hands as his fingers found their way up my back, pulling me closer.

We pulled our heads apart, both of us a little breathless, and his hands lowered to my waist.

He nearly whispered, "I've wanted to do that for weeks."

"So do it again."

He didn't hesitate. I lowered my hands and pressed his ass forward against me, and he groaned quietly as we kissed. I knew the spaghetti water was boiling, but I didn't care; the pasta wasn't in it yet, so it wouldn't boil over.

With a sort of shuffling gait, I walked Marshall toward a wall and pressed him against it. I kept our mouths together as I undid his belt and waist band, setting his erection free. I took the pulsing beauty in my hand, and as I lowered myself to my knees, Marshall's groans grew louder and were peppered with wordless exclamations.

Ordinarily, I would have teased him with my tongue, maybe even with my teeth. I would have massaged his balls and run a finger behind them. But there was no time for that, and I knew it. I barely had time to wrap my mouth around him before he released that tangy, salty milk I had learned to love. His hands were on my shoulders, and he leaned hard on me as he slid down, back to the wall, eyes closed, mouth open and taking in shuddering breaths, until he sat on the floor. My own erection had calmed with Marshall's release as though in a sympathetic connection.

I watched his face. He seemed so vulnerable, so emotionally exposed. A soft smile crept over that face and he opened his eyes lazily. "I have dreamed of this. So many times."

I chuckled. "I hope it lived up to your expectations."

"And then some." We grinned foolishly at each other. Then, "Shall I return the favor?"

I took his hand as I stood and he rose with me. "Perhaps later." I watched as he fastened his jeans, and we kissed again, gently but deeply. "Right now, I'm still hungry."

A pinkish tinge spread over the light, freckled skin of his face. I was beginning to find that quite charming.

~

That evening unleashed something in me, something I didn't recognize but which I found exciting and compelling. I was younger than Marshall by three years; I had seen the résumés of all the lay ministers. He had experienced much in life I could only guess at. And yet I was... well, not his superior, by any means. Maybe my relative stability, my self-confidence gave me a more solid place to stand, and I felt as though I provided a kind of emotional anchor for Marshall. It was heady.

In my past relationships, I had not experienced this dynamic. I had felt desired, wanted, even to some extent loved. But this, with Marshall, was different. With him, I felt needed.

No one in my life had ever needed me. Maybe if I'd had a pet, I would have had at least a little of that feeling. It wasn't that Marshall ever told me he needed me, but the feeling was powerful, and I believed it.

All that is not to say that the idea of a relationship with Marshall didn't give me pause. My last couple of years in New York, in addition to having a few short-term relationships, I'd experimented with a small number of what I'll call one-offs. These were sexual encounters not unlike what had happened with Marshall in my kitchen, with men I never expected (or, mostly, never wanted) to see again. Sometimes they occurred even when I was in a relationship with someone else. So no relationship I'd had since my very first, with Donald, had had to do with commitment.

A relationship with Marshall would, of necessity, be different. I had no intention of committing myself for life to anyone, at least not for the foreseeable future. But what I knew of Marshall told me that as long as I was with him, there could be no one else. And whatever developed with him would last. At least for a while. Would I come to love him? I couldn't promise. But I knew I had to be ready for him to love me.

The day after that spaghetti dinner was Halloween. For me, it would have been not much more than a series of doorbell rings and costumed kids expecting sugary handouts, except for Duncan. I had once told him I couldn't wait to see what his costume would be. It was around nine thirty, when the younger kids were mostly home digging through their take, when Duncan appeared.

In truth, I didn't recognize him. He was with two other teenagers, and each was decked out in truly ghoulish ways. I admit that when I opened the door, the realism took me so aback I started. The teen in front was nearly as convincing a werewolf as you'd see in any Hollywood horror film.

He grinned menacingly. "Hey, Rev. You afraid of me now?"

I laughed, and then Duncan laughed, and I gave the three teens everything I had left in my candy supply. As I watched them disappear into the darkness, I realized I had not seen any bloodied, tortured cats, black or otherwise. Adam and friends had done their job well.

Marshall brought another piece of music the Wednesday after the spaghetti dinner, a jazz classic titled "Blame It On My Youth." I'd heard the piece before as an instrumental, so I didn't know the lyrics until Marshall sang them. They confirmed my beliefs about how he would see our relationship. *If I expected love when first we kissed, blame it on my youth.* The whole song spoke to a naiveté, an almost childlike innocence that might accompany

137

someone's first love. *On my mind all the time. Forgetting to eat. Forgetting to pray.* If it hadn't been for the way he made love to me after dinner—no stranger to the art of foreplay, no hesitation when it came to rolling a condom onto my erection or to taking me inside him—I might have thought I really was his first relationship.

As accepting as our UU congregation was, we agreed it would be better to keep a low profile. Also, Marshall was sure it would be a problem if the school knew of our involvement. This meant our time together was limited to a couple of evenings a week—no sleep-overs—and to outdoor activities where it was unlikely we'd be seen together. To me, after being in New York where not only was it fairly easy to avoid being recognized, but also where I'd been mostly open about my relationships, this wariness, this vigilance, felt unnaturally confining. To be honest, it chafed.

It seemed to me that Marshall, with his background of outright torment for being gay, had less trouble with this subterfuge than I did. To me, it felt deceitful; to him, it probably felt like survival. Very soon, I wanted to be with him as much as he wanted to be with me. So I went along with his request for discretion despite not quite believing it was necessary.

Marshall lived in the lower floor of a two-family house not far from the school, and he felt too anxious about discovery for us to spend time there. My house, though, was only somewhat better; although it didn't happen often, there was always the possibility that someone in my congregation would drop by unexpectedly. Hoping to discourage nocturnal visitors at all times, I made a practice of not turning on any outdoor lights when I was home, and I drew curtains in every window each night, whether Marshall was with me or not.

Fortunately, he felt safe enough driving with me to get hiking equipment. Not long after that, he and Klondike took me hiking.

∼

The second Saturday in November was a cold day. It felt bitter cold to me, but Marshall assured me it was only cold, and he insisted that the thick clouds overhead were not snow clouds. I'd been wearing my new boots as much as possible, as instructed, so that I could break them in as opposed to having them break my feet, or so the store clerk had told me. There was snow on the ground, but not so much as to prevent us from walking.

Clearly, Klondike was up for a hike; when we stopped by Vanessa's to collect him, he was already jumping and excited.

"All I did," Vanessa protested, "was to ask if he was ready for his hike."

Marshall laughed and grabbed the fur on either side of Klondike's huge head, shaking it to the evident delight of the dog. He gave Klondike a solid pat on the back. "Let's go, boy!"

We took my Jeep; Marshall's little car was barely big enough for him and Klondike alone. I followed Marshall's directions to the trailhead, listening to the slight hissing sounds my tires made as they left tracks in the pale slush on the road, and feeling a pleasant anticipation with a slight undertow of anxiety.

After about half an hour we drove through another town, Little Boundary. It was larger than Assisi with charming New England style architecture—a lot of white clapboard and black or dark green shutters. As we passed a church built in the same style, I heard Marshall's sharp intake of breath. "What is it?" I asked.

"That church. It used to be Congregational."

"I had my eyes on the road. Couldn't read the sign. What is it now?"

"Assembly of God." His voice was tight, strained.

His family's denomination. The people who had tortured him. The people who had damned him and driven him to suicide. I didn't know what to say, so I waited until Marshall spoke again. It took him maybe ten minutes, and he spoke then only because we were nearing the trailhead.

Marshall was all business, getting out of the car, fastening Klondike's lead. I pulled out the backpacks and set them on the ground. Marshall still looked tense. Even Klondike knew something was wrong. He sat quietly, looking up at Marshall with what seemed to me to be concern. I wrapped my arms around Marshall and felt his head drop onto my shoulder.

"They can't get you," I told him. "You're safe."

His arms tightened around my chest. He gave two or three short nods and started to pull away, but I held him and planted a solid kiss on his mouth. Still tense, he responded as well as he could. Then, "Let's get going."

Marshall seemed less anxious once we were on the trail. He kept Klondike on the lead as we made our way along the lower section, which wasn't terribly steep. Once the trail became steeper with more large rocks to scramble over, he unfastened the lead from Klondike's collar.

"I'm not seeing any footprints, so I think we're alone on the trail. Klondike wants to run."

And run he did. Watching him, I laughed as well as I could, struggling for breath because of the effort of climbing. The dog was loving this. He ran up the trail, stopped and sniffed the ground, ran ahead again, and ran back to us, joy on his face, as if to say, "Why are you guys so slow? Come on!"

At one point Klondike disappeared into the woods along the side of the trail. Marshall, ahead of me, stopped and removed his gloves. With two fingers in his mouth, he made a loud, sharp whistle, and within seconds Klondike was with us again.

I grinned. "I've always wanted to be able to do that."

"You can't?"

"No amount of trying has worked."

Marshall laughed, and it felt so good to see him relaxed and enjoying himself.

After about two hours, the sun began to peek through the cloud cover. We stopped for a quick lunch on an outcropping of rock. There was a fallen tree to one side, and we brushed the snow off so we could sit as we devoured our peanut butter sandwiches. Marshall poured some water into an aluminum bowl for Klondike and gave him a few treats.

The view revealed many more mountains in the distance. Shadows moved across them as clouds obscured and revealed the wan sun. It struck me how much paler the sunshine was this far north than in the city.

Marshall decided we should descend right after lunch. "Going down will take longer, believe it or not."

I zipped the last of our lunch remnants into my pack. "Why is that?"

"Going up, you fought gravity using your thigh muscles, probably the most powerful muscles you have. Going down, the stress is on the front quad area, above your knee, and gravity tries to lower you faster than you want to go. If you slip and fall going up, you don't go very far. Going down, a fall can take you on a journey you don't want."

He was right, of course, and by the time we saw the Jeep ahead of us my knees were decidedly complaining, wobbling to prove their point.

Marshall gave Klondike more water as he watched me struggle into the car. "I'll show you an exercise to help you build up your quads. Tomorrow you might find it challenging to walk down stairs. If you do, just go backward until your muscles recover."

I noticed a small shaking in my left knee as I stepped on the clutch before turning the key. "I think I need a hot bath." I glanced at Marshall and noticed that he seemed tense again.

When he spoke, he looked ahead, and his voice had an edge. "There's a bed and breakfast in Little Boundary I like to stop at after a hike. They have a small restaurant where they serve hot chocolate, and they let me bring Klondike inside on his lead."

"Do you want to stop there today?"

He let out a sigh. "I want to. But that church…."

"Surely no one would recognize you, even on the off-chance someone from the church is there."

He nodded. "You're right. I'm being silly."

"I don't see it as silly at all. If you aren't comfortable, we can just go home and make hot chocolate."

"No. I need to face this." Now he turned toward me and grinned. "I have you and Klondike to protect me."

The small restaurant was charming. It was an extension of a huge old colonial house, white with black shutters of course. Inside there was pine paneling everywhere, and embedded in the white ceiling were dark beams. Only two of the eight wooden tables were occupied. Marshall chose a large one near the window, and Klondike settled under it, head on his paws, perhaps worn out at last.

A middle-aged waitress greeted us, a half-apron with bears in the pattern tied around her large midsection. "Hello, Marshall. Your usual?"

"Yes, please, and for my friend as well."

"Out for a hike?"

"Yes. It seemed a great day for it."

She eyed me as though hoping for an explanation as to who I was, but Marshall just smiled at her until she left.

By the time we arrived back in Assisi, dusk was upon us. We took Klondike home, where Vanessa proclaimed him sufficiently exhausted. At my place, from the refrigerator Marshall took the chicken casserole he had brought, so it could be starting to warm up until we were ready to cook it.

"Who gets to shower first?" I asked, hoping he'd say I would.

"You go ahead." I couldn't interpret his grin. I had just stepped under the steaming water when a hand pulled the curtain aside, and Marshall stepped in with me.

This was hardly the first erotic shower I'd had. Perhaps being unexpected was what made it seem more stimulating than usual, or perhaps I was just tired enough to be relaxed, but when I felt Marshall's hands on my back, and as he slid them down to my hips and pulled me toward his sheathed erection, my own dick jerked with anticipation. It wasn't often, in our love making, that he penetrated me. But now, after he'd introduced me to some-thing in which he'd taken the lead all day, it seemed appropriate. He wrapped his hand around my hard dick, both to protect it from the tiles and to make sure it got the attention it deserved.

"Do me real good," I told him, the side of my face pressed against the tiles.

It was not his tenor voice that responded. "Oh, yeah."

I came before he did, my limp dick pressed again and again in front of me as Marshall's thrusts continued. He kept one hand on the side of my neck, pushing my face onto the tiles. I'd never known him to be so rough, and I nearly came again as my dick rubbed harder and his grunts grew louder and deeper.

He came with a loud groan and stayed inside me as long as he could. Then he spun me around, still pressed against the tiles, and kissed me as though it would be the last thing he did before dying.

As he pulled away, his face changed from an expression of rutting lust to one of amusement. "I think we really need this shower now."

~

We put the casserole into the oven. I set my alarm so we could doze on my bed, in an embrace so tender as to refute the animal passion of our shower.

We spoke little during dinner, though we grinned at each other quite a bit. Instead of any dessert, we took glasses of cognac into the living room and sat close together on the couch as romantic chamber music from my stereo system washed over us.

I think it was around nine o'clock when Marshall sat forward, elbows on his knees, and turned his head toward me. "I'm not ready to go home yet."

"Then don't."

"I'm ready for something else. I *need* something else."

"Oh?"

"I need to feel you deep inside me. I need to be filled with you, with your confidence, your strength, your conviction that what we are is good and right."

There it was again. His need for me. I set my glass down, stood, and offered him my hand. "Come upstairs with me."

We undressed each other slowly, caressing each new area of skin as it was exposed. I kissed his chest, his belly, his thighs, everywhere but his genitals as he moaned softly. I wasn't entirely sure I could carry him, but I decided to try. I picked him up and carried him to the bed.

At first all went much as it had at other times when we'd made love here, on my bed, in the dark privacy of my bedroom. But tonight was different.

Marshall lay beneath me, his legs over my shoulders as I

pumped gently into him, feeling my way, not wanting things to end too soon. I kissed his neck, bit his tits, and listened carefully to his breathing. That's when things changed.

"Choke me."

I kept pumping slowly, not sure I'd heard right. So he said it again.

"Until I slap your arm. Choke me! Now! Please!"

"Marshall, I—"

"Now! Spencer, now!"

Hesitantly, I adjusted my position so I could place a hand on his neck.

"Harder! Until I can't speak!"

"How will I—"

He shut his eyes tight. "Harder! Harder! Hard—"

I pressed upward into his jaw just enough so that he couldn't get that last word out. I hadn't come yet, but Marshall was almost beyond ready. His entire body shook, almost in convulsions. He placed a hand over mine and pressed, or I might have released him.

I felt something hit my arm, and Marshall's body arched and then fell limp. I pulled my hand away. There was cum all over my belly. I felt my erection soften, and my dick fell away from him.

Confused, unsure of what had just happened, I fell to the side and watched as Marshall's breathing calmed and the tension on his face relaxed. Neither of us spoke for at least a few minutes as he lay there, eyes closed, and I watched, concern growing. This must be erotic asphyxiation. I'd heard about it. I didn't like it.

Finally, eyes still closed, he whispered, "Thank you."

"What *was* that?"

He opened his eyes and looked at me. "Seriously? You've never done that?"

"No. Never."

An odd laugh escaped him. "I'll do it for you sometime."

I got up and reached for my clothes. "I don't think so."

Marshall propped himself on one elbow, hand behind his head, and watched me. "Not if you don't want to, of course. But you don't know what you're missing." I said nothing. "Spencer?"

I sat on the side of the bed. "I'm not comfortable with that. Don't ask me to do it again."

I felt ridiculous descending my own staircase backward, but it was the safest thing to do as my knees were letting me know they were very unhappy. This absurdity might have lightened my mood after what had happened in the bedroom, but instead it served to darken it.

Marshall packed his casserole dish and put on his coat, clearly anxious. At the front door he turned to me. "Are we okay?"

"Sure. Good night." I gave him a light kiss and opened the door for him to leave.

CHAPTER 14

I spent part of Monday morning at the library. After assuring Mrs. Holland, the librarian, that I didn't need her generous offer of help, I wandered through a few aisles that had nothing to do with my mission. It would be better, I figured, if no one knew the UU minister was browsing for books about sexual practices. Gradually I made my way to the section about psychology and looked until I found a book I thought would help me. I stood there in the aisle, ready to replace the book quickly in the event I were discovered reading through it.

Erotic asphyxiation, I read, is the deliberate restriction of oxygen to the brain in the hope of intensifying the sexual experience. It's more common in men than women. It's also considered one of several types of paraphilia, which as a group has to do with arousal inspired by fetishes, fantasies, and other objects or stimuli.

Then there was autoerotic asphyxiation, in which one would do something to cause one's own oxygen restriction. Apparently this is even more dangerous than having someone else do it, because if one gets into trouble, there's no help nearby.

I placed the book back onto its shelf and chose another

psychology book at random. It didn't matter what it was; all I wanted to do was sit someplace and stare at an open book, pretending to read, while I allowed myself to calm.

In my mind, I had relived the choking event over and over since Saturday night, trying to understand why Marshall—why anyone—would want that. I had even masturbated and deliberately tried to stop breathing as I neared orgasm, which gave me at least a hint of what Marshall had wanted. But I quite enjoyed sex already, thank you very much, and I wasn't interested in having someone choke me, let alone doing anything to choke myself.

Sitting there in the library, elbows on the table and fingers pressed against my hairline, staring at a book whose title I didn't even know, I grew more and more angry with Marshall. What he had asked me to do was dangerous. I could have hurt him. I could have damaged his larynx. I could have prevented him from breathing for too long. Perhaps people who are prepared, people who know what they're doing, could do this thing without excessive risk, but I was not one of those people.

Marshall could have died. And he hadn't even warned me! He hadn't explained to me what he wanted or what the risk was for him and—damn it— for me! Imagine how I would go about explaining to the police that a local teacher was found naked and strangled to death in my bed!

I'd told him I wouldn't do it again. So on one hand maybe I didn't need to bring it up with him. But on the other hand, there was the danger he had put both of us in, without my knowledge or consent. I decided that had to be addressed. And if that weren't enough, I was now worried about what he might try on his own.

"Hello, Reverend."

The voice behind me startled me so badly I let out an odd sound. I turned and saw a woman from my congregation, but for the life of me I couldn't come up with her name.

I smiled as nicely as I could. "Hello! Fancy meeting you here. How are you?"

It seemed she was looking for ideas about garden plantings. "It'll be a while before I can plant anything, but I'm hoping to build a rock garden in the spring."

"Sounds lovely. I hope to see it when it's finished."

She smiled and moved away. I re-shelved my book, waved at Mrs. Holland, and left.

At home, I called Marshall and left a message on his home phone.

"Marshall, Spencer here. We, um, I need to talk with you about a couple of things." I barely stopped myself in time before referring to "Saturday night." He lived alone, but that didn't mean he never had visitors, and he would not want just anyone to know about our relationship. "Give me a call when you have a chance."

The afternoon got eaten up by a chore I'd been putting off: cleaning out a storage room in the church function hall. It was dusty work. Violet Verette helped me identify things that might be useful. We chatted about piano music while we worked, which made the chore less onerous.

I'd been home about an hour, having showered to remove dust, when my phone rang.

"Hey, Spencer." Marshall. "Oh, not those. The ones on the upper shelf."

"What?"

"Sorry. I wasn't talking to you." I paused, waiting to see if he'd tell me who he *was* talking to, but he said, "You called. What's up?"

He's calling me while someone else is there. I played along, bringing up something innocuous.

"I had an idea for the teen group. Food for thought, as it were. Something to get them curious and learning at the same time."

"Do tell."

"You know how Pope Gregory III co-opted the Celtic Pagan holiday of Samhain and turned it into a Christian holiday? All Saints Day? He kind of took half of Samhain and moved it to All Saints, and then other half became All Souls Day."

There was a pause. "Come again?"

"All Saints, November first, honors the dead who are now in heaven. The next day, All Souls, is when they pray for dead souls who are still making their way to heaven. You can see how these both draw directly from the tradition of Samhain."

His tone was tentative. "Okay, yeah, you did a sermon on that. But Halloween is behind us."

"And the same kind of thing happened around Christmas. All the typical traditions were originally Pagan. Many historians and scholars don't even believe Jesus, if he existed, was born in December."

Another pause. "I'll give it some thought. Anything else?"

I felt my back stiffen. "Yes. We need to talk about the other night."

"Okay, but not now."

"Apparently you aren't alone. So when would be a good time?"

"Can I get back to you?"

"How about tomorrow after the teen group?"

"I said, I'll get back to you. Bye now." And he hung up.

If I wasn't pleased with him before that call, I was royally pissed after it. He'd called me when someone else was with him, so he couldn't talk very long or about anything to do with us. He'd acted as if I'd suggested something that he didn't see the point of. And he'd refused to commit to a time when we could talk.

I decided to take a somewhat bold if not unreasonable step.

~

Teens for Truth met in the church function hall at four o'clock on Tuesdays. So that's where I went, only I arrived at four-thirty.

I shut the door behind myself very quietly. Marshall, who was talking to the group, didn't see me, but Jenny did. She looked surprised but not in a bad way. There were now nine teens in the group, I noticed, something Marshall had not told me. It might be a recent development, though, and he just hadn't told me *yet*.

Some of the kids saw me and looked my way, and Marshall stopped mid-sentence and turned.

"Oh," he said, his expression not quite friendly. "We didn't expect you."

I shrugged. "Just couldn't stay away any longer. I've heard you're all doing really good things here. I'll just sit over on the side and listen. Please; go ahead."

Hesitantly, Marshall turned back to his audience and continued. The subject today seemed to be whether the individual teens celebrated Christmas, if so how, and if not why not.

A couple of the kids said fairly predictable things, and I hoped my presence wasn't dampening their comfort level. Then a boy I'd never seen before stood.

"In The Forest, we celebrate Solstice, the start of Yule."

Marshall turned to look at me. Jenny said, "Yes, I've heard about that, Leigh. What does that celebration involve?"

Leigh looked at me. "We have lots of evergreen boughs and holly berries. We have fires that burn all night to encourage the sun coming back. It's the shortest day of the year, and after that the sun starts coming back. We sing songs. We dance. And if we want, we give each other gifts."

Darla was watching Leigh intently. "But that's just Christmas."

Leigh turned toward her. "It is *now*. But it was *Pagan* first, and we still do it." He turned back to me. "Solstice is the first night of Yule, and Yule goes for twelve days."

"The twelve days of Christmas!" Darla insisted.

Leigh's voice grew loud. "The twelve days of Yule. We were first."

Jenny spoke up. "I think this is very interesting, even if the twelve days of Christmas don't start until the twenty-fifth. The original Pagan holiday was so special and so wonderful that Christians adopted it. They just centered it on Christmas rather than on the Solstice. Does that sound right, Leigh?"

He shrugged and sat down, having made his point.

Marshall addressed the group. "I do see an important difference. It would seem that Yule celebrates something observable in nature, the turning of the year, while Christmas is centered on an individual. Jesus. Does anyone have other observations?"

No one did. Marshall continued. "Okay, so here's what I'd like to do. How many of you celebrate Christmas?" Four hands went up. "How many celebrate Solstice and Yule?" Two hands. "I'd like those who celebrate Christmas to imagine how you would celebrate Yule. You can write your ideas and impressions, or you can just talk about them at the next meeting. Maybe you know of some songs that come from the tradition you're representing—carols, that sort of thing. If you want to write a skit, that's great. Those who celebrate Solstice, you imagine what it would be like to celebrate Christmas. And everyone else, choose one or the other."

It seemed to me that a few of the kids weren't excited about this assignment, but the others seemed to accept it as at least interesting.

Marshall turned to me. "Perhaps Reverend Hill would like to say a few words, since he dropped in on us today."

I stepped forward, with no idea what I was going to say. It was not unreasonable for Marshall to put me on the spot, but I was already annoyed with him, so it felt like an imposition. But this was about the kids.

"I'm delighted to see so many of you here," I opened. "Mr. Savage and Ms. Pratt have been telling me what a special group this is, and I can see they're right. I love how open you are with each other, how honest. You're a wonderful group of people."

I smiled at them and turned toward Marshall. "Mr. Savage, I have a couple of things to discuss after this meeting. It'll just take a couple of minutes. I can come by your house, or you can stop by mine. Which works better for you?"

Marshall's smile was a lie. "I'll stop by you after we leave here."

I nodded to group. "I love what you're doing. Thanks for letting me listen for a few minutes." And I left.

So Marshall had taken my idea seriously. Or maybe he had already been planning to have the kids explore each other's midwinter celebrations.

~

"What's the idea of forcing my hand?"

Marshall stood in my living room, just inside my front door.

"It seemed the best way to be sure you wouldn't put me off."

"I wasn't 'putting you off.'"

"You were. On the phone. You could have agreed with my request for when to meet without revealing anything personal to whoever was there with you."

There was something sly in his expression. "Were you jealous?"

A slight coughing sound escaped me. "Of whom? Of someone who didn't know how to find something in your kitchen? Someone you didn't mind knowing you were calling

153

me?" I shook my head. "I don't think so. And stop trying to turn this around."

"Turn what around?"

I exhaled audibly through my nose. "Will you sit down?"

"I don't have time for dinner."

"I said, will you sit down?"

Jacket still on, he flung himself onto a chair and glared at me.

I sat on the couch at the end nearest him. "We need to talk about what happened Saturday night."

"You mean *you* need to talk about it."

"No, *we* do. Because you owe me an explanation. What you asked me to do was dangerous. Even when someone knows what they're about, it's dangerous. It would have been easy for me to accidentally hurt you, perhaps worse than hurt you. And if I'd needed to call an ambulance, or the police, then not only would your secret be out, but also I would have had some nasty explaining to do. You put me in an untenable position." I stopped and watched Marshall's face.

His arms were crossed over his chest, and one leg was crossed over the other. It was an intensely protective posture. "What do you want me to say?"

"An apology might be nice. An assurance that you won't make that request again." We stared at each other. I added, "And maybe a promise that you won't try to do anything like that when you're alone."

"Seems to me you know a lot more about this than you pretended on Saturday."

"I know more than I knew on Saturday, thanks to some research I did yesterday. Saturday, I was totally nonplussed. Caught by surprise. However you want to think of it. Saturday, I knew nothing about this phenomenon. If I had, I would never have done as you asked."

More staring, and then Marshall stood up suddenly, turned

his side to me, and ran a hand through his hair. When he turned toward me, he seemed just this side of desperate.

"Look, Spencer, sometimes I need that, okay? Sometimes just the regular release is not enough. Can't you understand that?"

"Why?"

"What?"

"Why do you need that?"

"I just do, all right?"

I watched his face, knowing what I had to say, not wanting to say it. "And if I can't give it to you?"

"Shit, Spencer, I don't know. I don't know."

He sat down again but wouldn't look at me, his gaze glued to the carpet.

My voice was tense with emotion, and if I heard that I'm sure he did, too. "We have so much going for us, Marshall. We have music. We have a common spirituality. We like and respect each other. And we have really great sex, or so I thought."

I paused, but he said nothing, so I went on. "I'm not telling you we're destined to be life partners. I'm nowhere near ready for that with anyone yet. But—Jesus, can't we keep what we had for more than a few weeks? Or is this—this practice not the only thing in the way?"

He raised his eyes to mine. "I think I'm in love with you, Spencer. I want this to last as long as it can. I'm just having trouble seeing into the future if you won't help me once in a while."

"If I won't help you? If I won't do something that could damage you or kill you and put me in a wildly compromising situation?" I shook my head and forced myself to say what I had to. "If that's the make-or-break, Marshall, then it's a break. Because I won't do that."

Eyes on the floor again, he said, "At least you didn't say something like 'Am I not enough for you.'"

I waited. I needed him to tell me where he stood on this issue.

He looked up. "I know I want you. I want to be with you. I want your arms around me, your mouth on mine, your dick in my ass, mine in yours sometimes. I—" His voice caught as though he were fighting tears. "I want you."

"You have me, Marshall. And I want you, too. Just not like that."

"I don't know if that's enough."

I stood. "Then you have some thinking to do."

He stood and moved toward me, but I stepped back. I thought he might cry. I went to the door and opened it; there was no way he would do anything that revealed our relationship, in view of the world, and I couldn't bring myself to embrace him.

Marshall stopped and looked at me before stepping outside. I said, "I'm here if you want me. Just let me know what you decide."

If it hadn't been for the things that kept me busy, I think I would have been a bit of a basket case over the next couple of weeks. Duncan was actually making progress in his lessons, and he'd even gotten permission to practice on the school's piano in the music room there, when it wasn't otherwise in use. He was tending toward music in the rock genre, and he'd gone so far as to procure music scores for some songs. For some of them, we mixed things up; I played, and he sang. It was actually fun. I asked him, the week before Thanksgiving, whether he'd told his folks.

"I will someday. Maybe when hell freezes over."

I saw Marshall at Sunday services, though we didn't speak. It surprised me how much that hurt.

~

Thanksgiving week was very busy. Because Thanksgiving is nondenominational and nonreligious, it was seen by the congregation as an opportunity to share the goodwill and loving connection that is Unitarian Universalism without worrying about stepping on someone's religious toes. I had to help prepare for and then attend a number of gatherings, including one in Little Boundary on Tuesday in which ministers and priests from several towns met to explore innovative ways to celebrate Christmas. While I was there, I'm afraid I surprised a number of attendees by asking whether anyone from The Forest had been invited to participate.

At that gathering, I met Alan Jermin, the minister at the Assembly of God church in Little Boundary. Probably in his late thirties, he was slender and not very tall. His light brown hair seemed anxious for everyone to see what his scalp looked like. I watched for an opportunity to speak with him, to get a sense of whether his congregation was anything like what I understood about the one in Marshall's home town, but he seemed to be avoiding me.

Finally I managed to corner him just as the one-day event was wrapping up. He was putting his coat on, and I walked up behind him.

"Pastor Jermin," I said, extending my hand as he turned toward me.

He took a sudden step away from me and stared at the hand I held toward him. I barely heard him mumble, to himself more than to me, "Get thee behind me."

"Pardon?"

Now he looked at my face. "Sodomizer."

I was so stunned that I just stared at his retreating back. And that, I decided, was all I needed to know about him and his church.

There were entirely too many of my generous parishioners who insisted that I join them for their Thanksgiving celebrations. I managed to visit several homes before or after their meals, and my own turkey feast was with several other single people at Jenny Pratt's house. As I was helping her clear the table at one point, she told me she had invited Marshall.

"He said he'd be here, but this morning he called to say he wasn't feeling well. I hope he's all right."

"I'll check in on him."

I stopped by his place on my way home around nine-thirty that evening. There were lights on, so I rang the bell. When he came to the door, I saw his jaw grind.

"Oh. It's you." He didn't invite me in.

"Jenny Pratt was worried about you."

"I'm fine."

"Why didn't you—"

"I found out you would be there. I'm not ready to talk to you." He backed away and closed the door, leaving me on the cold porch, unsure whether to be concerned or pissed off.

When I got home there was a voice message from Ruth.

"Spencer? Can you give me a call back? I need to let you know about something."

Cryptic. I poured a glass of single malt Scotch, lit a fire in my fireplace, and sat watching the flames for a few minutes before returning her call.

"Did you have a nice Thanksgiving?" I asked.

"It was good, if a little strained. Just the three of us."

"You mean Donald? He wasn't with Bruce?'

"That's what I want to tell you about. Donnie broke it off with Bruce a few weeks ago."

"Really? That's good, right? I have to say, I did not warm to the fellow."

"Oh, that part's great. Nelson and I were so glad. But Bruce...."

"What about him?"

"He seems to think you had something to do with Donnie's decision. It might not be going too far to say he blames you."

"Blames me? I didn't do anything."

"I believe you, but at the same time I think this break kind of got started when you came for the wedding. I don't know if there was something you said to Donnie, or to Bruce, or maybe he just didn't like that Donnie was glad to see you. I don't know. But he keeps calling Donnie, and now he says he's driving up there Saturday."

"Why?"

"He seems to think he's going to... I don't know, have it out with you, or something."

I sat up straight. "Have *what* out with me?"

"Well, as I said, he blames you."

"Does he even know where I am?"

I heard her exhale. "I'm pretty sure he knows you're in Assisi, and it's a really small town, right?"

"It is. I suppose if he shows up here, he'll find me."

"Is there someplace you could go? Like, for the weekend, or something?"

"Ruth, I'm not running from the guy. And I have a sermon to give on Sunday. The term 'weekend' doesn't mean the same to me as it does to most people."

"Spencer, you've met him! He's a big guy with a bad temper!"

"I'm taking what you're telling me seriously, honest. I'll do my best to be unavailable on Saturday. Sunday will take care of itself."

So Donald had broken up with Bruce. And for his sake, I sent up a prayer of thanksgiving.

CHAPTER 15

Saturday dawned sunny and, with forty-one degrees the expected high, it was almost warm, at least for this part of the world. I had an early breakfast and then phoned Vanessa. If Bruce showed up, it might be better to be hard to find.

"Good morning," I said when Vanessa answered. Her voice seemed thin, and I wondered again about her health. "D'you think Klondike would enjoy a hike today?"

"Oh, yes. That would be marvelous. I haven't had the energy for much more than short walks lately. I'll make you a packed lunch for your trouble."

"No trouble, really. But yes, please!"

Klondike was clearly thrilled to be going on an adventure. He peed three times before getting into my Jeep. Vanessa handed me a full water bottle, an aluminum bowl, and a small package. "There's a whistle in there in case you lose sight of Klondike."

Not knowing a lot about trails yet, I decided to go back to the one I'd been on with Marshall. At least Klondike would be familiar with that one.

The roads were pretty clear today. I sang hymns to Klondike on the way to Little Boundary, and he made noises that were not quite howls and not quite growls. I decided to assume he was joining in rather than complaining.

Near the Assembly of God church, I slowed down. There were maybe twenty cars parked there. I knew their services were on Sundays, so I presumed today was some kind of gathering in honor of Thanksgiving.

At the trailhead, I parked in the same place I had with Marshall, leashed Klondike, and hefted my pack onto my shoulders. "Okay, boy. We're off!"

The trail was a little easier today. It had snowed only once, lightly, since I'd been here two weeks ago. I was a little anxious about letting Klondike off his lead, so I tested the whistle even before he went out of sight. He came back immediately each time, so I let him wander a little.

Klondike and I had our lunch on the same outcropping as before. I gave him some water and the treats Vanessa had packed for him. By the time we'd both finished eating, it was only about twelve thirty. I looked at the dog.

"Whaddya think, boy? Should we go a little higher this time?"

Klondike watched my face eagerly, and I took him to mean Yes. So we did.

It was close to three o'clock when we got back to the Jeep. I noticed my knees were in better shape than they had been last time.

We stopped at the same place as before, and the same plump waitress brought cocoa for me while Klondike lapped from his bowl. She didn't leave right away. I noticed her half-apron today had turkeys on it. I introduced myself, as Marshall had not done when we'd been here together.

"But that's not your dog," she said.

"He belongs to someone in Assisi. I just borrowed him for the day."

"Would he like a bit of meat?"

I glanced at Klondike as if he knew what was said, and I was waiting for an answer. "I don't see why not."

She came back with a large bone that had some bits of beef clinging to it. We both watched him gnaw on it for a moment. I told her, "He says thanks very much." She smiled and left, never asking about Marshall, never asking why Klondike was with me today.

This time, at the Assembly of God church, there were only two cars. I couldn't have said whether it was Pastor Jermin's rudeness when we'd met last time, or the idea of a confrontation with Bruce, or some protective feeling for Marshall—maybe all of that—but I pulled into the lot, ready for a confrontation.

I cracked a window and told Klondike to stay put, as if he had a choice. I was beginning to understand people who talked to their animals.

Inside, the church looked as expected: white walls with some stained glass, wooden pews, an altar, and behind that a couple of rows of wooden benches where choir members might sit. In one of the pews, close to the altar and on the right side, was Pastor Jermin. He was speaking to two people, possibly a husband and wife, in hushed tones. I stood just inside the front doors and waited to see how long the discussion might take, trying to come up with a credible reason why I was here, hoping my brain would land on what I wanted to say to this man.

After maybe ten minutes, the couple stood, embraced Pastor Jermin, and headed toward where I waited. He caught sight of me.

I walked forward, doing my best to appear deliberate without expecting confrontation. His face told me he felt no such compunction.

His voice fairly boomed, a lot of sound for a small man. "What are you doing here?"

I stopped and waited for him to approach, my hand out in greeting as before. And, as before, he ignored it. I dropped my arm. "We didn't have an opportunity to talk at the conference this past week. I was hiking nearby and thought I'd take a chance, so I stopped."

His glare was scorching. "You're from Assisi?"

"Unitarian Universalist of Assisi."

More to himself, he repeated the words I had just said, spitting them out as though UU was already halfway to hell.

"I've heard about you," he told me, "and your crazy *church*. Wouldn't surprise me if some of those hellish Pagans showed up there."

"If you mean the Forest Dwellers, you'd be mistaken. They like to keep to themselves."

He snorted. "Forest Dwellers. Too bad that place wasn't completely burned up."

"Burned up?"

He laughed, a humorless barking sound. "You don't know? Turn of the century, I think. Group of men took torches to that den of heretics. Too bad they didn't destroy *all* their homes."

I was stunned nearly to silence. Why had I heard none of this? "Men from Assis, or from here?"

"Here. Little Boundary. Folks here are more committed to Christ than you lot."

So many thoughts ricocheted around my brain that I couldn't think of more to say than, "It's a shame we have so little in common. I was hoping we could have a meaningful conversation."

"Don't see that happening. Now git."

"I will. Just so you know, the word heretic comes from the Hairetikós, meaning able to choose."

"And that's the problem."

I shook my head and turned, lifting first one foot and then then other to shake off the dust of this horrible atmosphere. I hoped fervently that Pastor Jermin witnessed that action and knew what it meant.

All the way back to Assisi I talked to Klondike.

"What the fuck, Klondike? Why didn't anyone tell me about that? No wonder the Forest Dwellers are a little reluctant to throw their proverbial doors open. But what do they have against Assisi? It was Little Boundary assassins who attacked them. Have they written off all non-Pagans?"

Klondike, very sensibly, didn't try to answer me, just watched me carefully, releasing an occasional whine in apparent concern.

As I approached Vanessa's door, I noticed all her blinds were drawn, though dusk was only threatening and had not arrived. Her voice sounding a bit strained, she said, "Come in. Come in. Did you boys have a good time?"

"The hike was great. We tuckered each other out."

"Can I offer you tea or coffee as a reward?"

"Coffee would be great. Black, with just a smidge of sugar."

I sat at her kitchen table as she busied herself, preparing coffee and giving Klondike fresh water and a snack.

"Oh," I said, "someone at a restaurant where I stopped gave him a beef bone. I'll bring it in before I go home."

"About that." She stood still, watching me as though not sure how to say what she needed to say. "I hope you'll forgive me, but I used an old key I still had to go into your house. I brought you clothes and toiletries, and I found your notes for tomorrow's sermon. I think you should stay here tonight."

I blinked stupidly at her. "Whatever for?"

She turned back to her coffee preparations. "Seems there's this fellow in town looking for you. He kind of had an air of death and destruction about him. He was going around asking for you, and I sneaked over and grabbed your stuff. I went out again a little later, just drove around, and he was camped out on your doorstep."

"Christ." This explained Vanessa's closed curtains.

"I've told Ben Marks, the police chief, about him, and I know a patrol car has driven by your house a few times." I was lost for words. She asked, "What do you know about him?"

"His name is Bruce Cobb. I think I mentioned him after my New York trip. He was seeing Donald Rainey, someone I used to be with."

"Ah, yes. I recall."

"My friend Ruth, Donald's sister, said they'd broken up, that Bruce blames me, and that he's planning to have it out with me."

"And are you to blame?"

I shook my head. "I disliked the guy, and I'm certain he picked up on that, but that's the extent of it. I'm delighted Donald's rid of him, but I had nothing to do with it."

"So Donald is not competition for Marshall, right?"

"He's not. No. Why?"

"Because Marshall is driving around to be sure he keeps tabs on the guy."

"Holy fuck." I waved a hand. "Sorry. I just can't believe this. I need to go get this settled."

"I don't think you should. But if you think you must…. Have your coffee first." She set a mug in front of me.

"Well, I will, but only because I have to ask you about something I learned today. It seems that at one point, a group of people raided The Forest and nearly burned it down."

Vanessa sat back in her chair, clearly not pleased that I'd brought this event up to her. She said nothing.

I asked, "Is this why they are so very reluctant to have anything to do with us?"

She let out a long breath. "It is."

"Why didn't anyone tell me? You obviously knew about it."

Her face went through a few different expressions I could make no sense of. Then, "It's probably because we are so very ashamed that anyone here would have done something like that."

"From here?"

"From Assisi."

"But—that's not what I heard. I heard it was a gang from Little Boundary."

Her face froze. "Who told you that?"

"A pastor from the Assembly of God church there."

"Why on earth were you talking to him?"

"Vanessa, don't change the subject. Are you telling me that everyone here has avoided telling me about that because you thought the perpetrators were from here, and there's still so much shame attached to it?"

She shook her head several times. "No one here will talk about it. To anyone. Not just you."

"Well…. What made anyone think these people were from Assisi?"

"There was a man whose home was burned. His wife and two children were killed. He was sure one of the raiders was a man from Assisi. If anyone else was recognized, we never heard about it."

Every one of the times I'd felt resistance from a Forest Dweller played behind my eyes, and I cringed. "So you all just let me go forward and make a fool of myself."

"I'm sorry."

"When did it happen?"

"It was nineteen-o-four. Spencer, if it was men from Little Boundary, I don't know how much difference that will make to the Forest Dwellers."

"It might make all the difference in the world! That is, as long as no one from Assisi was known to be so full hatred for The Forest."

"As far as I know, we were just neighbors. I think that's one reason the event had so much effect on us. We couldn't fathom it. So it was a horrible shock here. It still kind of is."

My coffee grew cold. I'd drunk none of it.

"Spencer, I'm so sorry. Truly. I should have said something."

"Yes. You should. And I think it's about time we got to the truth." I stood, feeling a slow-burning anger I didn't want to vent at Vanessa. "I'm going to go and face this idiot. And then, maybe starting tomorrow, we need to come up with a way to figure this out."

"Spencer? I don't think you should go."

"I don't either. But I'm going. This is not your battle, or Marshall's." I grabbed my jacket and headed toward the door, shutting it behind me.

As I climbed into my Jeep, I heard Vanessa call to me from her open door. "I'll call Ben Marks."

I didn't respond.

I also didn't notice that Klondike had escaped Vanessa's house and was following me the short distance to mine.

Sure enough, there was a hulking mass of a man sitting on my front steps. He stood as I shut the door of the Jeep, and that's when I saw Klondike.

"Home!" I shouted at the dog, pointing in the direction of Vanessa's. "Go home! Now!"

The dog stood still and then sat on the ground, immovable. His white fur stood out vividly in the gathering dusk, making him look even larger than he was.

I turned toward Bruce, who was headed toward me. My fists clenched hard. All the anger I'd been collecting, anger I hadn't allowed myself to release on Alan Jermin, coalesced into a fury the likes of which I don't think I had ever felt.

I opened the exchange. "What the fuck do you think you're doing here, frightening everyone on some ridiculous mission of misplaced vengeance?"

"Fancy words, Father Hill. I'm here to make you eat them."

I'd never struck anyone with a fist in my life. Bruce outweighed me by maybe twenty pounds of muscle. I didn't care; I wouldn't strike first, but I was ready to defend myself. My fury turned to sharp ice, and I wanted it to be hard enough to cut this man to shreds. "Get out."

Bruce stalled just slightly, as if he wasn't quite sure what to do next. "You told Donald to leave me."

"I did no such thing. If he left, it was of his own accord. I'm very glad he did, but I had nothing to do with it."

"Liar! You want him for your own."

I heard a car approach, stop, and go silent; someone got out. I didn't look.

"Wrong. I'm with someone here. Donald is a free agent."

Bruce took a step forward. Klondike stood, growled at him, and bared his teeth. Bruce froze in his tracks.

"He's not lying." The voice was Marshall's. He stood beside me, facing Bruce. "Spencer is in love with me. He doesn't like you, but he doesn't want Donald."

We stood there, three men and a dog, in the growing darkness, regarding each other, until another car pulled up, lights flashing on its roof. Ben Marks, along with his deputy, approached.

Ben, hands on his hips, gun prominently on display there, spoke to Bruce. "You'd best be on your way, mister. We don't tolerate your type here." He pointed to a car I didn't recognize, parked near the house. "That yours?"

Bruce ground his teeth.

"Get in it and drive on out of here." No one moved. "NOW!" Klondike growled again and lifted a paw.

That was enough for Bruce. He backed away and walked quickly to the car Ben had pointed to. We all watched as he drove off, turning our bodies and heads as necessary to follow him as long as possible.

Ben nodded to me. "We're just gonna follow him. Make sure he's gone."

"Thanks."

Marshall and I stared at each other for several seconds. Then I grinned at him. "So I'm in love with you, am I?"

"I hope so. I'm in love with you."

"Even if...."

"Even if."

We walked Klondike home, where Vanessa stood in the front yard, arms around her ribcage. Marshall ran forward.

"Vanessa! You shouldn't be out here in the cold. Let's go inside."

Marshall and I stayed long enough to describe to Vanessa what had happened. I collected the things she had brought from my house, and Marshall and I walked back in the near darkness.

Just before reaching my front door he asked, "So who's Donald?"

I chuckled. "Someone I was with in New York. It ended three years ago."

"Good. Invite me in?"

"Please. Come inside. Help me put a dinner together. And then allow me to make wild, passionate love to you."

He grinned. "Reverse the order of dinner and passion, and I'm there."

∾

From the pulpit the next day, I strayed wildly from the material I'd given Deena.

"What I'm going to talk about today will be different from what Deena Cunningham has so conscientiously put into your programs. Don't blame her."

I gazed around at the faces before me, some confused, some curious.

"Instead, I'm going to talk to you about blame. Misplaced blame. And what damage that can do."

I reminded them of the story from Genesis, of Eden, of Yahweh God creating everything from plants to animals, to water in the streams, to trees and grass, to humans. I stressed the supposed omnipotence of Yahweh, and his omniscience, and how those things together allowed him not only to create every-thing but also to know exactly how everything he created would behave, what everything would do. I pointed out that not only had he created the tree of the knowledge of good and evil, and the serpent that waited in the tree, but also he had imbued the humans with curiosity and the capacity for boredom, and then he'd pointed them right at something he'd known they couldn't resist.

"Don't think of a blue horse," I told them. "Consider where your mind went when I said that, and then consider Adam and Eve's likely response when Yahweh told them, 'My children, you may have anything here in this paradise. It is all here for you. Take and use anything you want. Except,'" and here I paused significantly, "'except for one thing. Just *one thing*.' Is it any wonder that they found themselves in front of that tree? Is it any wonder that they both—not just Eve, for Adam was right at her elbow and never tried to stop her—they both found it impos-sible to resist the temptation that Yahweh himself had set them up to experience?"

I stood as tall as I could and raised my voice. "And yet who was blamed? Who was blamed for the plan Yahweh himself put into action? Who was labeled as a creature with sin so original that humanity would carry it forward to eternity? It wasn't Yahweh who was blamed. And it wasn't Adam. It was Eve! Eve is blamed by orthodox Christianity for having brought on the downfall of man from paradise to the mundane existence we know today.

"And here is perhaps the cruelest part of all. Neither Adam nor Eve had ever known anything but ease, and goodness, and plenty. They knew nothing of pain, or suffering, or death. So when Yahweh the Omniscient threatened them with death if they ate of that tree's fruit, what did that mean to them?"

I nearly shouted. "Nothing! Death meant nothing to them. In any way that is fair and just and ethical, they are blameless. And yet they are blamed for the suffering mankind was doomed to experience on earth. Man was cursed in that he was to toil all his life and know what it was to eat dust. Woman was cursed with the agony and potential death of childbirth. And they were both cursed with enmity that would come between them, yea unto the very children they would bring forth."

I paused, taking in a few deep breaths, and then bowed my head. The church was so quiet that if I hadn't seen all those people, I might not have known they were there.

I raised my head, my voice quiet now. "Blame. Blame has its place, to be sure. But, people, let us be certain—absolutely as certain as we can possibly be—where it belongs before we cast it. Before we hold some horror over the heads of people who do not deserve it."

It was a self-indulgent speech, I knew that. I didn't care. The message might be lost on many members of my congregation, but others would understand. But the worst of it was that I wasn't speaking to the people who had cast the blame for the devastating fire. Nor was I speaking to the people who'd done something to be blamed for. Assisi had been caught in the middle. And I was determined to set the record straight.

CHAPTER 16

Marshall came for dinner and passion on Monday evening. Or, passion and dinner, which was the order we both preferred. Over dinner, I told him about my recent hike with Klondike, and then I described what I'd found out about the fire.

"God in heaven," was the first thing he said. "I had no idea. I've been here a few years, and I never heard anyone talk about it."

"I gather there's enough shame, and there was enough shock, that no one who knows about it mentions it. But if the Forest Dwellers are also convinced the raid was from Assisi, it's no wonder they aren't jumping at the chance to make nice with me."

"Are you thinking you can do something about it?"

"I *have* to do something about it. And the first thing is to verify what that man told me."

Marshall actually giggled. "What on earth possessed you to stop there, anyway?"

I shrugged. "I was mad at you, I was mad at Bruce, and I was mad at the way Alan Jermin had treated me at the conference. I guess it was a perfect storm of anger."

"What's your first step?"

"I'm thinking I'll go back to that restaurant where we got cocoa. I introduced myself to the waitress Saturday, and she gave Klondike a bone. I'll bet she's been there long enough to know. If not, maybe she knows someone who has. Because I don't want to take Jermin's word for it. I want to be as sure as I can what really happened."

"Mmmm. Like you said in your Sunday sermon."

I chuckled. "Yeah. I think I took some folks by surprise."

"Well, you did give us all a bit of fire and brimstone. Didn't think you had it in you."

I gave him a wry grin. "You once told me you had a monster inside you. I think there's one in me, as well."

He looked down at his plate. "Um, Spencer, I, uh, I'll help you with this mission any way I can, except don't ask me to go to Little Boundary with you. I'm still creeped out by that new church."

"Fair enough."

～

And I did go back. I took Klondike to be sure the waitress would recognize me, and she did. I arrived mid-afternoon, when I hoped the restaurant wouldn't be busy, and it wasn't.

Now with Santa Clauses on her apron, she greeted me with a smile. "Here for another bone?"

I laughed. "I'm sure he wouldn't say no."

When she came back with the cocoa and the bone, I asked, "Do you have just a minute? I was hoping to ask you something."

"Sure." She sat across from me. "I'm Maggie Downing, by the way, Reverend. What is it you wanna know?"

I took a breath. "This might be a sensitive topic, so if you're uncomfortable with it, I'll understand. I'm hoping to find out what I can about something that happened in nineteen-o-four."

"Oh. The raid. That was horrible. I wasn't born yet, but my aunt told me about it. Of course, the group in the woods was different then. What she told me was the people who started that community had been witches, or accused as such. Couple hundred years went by, and those weird Perfectionist types came on the scene. Somehow, they all got along. Now it seems like it's a bunch of Pagan types. But when the raid happened, it wasn't long after the Perfectionists had shown up."

"So what prompted the raid?"

"Zealots. There was a lot of them in those days. I think there was some competition about land claims, and some livestock went missing, and that settlement got blamed. Not too sure any more. Plus there was that weird Perfectionist thing. Did you know they shared their wives?"

"I believe they shared everything. So, who did the raid?"

"Got started by the Burgos brothers. Their land bumped up against the community, and they always held that when the Perfectionists showed up, they took over some Burgos land. I also think some Burgos livestock went missing. Anyway, they got some other people all fired up." She shrugged. "The rest is history."

"I heard someone in the settlement thought he recognized one of the raiders as a man from Assisi."

"Yeah, I guess there's been some confusion since. But I don't know as anyone from Assisi joined in. Seems unlikely. I don't know of any beef Assisi had with the community, and I do know the Burgos family hated those people."

I thanked her for her time and information and asked if she'd be willing to sell me an entire pumpkin pie. She brought it over, all packaged, and set it on the table.

"Truth is, I'm glad to be rid of it. People are all into Christmas, now. Tired of pumpkin anything." She grinned. "By the way, why are you so interested in that raid?"

"I live in Assisi, but I'm new to the area. People there seem to know about what happened, but there's some doubt as to *how* it happened. And somehow, I thought you would know." I gave her a big smile and a bigger tip.

~

That week I contacted the priest of Assisi's Catholic church and the minister of the Protestant church and asked for a meeting "about a matter of local importance." We met in the UU function hall mid-afternoon on Thursday.

I opened the meeting by asking how much they knew about the fire. David Foster, the Protestant minister, was young and fairly new in town, and he hadn't heard anything about it. But Father Milton Bryant, who was in his sixties and had lived in Assisi for many years, had.

"A horrible thing," Milton Bryant said. "It was a shameful time for Assisi. I don't think you'll do anyone any favors by bringing it up."

I nodded. "I would agree with you, except for one thing. It turns out the instigators were not from Assisi. In fact, it's unlikely anyone from Assisi participated." I told them what I'd learned so far, adding, "Since then, of course, things have changed, and that community identifies as Pagan."

Milton Bryant looked stunned. "How do you know this? What's your source?"

"Two people in Little Boundary. One is a newcomer, the minister at the Assembly of God. But the other's family has been there for a few generations, and they were there when it happened."

David Foster looked confused. "Why have I never heard about this?"

"I hadn't either," I told him. "In fact, before I knew any of this, I'd been trying to connect with the Forest Dwellers, just to get each side to know and understand each other better, and I couldn't figure out why they were resistant. I found out about the fire only this past weekend."

David was still confused, as I had been. "But why is it such a secret?"

I looked at Milton, who seemed reluctant to say anything, and waited.

"The people of Assisi," he said finally, "pride themselves on being open-hearted, and accepting. We're a very liberal community, as *you've* no doubt perceived." He gave me a meaningful glance, which seemed to confuse David.

So I told him, "I think Father Bryant refers to the fact that I'm gay."

"So," he continued, "for the residents to be convinced that some of their neighbors had committed that heinous act was a matter of deep shame. But they couldn't determine who from Assisi had been involved. It's my understanding that some Assisi men were recognized." He looked at me. "What do you know about that?"

I shook my head. "Nothing useful, I'm afraid. I suppose it's possible. But from what I understand, there was only one man someone thought they recognized from Assisi. And keep in mind that there's never been much mixing between the two towns, and at the time they would have seemed geographically even more separate as well, so it seems unlikely there would have been any collusion. But if it was one Assisi man, it seems that would have been the extent of it. The real culprits were all from Little Boundary."

Milton leaned back in his chair and exhaled. "What's your plan? You brought us here. What's next?"

"I'm the new guy in town," I said. "Been here only since September. I'd love to go through the streets with a megaphone and let everyone know this shame isn't theirs, but who am I to do that? I'm open to any ideas you might have to try and get the word out."

"Town hall." David spoke up. "We need some kind of town meeting. So we need to get the town leaders involved, not just the religious leaders. There are people here who don't go to any of our three churches."

Milton nodded. "I agree. But first I think a little more research is indicated. I don't imagine Maggie Downing lied to you, Spencer, but we need more. Let me speak to the Catholic priest in Little Boundary. And David, can you do the same with your colleague?" He looked at me. "I don't think there's a UU there."

"No," I said. "There isn't. How do we get the town leaders involved?"

Milton knew. "Start with Vanessa Doyle. She's been here all her adult life, and she knows everyone."

"I can do that. I speak with her frequently." I couldn't promise that I'd have any success, based on her reaction to our first conversation about this raid.

There was a deep silence, as though we were somehow conspirators. Then Milton said, "This might do no good at all. It might change nothing. We need to be prepared for that."

I nodded. "You're right, of course. And I'm thinking David and I should probably take a back seat as newcomers to the area. I'll do what I can to get Vanessa on board, but then I'll back off and let her run with it or not."

Milton seemed to agree. "And as good an idea as a town hall would be, I think it should happen more organically than we might like. That is, it should happen because enough people in Assisi are questioning something they've always held to be true, not because a few of us want to convince them otherwise."

"Frustrating," was David's comment. "But probably wise."

I chuckled. "I've already delivered a sermon on inappropriate blame, though I said nothing about this situation." I looked at Milton. "If you're right, then a lot of the shame could be coming from people not knowing whom to blame when it happened. So they probably all looked at each other with suspicion."

David sat up straight. "And that's what we can do. We can highlight behavior that brings people together and compare it to what separates us. And we can stress forgiveness. The Little Boundary raiders are all long dead." I tapped my fingers absently, and David looked at me. "You disagree?"

"Not at all. I'm just remembering a conversation I had with the pastor at the Assembly of God church recently. He seemed to think that the whole community should have been obliterated."

Milton sighed. "Let's hope he's in the minority."

Duncan noticed that I was distracted during his piano lesson that afternoon.

"Hey, Rev, you with me here?"

"Yes. Sorry. I'm a little preoccupied with something."

He sat back on the piano bench, hands on his thighs. "Feeling a little uninspired, myself. Spill."

Curious. Duncan Beale wanted to know what was on my mind? I decided to test it.

"What do you know about the raid on what's now The Forest, the one just after the turn of the century?"

He lifted a shoulder and dropped it. "Not much. Mostly folks don't talk about it. I don't really know what happened, cuz all I ever hear are these vague references to it between grown-ups. You know how they look when they think they're speaking in some kind of code that kids don't understand? It's something about burning people's homes, is all I know."

"So you don't know anything about who might have done it?"

He gave a snort. "Alls I can say is it must be someone bad."

"You don't study it in school?"

"Nope."

So Duncan, and probably all of his generation, were pretty much in the dark. This told me that the adults were still very much ashamed of something they think their neighbors did, something for which it seemed no one was ever held account-able. No specific individual received the blame, so everyone assumed the shame.

Duncan shocked me out of my ruminations, in a good way. "So that Teens for Truth thing."

"Yes?"

"Not as lame as I thought."

"Yeah?" I was afraid saying any more than that would serve to make him think twice.

"Couple of kids from The Forest are teaching us some of their Pagan routines. Pretty interesting stuff."

I had to stifle a laugh. Seems the children were accom-plishing what the adults could not. "That does sound interesting."

"I went with them on a cat rescue mission. Black cats."

"Did you really? This was right before Halloween, yes?"

"Yeah. Those guys are committed."

I was dying to ask whether Adam Cooper had led the group Duncan was in, but I didn't want to take any of the glory from him. So all I said was, "They do seem determined, don't they? I rather admire that. And I admire you for helping them."

The last thing Duncan said to me before he left was, "Y'know, I think I'm gonna bring that thing up in Teens. That thing about what happened in that raid."

I invited Vanessa for lunch Friday, letting her know in advance I had an agenda. We sat at my kitchen table by the window, where soft snow floated past the glass panes.

"Something I can help with?" she asked over her bowl of tomato bisque soup and plate of grilled cheese sandwich.

"I'm afraid it's a topic you might not want to talk about. But I think revisiting it is important, and I hope you'll agree."

I told her I'd met with Milton Bryant and David Foster. She liked hearing that. Then I told her why. She sat, still as stone and not eating, while I reminded her about my brief encounter with Pastor Jermin and related my conversation with Maggie Downing.

Her tone as icy as the outdoor temperature, she said, "So you're determined to drag this out into the open?"

"Drag... what do you mean? What I want is for Assisi to stop kicking itself in the butt for something it didn't do. By all accounts so far—though Milton Bryant and David Foster are talking with their Little Boundary counterparts for verification— the act was done by men from Little Boundary, not from Assisi. It seems unlikely anyone from Assisi was involved, and the supposed recognition that took place in the dark, in a state of panic, was wrong."

"You're messing with history, Spencer."

"I'm hoping to correct false history."

She was silent for a few moments as she consumed perhaps half of her lunch. Then, "Spencer, you're new here. I believe your intentions are commendable, but this is a long-standing—"

"Too long-standing," I interrupted her. "I get the impression that the adults have tried to keep it from the younger generation, but I happen to know it isn't working. They've picked up that there's something the adults are ashamed about, something they speak of in code words and whispers to try and protect the kids. The kids know there's something shameful, they don't know what it is, and they're making up their own stories about it. In fact," I pushed my plate aside so I could lean forward toward Vanessa, "the teen group is starting to talk about it. And I'm terrified that the Forest Dweller kids in the group, who probably believe the same thing the Assisi adults do, will lay the blame on the Assisi kids. Do you really want that to happen?"

Vanessa's face was stern, bordering on angry. "You realize you're the one who's stirred all this up. You're the one who kept poking at the Forest Dwellers. This teen group might be led by Marshall and Jenny, but it was your idea."

"It was *our* idea! Yours *and* mine! We talked about it right at the beginning of my tenure."

"*Assisi* teens!" she nearly shouted. "I never suggested you involve Forest Dwellers." Elbows on the table, she propped her head up with her fingertips.

I sat back, regarding her, wondering what it was about the truth that bothered her so much.

"Vanessa, you know the story of Pandora's Box?" She raised her eyes to mine without lifting her head. "All kinds of bad things came flying out, things that had been kept secret until the lid was lifted. One flying evil thing after another took to the air to renew whatever torment it had perpetrated before being captured in that box."

"You seem to be the one who has opened it."

"Maybe. But keeping those evils in the box didn't destroy them. Didn't render them impotent. And once they were all out, the box wasn't empty."

I waited. Would she remember what was still in there?

She sat back, hands in her lap, and closed her eyes briefly. "Hope."

"Hope," I echoed. "Beautiful, golden, sparkling hope, full of promise. Hope is what we need to keep going. Hope is what we'll need to lift the shame from Assisi, not only from people who did no harm themselves, but also from people who didn't do it seventy years ago. And we can't let that misplaced shame fall onto people who are young and impressionable and who should bear no weight of the shame that doesn't even belong to their parents or grandparents."

Her gaze was steady. "And who gets the blame now?"

I shook my head. "No one. This isn't about blame. It's about history. The men who conducted that raid are dead by now. The Pagan community that grew out of the accused witches and Perfectionists has coalesced into something that bears only a passing resemblance to what it once was. We don't need to blame Little Boundary to exonerate Assisi."

Vanessa was silent for several seconds.

"Vanessa? Let's do what we can to pave the way for brotherhood between Assisi and The Forest. It might lay the groundwork for brotherhood between The Forest and Little Boundary. My impression is that not many Little Boundary folks liked what happened. I think they'd be glad to leave it behind. And isn't that what our calling would have us do?"

"What do you want from me, Spencer?"

"As the new guy in town, I don't have a place to stand on this. I can't show up on the scene and say things that might be taken as criticism. David and Milton and I will begin to tailor our sermons around concepts that clear the path for the truth, doing everything we can to avoid laying any blame anywhere. But that's probably the extent of what I can do openly. The change, if there is to be one, must come from people like you. People who've been here long enough to know the effect this burden has had on the town. Maybe, once word has started to get around, there could be a town hall meeting, something like that, to address people's questions and concerns and to get things moving forward in good ways."

"Spencer, I have nothing to work with."

"Well, there's the information I've told you about, and Milton and David are collecting more. When we put it all together I hope we'll see the way forward and give you the facts you need to talk to other people—individually at first, I imagine, though you'll know better than I would the best way to move forward."

"Andrea Beale writes a column in the weekly town newspaper."

"Excellent! Between you, perhaps you could decide how to begin rolling out the new information."

More silence. So I said, "So you'll do it? You'll help?"

She sighed. "If this thing has been a lie all these years, then yes, I'll do my part. But Spencer, I'll need to be convinced. And, by the way, ideally we'd want to convince the Forest Dwellers. I can't imagine that they don't still blame us."

"Fair enough. And if we discover that I've been misinformed, I'll eat my vestments."

She laughed. "And I'll sell tickets to that."

CHAPTER 17

After Vanessa left, I ran some errands and then sat down to flesh out the notes I'd already given to Deena for Sunday's sermon, determined to carry forward with the themes my colleagues and I had agreed upon. I spent a bit of time thinking, but I'd barely put pen to paper when my phone rang at around four thirty. I almost ignored it, but my thoughts weren't yet ready to be expressed, so I picked it up.

"Spencer?" It was Marshall, his voice a strained whisper. "Something horrible just happened."

"Are you all right?"

"No! How can I be all right? Two people just rang my bell, and when I let them in they told me they were from the Assembly of God!"

"From Little Boundary?"

"Yes. They were here to proselytize."

"Didn't you send them packing?"

Silence. Then, "Spencer, I don't think you understand how traumatic it is for me even to talk to them. And what if they recognized me? What if they figure out who I am?"

"How would they do that?"

"These people are connected! They might recognize my last name! Christ, why didn't I change that? They might know things about me I don't want anyone here to know! I could lose my job!"

"Well...."

"That camp my folks sent me to was in Massachusetts. Not that far away." He sounded near tears.

"Do you want to come over?"

"What if they come to your house next?"

"I won't let them in. They won't know you're here. Stay there, Marshall. I'm coming to get you." I hung up.

Marshall was watching for me. He scrambled quickly into the Jeep and hunkered down, anxious not to be seen. When I parked the car at my house, he waited until I had the front door open and had looked all around to be sure the proselytizers were nowhere in sight, at which point he dashed into the house.

Inside, he collapsed onto my couch and curled into a ball. I wrapped my arms around him as best I could, rocking gently to try and calm him. It was several minutes before he spoke.

"They'll find me. I'm sure of it."

"Sweet man, I know they did horrible things to you. I know how much they hate who and what we are. And I understand that you're afraid because of your job. But do you *know* that you need to be? Afraid for your job, I mean?"

He raised his head. "I can't afford to find out the hard way."

"I'll bet I could find out."

He pulled away from me. "Don't you dare!"

I stifled an exasperated sigh. "Marshall, I wouldn't let on that I was talking about anyone in particular. But because I'm out, it's the sort of general question I'm in a position to be able to ask with impunity."

"Spencer—"

"Even Father Bryant at the Catholic church—*Catholic*, Marshall—was telling me how Assisi values its openness and progressive attitudes. He looked right at me when he said it. He knows I'm gay."

Marshall pulled away from me, stood, and began to pace the room. He couldn't go far; the piano took up too much space. He kept saying, "You don't understand. You don't understand."

"Tell me what I'm not understanding. Please."

He stood in front of me, his hair a mess where he'd been gripping it, his eyes wide and unfocused. I felt fear, not for me but for him.

"The threat to my job is huge, okay? It's huge. But that's only part of it."

He began to pace again, so I stood and blocked his path. "What's the other part, Marshall?"

He nearly fell onto the couch, elbows on his knees, head in his hands. When he looked up, he said, "It wasn't just the one time."

"What wasn't?"

"In the camp. When I tried to drown myself. That was the first."

My brain wouldn't work. Was he telling me he'd tried to kill himself again? I willed myself to be calm, to speak in quiet, even tones. "When was the second?"

He took several deep breaths. "In college. I was a senior when Robert died."

"Robert?"

"The medieval music professor. He—we were lovers. And he died. A car accident. Someone else was driving. It felt so sudden. So sudden." Marshall's voice grew so soft I had to strain to hear the words. "So sudden."

Words failed me.

"I couldn't go on. It was like my world collapsed. I found the keys to his car and drove it into a tree."

I nearly stumbled to the couch and sat beside Marshall. I didn't touch him. I didn't speak.

He dropped his hands, dangling them between his knees, head bowed. "I didn't know how to tell you."

"I don't know what to say."

"No need to say anything. Just please understand how vulnerable these people make me feel."

What I was beginning to understand was that Marshall was not just vulnerable. He was also fragile. I knew it would do no good to point out that the second suicide attempt had nothing to do with his old church, at least not directly; somehow he was connecting the two. But why? As far as I could see, the only connection was Marshall himself. And perhaps that was the most concerning.

My feelings bounced wildly between wanting to protect him and keep him safe, and knowing I would always be terrified of failure.

Marshall spent that night, for the first time, at my house. But not in my bed. He slept on the couch, terrified to go home. He was still there Saturday morning, dead to the world, when someone rang my doorbell at nine-thirty. He sat up when the sound woke him, groggy but still terrified.

"Stay there," I told him. "It's obvious you slept on the couch."

I opened the door to Loraine.

"I have to talk to you," she said, brushing past me but stopping when she saw Marshall. "What are you doing here?"

"Come into the kitchen, Loraine. I've just made a pot of coffee." I chuckled quietly; Loraine, so out about her orientation and so pleased with mine, hadn't guessed about Marshall and me.

I poured a mug for each of us and set cream and sugar on the table. "What can I do for you?"

"Have you seen those proselytizers? They're all over Assisi."

"Really? Well, as it happens, that's why Marshall slept on my couch last night. He grew up in the Assembly of God and hated them. They tried to conscript him yesterday afternoon and it kind of freaked him out. But I haven't seen them."

Marshall's voice came from the doorway where he stood, a blanket wrapped around himself. "They went to your house?"

Loraine barked out a laugh. "They did. But I sent them packing."

Marshall managed to sit in a chair without dislodging the blanket. "How did you do that?"

"Easy. I pretended to be all excited to see them. 'Wait here for a second, will you?' I said. I ran and got a pair of scissors. I looked at them, eyes wide, all excited. 'Will you each give me a lock of your hair?'"

It took Marshall a few seconds to join me in laughter. She added, "They won't be back. But, Spencer, I thought we should talk with the other lay ministers in case they get calls from people about this."

"You're absolutely right." I should have thought of it, actually. Perhaps I would have, if not for Marshall's distress.

"Good, because I've told them to meet us here at ten."

Marshall looked alarmed again. "Why not the church?"

Loraine shook her head and stood. "Take too much time to warm the place up. Too expensive, too. I have a box of donuts in the car. I'll fetch that."

Marshall was still not comfortable. "I should probably leave."

"If you feel you need to," I said. "You have a way to get rid of them now, if you're willing to follow Loraine's lead. But as a former lay minister, it would also make sense for you to take part in this meeting."

He decided to go upstairs and freshen up.

∾

While Loraine and I waited for the others, I called Vanessa to see if she wanted to be involved or if she had any insights.

"That's very thoughtful of you, Spencer. I wish I could, but I had kind of a bad night. I need to stay here and rest."

So I'd been right; her health was not improving. "Someone will come by later to walk Klondike, if that would help."

"Yes. Please."

∾

Of course our meeting didn't help us come up with any way to rid Assisi of the Assembly visitors. But we did decide that Andrea would write an article for the town newspaper about the situation, and that I would make a brief announcement about them during services the next day, just to remind everyone that it was perfectly fine to smile, say nothing, not invite them in, and shut the door. On Sunday, from the rustling and hushed conversations in the congregation after I spoke about it, I gathered many people had already been visited.

∾

Loraine had walked Klondike twice Saturday. I stopped by after church to take a turn. When I did, Vanessa looked positively haggard.

"I'm sorry, Spencer, but I haven't done anything about the situation with the fire. Getting anyone involved, that is."

"I completely understand," I told her, trying not to look disappointed.

"You know who you should talk to? Ben Marks."

"The police chief?"

"Confidentially, he's always thought it might have been his uncle who was recognized. He was going to be my first contact, actually. You can tell him I suggested him."

Monday afternoon I took a break from my ministerial rounds to grab a cup of coffee in the diner where Loraine and I had met back in September. I sat alone at a table near the window, coffee and a donut in front of me, and had a moment of mournful nostalgia. In New York, there was no end of coffee shops, little cafés, and similar places where one could get really great coffee and a huge variety of pastries to go with it. And there were bagels. Oh, the bagels! I gazed at my donut and knew, as good as it might be, it couldn't compete.

I had just resolved to accept this substitute and had picked the thing up when someone spoke my name. David Foster stood beside my table, with coffee and his own donut.

"May I join you?"

"Please do. It's good to see you again."

We chatted about the weather, the challenge of getting younger folks to services, and finally got around to the topic on my mind which was, of course, the fire. He told me he'd centered his sermon the day before on how neighbors mend fences.

"Odd expression, isn't it?" he said. "I mean, fences are built to keep things separate."

"Ah, but there's that expression that good fences make good neighbors."

He laughed. "True." He sipped his coffee and took a bite of

donut. Then, "Did you say you'd met with Alan Jermin, the Assembly of God minister?"

"I'm not sure I'd say I met with him. I tried to talk with him at the conference before Thanksgiving. And I stopped by the church about a week and a half ago, on my way back from a hike. Why do you ask?"

David gave me an assessing glance. "I take it you did not exactly get along famously."

I gave him a wry grin. "Notoriously might be a better descriptor. Have you spoken to him?"

"Like you, I tried to talk with him at the conference. He was dismissive of most of what had happened there and seemed more focused on… shall we say, the more disciplinarian aspects of religion."

I chuckled. "Then you got further than I did. He mumbled 'Get thee behind me' when I held out my hand, and then called me a sodomizer."

David shook his head slowly. "He's a character. Have you met his wife?"

"I know nothing about his family, so, no. Have you?"

He nodded. "Pretty thing. Probably about ten years his junior. They have two children, a boy of six, I think, and a girl maybe a year younger. He's got money from somewhere. Maybe from his wife."

"Oh? What makes you say that?"

"He bought this big old barn of a place up on the hillside, not far from the old Burgos farm. Put in a swimming pool. They have horses, too, according to someone I know who's been there."

"A swimming pool? In this climate?"

I saw one of David's cheeks recede into the side of his mouth. "Perhaps," he said slowly enough for sarcasm, "he uses it for baptisms."

I laughed. "And if it's frozen, and he throws someone into it and the ice melts, they're a witch."

"And if it doesn't, and they die, they're exonerated."

We laughed hard enough to draw the attention of the people at two other tables.

David held a finger to his lips. "We are being dreadfully uncharitable."

"Indeed we are. If only irreverence weren't so much fun."

My conversation Monday evening with Ben Marks was difficult. But it turned out to be exactly the right thing to do, though he was certainly surprised that I wanted to talk with him.

"I can't believe it," was the first thing he said on hearing what I'd discovered, but his tone told me he wasn't denying it; he sounded incredulous, with perhaps a note of hope. We were in his living room, and his wife Mona was in the kitchen putting dinner together.

"We're still verifying things," I said, "but it's beginning to look very much as though Assisi wasn't involved."

"Who's 'we?'"

"I've spoken to Father Bryant at the Catholic Church and your minister, David Foster. They're both talking to their counterparts in Little Boundary, and with any luck we'll have more validation."

He got up, and from his fireplace mantle he lifted a picture frame. After gazing at it for a few seconds, he handed it to me. "That's my uncle and his wife. My sister and I always thought he was the one who was recognized." He turned away from me as I regarded the photograph. "Damn, but I wish I could ask him!"

"He's passed?"

"Yes."

"Did he know he was suspected?"

"Don't think so. I never said anything to anyone, and I never heard anyone else speculate, besides my sister. But he was an ornery old coot, and he had nothing good to say about the Perfectionists."

"Are you willing to help us figure out how to move forward with this, provided we get the information I'm hoping for from Little Boundary?"

He sat on the couch again, at first looking defeated as he gazed at the carpet. But it took only a few seconds for him to lift his head. "I am. God damn it, I am."

We agreed his best approach would be to ask some of his relatives, quietly, whether they had shared his suspicions. He said, "We've all been silent too long. Hiding too long. And if what you've learned is true…."

Marshall, Loraine, and I took turns walking Klondike, with a few others pitching in at times. Marshall mostly walked him in the late afternoons, unafraid of anything as long as the dog was with him. After all, he'd seen how Klondike had reacted to Bruce Cobb's threats. I offered to walk with Marshall, but with the Assembly of God making inroads, he was even more worried—and even more cautious—about being seen together.

By the end of the week, Vanessa had improved quite a bit; clearly, rest had helped. But then, as if to justify Marshall's fears, the week after my conversation with Ben Marks the proverbial shit hit the fan in another quarter.

Marshall called me that Tuesday around eleven in the morning, barely able to speak.

"They fired me," he said.

"What? Who?"

"The school." I waited while he made an effort to control his breathing. "They found out."

"Marshall, what—"

"Can I come over?"

"Of course." While I waited, I made a couple of calls, postponing some parish visits I'd scheduled.

Marshall fell into my arms as soon as I opened the door, unable to speak for his sobs. Without releasing him, I moved farther into the room and pushed the door shut with a foot.

"Sweet man, sweet man," was all I could think of to say. Finally he pulled away and collapsed on the couch. I handed him a box of facial tissues.

"It was them," he said, his breath catching. "Someone recognized the name Savage and went digging."

"Are you sure? How do you know?"

He blew his nose juicily. "The vice principal has never liked me. I've always suspected that he had an idea that I'm gay. He told me they knocked on his door, too, only they weren't there just to proselytize."

I sat beside him, stunned. So many thoughts ran through my mind, but the one that kept surfacing was to wonder whether my brief conversations with Alan Jermin had spurred him into action, digging into my life and stumbling upon Marshall in the process. They wouldn't even need to know about my relationship with Marshall; all that would have to have happened would have been for them to decide to come here because of me and look into their own rosters for a match with someone in Assisi. It would be an incredibly vindictive thing to do. Surely, not everyone in the Assembly denomination would do something like this, but it would take only a few. A few zealots. And an especially venomous vice principal.

Sitting there, wondering how I could bring any comfort to Marshall, I told myself my imagination was running wild, that the whole thing was preposterous. But I couldn't shake it. And what Marshall said, that the Assembly people hadn't gone to the vice principal only to proselytize, made it more likely. And he'd been right about what would happen if they found out he was gay.

So this was very possibly my fault.

~

Marshall stayed with me all day, through a dinner he barely picked at, and through the night, curled against me in bed. He said there was nothing to lose at this point.

Wednesday morning he asked if he could stay with me for a few days, and he went to get some clothes and a few items from his house. Afraid for him, afraid of what he might do, I went with him. Then, back home, I was terrified to leave him, but he insisted he'd be fine while I went about my ministerial chores.

One of those chores was to visit Vanessa.

"How could this happen?" I was practically moaning to her. "In Assisi? Even the Catholic priest doesn't seem to care that I'm gay!"

Vanessa eyed me from a large overstuffed chair where she was ensconced, wrapped in a quilt and sipping tea I had brought from the kitchen. "Spencer, dear boy, the priest is one thing. The congregation is quite another. Now, I'll admit I'm a little surprised that the school would act so—oh, I'll just say it—so violently. And it's true we're pretty progressive here. But not everyone in Assisi is in our church."

I just shook my head.

She added, "And I'm sure Marshall had a morals clause in his contract. It might or might not have specified homosexuality, but if the school board agreed the clause had been violated, that would be reason for dismissal."

"The school board…." I echoed. "Who's on that?"

"I couldn't tell you. Marshall probably could. But if you're thinking of accosting them, don't."

"Why not?"

She sighed loudly. "Use your head, Spencer. Even if you were able to change their minds, how would Marshall be able to face his students? There would be new students every year, and he'd have to go through it over and over again. What would parent-teacher conferences be like for him? Maybe someone like you could weather that storm. But could Marshall?" She shook her head. "I don't think so."

I got up and paced the room, nearly treading on Klondike's tail. Then I wheeled on her.

"You're the one who encouraged me to be in a relationship with him!"

"No. All I did was tell you not to leave him hanging."

I stretched my mind back, trying to remember who had said what, and I had to admit she was right. If I could fault her, it would be only whether she should have discouraged me, and him. But I knew that was absurd. I might be young, but I knew enough to realize that telling people not to get involved with each other was futile at best.

I sat heavily on the couch. "What a fucking mess."

"I think you should encourage him to see a therapist. Not here in Assisi, and of course not in Little Boundary. The right therapist could help him get over this crisis and start exploring what his future should be."

I looked up at her and echoed her words: "Not here…."

"No. I think we need to encourage him to leave Assisi."

This was not my fault, I told myself over and over as I drove home. *This was not my fault.*

If I had known how bad the consequences for Marshall would be if he were outed, I would never have started this relationship. But I didn't think hard enough about that. I should have realized that the UU church, with its progressive attitudes, did not represent everyone in Assisi.

At the same time, though, didn't some of the blame (there was that word again) belong to Marshall? After all, if he *had* known how severe the consequences of discovery would be, why did he allow our relationship to progress? Oh, sure, he tried to avoid me, but after he'd told me how he felt, that's when he'd started showing up at my house. First it was to talk about the teen group. Then (and, all right, I encouraged him) he started bringing over music.

And then there was that morals clause. If one existed, and Vanessa was probably right, he would have known about it.

Stop it, Spencer. This is not about blame.

What Vanessa had said, almost in so many words, was that Marshall's life here was over. In having a relationship with me, he had essentially committed a kind of career suicide in his chosen town. And there was nothing I could do to help him.

God, but my heart ached!

When I arrived home, I sat in my parked Jeep, trying to summon the courage or whatever it would take to face Marshall's distress and suggest the only way out I—or Vanessa—could think of. Only after about five minutes did it occur to me that all my own distress was for him. That is, the idea of him leaving was not what tore at my heart. And that made it worse; he had sacrificed his life here in Assisi for his regard for me, which I was beginning to realize exceeded mine for him. If he loved me, of course I had no control over that. But despite what he'd told Bruce, the fact was that although I cared deeply for him, although I enjoyed his company, including the sex, I did not—and probably never would—love him.

And as horrible as it would be for him to know that, it might be just the thing to get him to leave.

I sat up straight and shook my head rather violently. It was not up to me, or to Vanessa, or to anyone else to decide what Marshall should do.

He was lying on the couch, his eyes red from weeping, his skin blotchy and his hair a mess. The sight tore at my heart. I sat on the edge of the coffee table.

"Sweet man, you can stay here for however many days you need to. I don't want you to be alone before you're feeling stronger."

"Thanks." He said nothing else, just watched my face with his sad eyes.

"And when you're ready to talk about what comes next, I'm here for you." There was no way to broach the subject of therapy or relocation right now. I wondered how I would know when it was time. And I wondered if I would ever actually tell him how I felt.

CHAPTER 18

There was only so much I could do for Marshall in the near term, other than be with him, comfort him, and wait for the right time to broach the direction Vanessa had suggested. Meanwhile, as best I could I needed to refocus my efforts on clearing Assisi of blame for the fire.

By Saturday, both Milton Bryant and David Foster had been able to talk to their Little Boundary counterparts. We met at the Protestant church's function hall.

The Methodist minister in Little Boundary had been surprised to learn that Assisi blamed itself for the fire. David told me, "He's been there about twenty years. He hasn't heard a lot about the fire, but he did say that if anyone was to blame, it was the Burgos family. So I checked with the town librarian, and she also seemed surprised that there was any confusion. Her grandparents had owned land adjacent to the Burgos farm, and what she'd heard about that family was that they were exactly the sort of people to do something like that. Or, they had been at the time. And she was as sure as she could be, without actual documentation, that it had nothing to do with Assisi."

"Is the Burgos family still around?"

"I didn't ask, and I didn't seek them out. We might want to consider doing that."

Milton Bryant had less solid confirmation from his counterpart; the Catholic priest in Little Boundary had been there only four years. "However," Milton told me, "he put me in touch with the son of the man who had been the sheriff at the time. He told me that the town had essentially turned a blind eye to the perpetrators, and he suspects that the reason for it was that a lot of people at the time thought maybe the Perfectionists had it coming."

"Good God," I said, sitting back in my chair. "People died!"

"Yes," said David, "but not anyone from Little Boundary. Or, I'd guess, from Assisi."

"Right. Just people who had already been persecuted."

"Well," Milton said, looking a little sheepish, "the Perfectionists were pretty out there, as the saying goes. And it's possible they did confiscate some land."

My hand hit the table a little harder than I had intended. "Speaking as someone who has been persecuted, someone in a group of people who have been beaten and fired from their jobs and *burned*, I will tell you what you already know: There is no excuse for what they did!"

David, clearly startled, sat back away from the table, but Milton didn't flinch. "Oh, absolutely. I completely agree. But what we need to do now is figure out the next steps."

"Okay," I said, forcing myself to calm down, "I've spoken to someone here who's willing to bring the tragedy up quietly with people he thinks might have some memory of that time. He believes it's been obscured for too long."

"He?" Milton asked. "So it's not Vanessa Doyle?"

I shook my head. "I did ask, and she was willing to help, but she hasn't been feeling well recently."

"Who is it?"

"I'd rather not say just yet. Let's see whether he has anything to report."

～

Ben had moved quickly. He called me that night.

"I haven't actually mentioned the fire. But I asked my cousin, Uncle Jerome's daughter, about her dad and what he did in general. Seemed glad to talk about him. And I'm pretty sure that on the night in question, he was away. One of the things he did was supply firewood to different people, and that night he was almost certainly on his way back from a delivery over three hours away."

"That's great. So unless we hear about someone else, we don't have a suspect here."

"Correct. And I've never heard any names mentioned."

So far, so good. But I took only so much assurance from that. "It would be even better if we could be sure no one else was suspected, but we probably won't know that unless people start talking about it."

"I'm on that as well. My wife's brother perked up when I mentioned it casually over dinner tonight. He got a couple of hard stares from my wife and his, like they wanted to let sleeping dogs lie. He seemed not to notice, though, so I've planted a seed there. And there are a few other people I can bring it up with. Casually, of course."

"Get them talking. Good. Do you think they'll just talk about it, or might they begin to wonder who started it?"

"Don't worry. I planted that seed, too."

I laughed. "You're a one-man public relations expert."

"I'll do what I can. I can't thank you enough for kicking my butt, get me looking into this. With my line of work? You can imagine how it hung over my head that my uncle might have been the culprit."

"What puzzles me the most, I guess, is how it's gone on so long, and no one from Assisi talked with anyone from Little Boundary about it enough to figure this out before."

"Ah, well, there's a bit of history there, too. You might not know that before the fire, toward the end of the last century, gold was discovered on land that hadn't yet been claimed. Both towns vied for ownership. Little Boundary won the battle, but they lost any goodwill Assisi might have had for them. The gold didn't last long, but the rancor between the towns is still hanging on. Plus, at that time, it took a lot longer to travel the distance between the towns, so communication between them was sparse for that reason, too."

"You, sir, are a gold mine yourself. Thank you." I shared with him what I'd learned from Milton Bryant and David Foster.

"Well, Reverend Hill, I might be a gold mine, but you are an angel if you can help us get over this thing."

"We make a great team."

Marshall did not attend church on Sunday. He was still staying at my place, and I did my best to encourage him to come with me, but he said he couldn't take it.

"Marshall, you know you have nothing to be ashamed of, don't you?"

"I was fired. Have you forgotten that? I don't want everyone's pity."

If I was surprised that he didn't come to church, I was even more surprised not to see Vanessa there. It made me worry about her health. But when I walked home through a mild snowstorm after services I found her in my kitchen, talking to Marshall.

Vanessa's arms were on the table, reaching toward Marshall, holding his hands in hers. His head was bent forward, and his face streamed tears. Neither spoke.

As I walked into the room Vanessa looked up. Her eyes were not dry, either. She released Marshall and stood. "I'll get on home, now. You two might want to talk." I watched Marshall as Vanessa put her coat on. "Loraine's going to walk Klondike. He does love the snow."

I let Vanessa show herself out and sat in the chair she had used. "Marshall? Sweet man? What did you talk about?"

He pulled tissues from a box on the table, used them, and added them to a pile beside him. "She thinks I need professional help." I thought he'd say more, but he fell silent.

"Do you disagree?"

He looked at me, his expression unreadable. "Sounds like you think she's right."

"All I can say is that therapy helped me immensely."

"When were you in therapy?"

"My first year at General Theological Seminary was when I realized I couldn't deny that I was gay. But the Episcopal Church hasn't come into the twentieth century far enough to allow me to live a life like that of straight priests, and I couldn't accept that. On top of that, my mother died. We were very close. I kind of fell apart."

"You never told me."

"I'm sure I would have, at some point. Anyway, my advisor at General referred me to someone who helped me face things about myself I hadn't wanted to face, and she helped me put things into perspective in a way I could never have done on my own. The decision to see her was one of the best things I've ever done for myself."

He looked down at the table, fretfully tearing a tissue apart. "You were in New York. Lots of therapists to choose from." He looked up at me. "Plus, how am I going to manage, with no income, and pay for a therapist at the same time? And if I saw someone near here, how many people would find out? I couldn't stand that."

For one wild and crazy moment, I came close to suggesting he could live with me, and that we'd find someone far enough away. But Vanessa's voice in my head said, *Don't lead him on.* Maybe I wasn't ready to tell Marshall I didn't think I would ever really love him, but I had to admit it to myself.

But then I had a brainstorm.

"You could go to New York."

"What?"

"Maybe you could even see Kathleen Connolly. My therapist."

"Spencer, I can't afford to live *here* without a job. What would I do in New York?"

"Give me some time. If I can come up with a plan, would you consider it?"

His face crumpled. "I'd have to leave you."

My voice soft, I said, "Yes. That's true. But I'm hearing you say you can't stay here, anyway. But if it's the difference between you getting on your feet again, finding a way to get through this and restart your life, I wouldn't want to keep you here."

It hurt so much to say that. The idea of not seeing Marshall, of ending the relationship even for such an important reason, made my breath catch and my chest clench. Maybe this wasn't true love for me, but I was very, very fond of this man.

He sat silent for maybe a minute. I prodded, "Would you consider it?"

He stood so suddenly the chair nearly went over backward. He grabbed his coat from the front closet and headed out into the storm. I didn't know whether to follow him or not. I got up and watched from my front window as he walked away, head down, arms around his body, snow in the air slowly filling the space between us. I decided he needed to be alone.

~

By four thirty, the snow had intensified, and the sun—wherever it was behind the clouds—had set. I was almost ready to call Ben Marks and head out on a search. Anxiety ate away at my stomach; he might attempt suicide again, and that made me realize that whatever his decision might be, I couldn't go on much longer in this relationship. No amount of fondness, no amount of love even, would be enough to keep him safe. Marshall needed to find himself. I couldn't do that for him.

But I did have to go and look for him. And I figured I could use some help. I called Vanessa.

"Do you think Klondike would like to play in the snow a little more?" I didn't tell her I was hoping he could help me track Marshall; I didn't want to worry her.

"I'm sure he'd love it. Is Marshall walking with you?"

"Not right now. He needs some alone time."

I grabbed a flashlight and the T-shirt Marshall had slept in for two nights, drove to Vanessa's to get the dog, and drove home again; I figured Klondike should start where Marshall had.

At first when I gave Klondike the shirt to sniff, he seemed confused. But when I started walking in the direction Marshall had taken, dismayed that new snow meant I could no longer follow his footsteps, Klondike took the lead.

I was hard pressed to keep up with the dog. He didn't seem to pay any attention to the ground—that is, the snow—but he did seem to know where he was going, so I just followed, the leash nearly straight out in front of me.

It seemed like forever, trudging through ankle-deep snow, wind-swept flakes bouncing off my face, but finally we ended up near the school.

"Klondike, buddy, I think I know where you're headed. I sure hope you're right."

I followed the white dog, not quite invisible in the darkness on the white snow, up the wooded lane where I had first walked with Marshall, the day I had accosted him in the school parking lot. Other than the beam from my paltry flashlight, there was no light out here except the white of the snow.

We'd gone about a quarter of a mile when Klondike's excitement intensified, and he bounded to the side of the trail toward what looked like a tangle of fallen trees, and then he stopped and nosed into the tangle, sniffing and whining.

There was someone in there. It was Marshall, lying on his side in fetal position. Protected partially by the fallen trees over him, he had only a little snow on him. The space he was in looked kind of like a woodland nest, very likely a place Marshall had come many times before with the dog. I dropped Klondike's lead and reached for Marshall.

"Hey!" I nearly yelled. "Marshall! It's me. Come out of there, will you?"

He was shivering violently, and he could barely move. I pulled one of his arms. He didn't exactly resist, but he didn't seem to be cooperating, either. I couldn't figure out if he was too cold or if he'd been hoping to freeze to death and hated that I'd found him. Whichever, I realized that even if I managed to lift him out of that nest, he wasn't going anywhere in this condition.

I stood upright again, desperate to know what was best to do.

"Klondike? You need to watch him. Stay here." Unsure how much Klondike understood, I fastened his leash to a branch.

But the dog did seem to know what he needed to do. He crawled into the space with Marshall and huddled against him. A crazy thought came to me of something I'd heard about how some Aboriginal Australians would survive a cold night, cuddling with one or more dogs depending on how cold it was.

Supposedly it was the genesis for the name of the band Three Dog Night. I turned and ran.

Thank God I'd bought a Jeep for my life up here in the frozen North. With its four-wheel drive, it was able to follow the narrow, rutted trail, despite three or four inches of snow, to where Klondike and Marshall waited. I had the heat on high, and although it wasn't very warm inside yet it would be better than where Marshall was. I got out and left the engine running.

"Marshall, you need to help me, here. Klondike and I can't do this alone." I'd carried Marshall to my bed once, but getting him out from under that make-shift shelter was much harder. I pulled on one arm while Klondike yanked on a leg of Marshall's jeans, and together we managed to pull him into the open.

"Go away." His voice was thin and weak.

"No. You're not dying here. Not today."

I heaved and struggled to get him into the back seat of the Jeep. He was too weak to fight me. Klondike jumped in with him. It was another struggle to get the Jeep turned around, and at one point I thought for sure it was stuck in a rut on the side, but somehow I got the Jeep free and back to my house.

Marshall was slightly more alert by then, and he must have realized there was no negotiation; he was going into the house one way or another.

We shuffled upstairs together and into the bathroom, where I stripped him as the tub filled with warm water. Klondike watched from the doorway. Marshall didn't fight as I helped him into the tub. He wasn't shivering as much, which actually worried me a little; I was pretty sure that once someone gets truly hypothermic, they stop shivering.

He wouldn't look at me. He just lay there in the warm water, not moving.

I turned to the dog. "Klondike, stay." He sat obediently and watched Marshall, tongue hanging out in a friendly pant.

I ran downstairs, heated some water, and put it into a thermos. It didn't need to have anything else in it; it just needed to be warm. Upstairs again, I poured a cup.

"Drink this," I said, but Marshall didn't respond. So I kneeled, and with one hand behind his head I fed the water to him. He took it, at least, so I poured more. After two more cups he began to weep. I sat on the closed toilet and waited.

Finally he spoke. "I didn't mean to die. Honest. I just didn't know what to do. Where to go. I felt so empty inside."

"Marshall, I—" He looked up at me. I shook my head. And then I grinned. "Thank God for Klondike. He seemed to know right where you'd be."

"It's a favorite spot of mine. A nice place to hang out, just me and the dog, sheltered against the world." He looked up at me, eyes still tearing. "I can't stand the thought of not being with you. I can't stay here, and you can't leave. And I know you didn't sign up for this."

"I didn't sign up or not sign up. That part's irrelevant. But I can help you, sweet man. I can help you get someplace where you can get your feet under you again."

"Can you help me learn to love myself?"

There was no answer to that, or none I wanted to voice. I reached for the tap and ran more hot water into the tub, and then I poured from the thermos again. "Here. Drink a little more hot water."

Maybe an hour later Marshall was in clean underwear and a warm bathrobe, lying on my couch with a pot of tea on the coffee table. I had called Vanessa earlier to let her know I'd be bringing Klondike home soon, but I didn't leave with him until I was sure Marshall was safe and warm. When I got back from taking the dog home, Marshall hadn't moved. He gave me a wan smile as I sat down in a chair near him.

"Are you going to send me to New York?"

"Unless you have a better idea. I know people there who can help you."

"Like who?"

"I'll tell you once I've spoken to them." I stood. "I'm going to heat some soup for dinner. Would you like biscuits or toast with yours?"

He waved a hand. "Whatever is easier."

As I worked in the kitchen, I kept one eye on Marshall. When I saw he'd fallen asleep, I picked up the kitchen phone and called Ruth. With money she'd inherited a few years ago, she'd bought a nice condo in the city. Three bedrooms, as I recalled.

"Hey, Spencer. I hear it's snowing up there. Are you making snow angels?"

"Not exactly. Listen, I have a favor to ask. A big one."

She laughed. "You can ask."

"There's someone up here I've grown really fond of."

"Oh?" Her tone was teasing.

"All right, yes, someone I'm in a relationship with. But here's the thing. He needs to get out of Assisi for reasons I won't go into right now, and he also needs to talk to a therapist. I can help with the therapist end, but he has little money and no place to stay." I paused, hoping Ruth would get my drift.

"For how long?"

"Oh. Um, I hadn't thought of that."

I heard her exhale. "Well, that could make a difference. Would I like him?"

"I think so. He's got a heart of gold, but he's kind of fragile emotionally right now." I think it was at that moment that it occurred to me I was asking Ruth and Nelson to live for some unspecified amount of time with someone who was possibly suicidal. "You know what, never mind. It's too much. This is a silly idea. Sorry I asked."

"Don't be so hasty, Spencer. Why is it too much?"

I glanced in at Marshall; still sound asleep, snoring lightly. "Well…. I don't think he's actually suicidal, but I can't say it's out of the question. That's too much to lay on you."

"That fragile, is he? Let me talk to Nelson."

"Ruth, I said never mind."

"I heard you. I'll call you back. I'm sure we'll have a few questions."

Marshall decided to go to bed right after dinner, which didn't surprise me. I'd given him one bowl of soup and a single piece of toast, and he almost couldn't keep his eyes open long enough to finish.

Ruth called back around nine thirty with Nelson on the other line, and I felt a little freer to give them at least some details of what had happened.

"It's not that he needs to be in New York specifically," I said. "I just don't know where else he'd go, and neither does he. Plus I want to get him into therapy, either with my therapist or someone like her. I'm expecting to pay for that, if he'll let me."

Nelson said, "So we'd be taking on a boarder—a roommate, really—who's in a fragile emotional state, who needs therapy, and who might be suicidal, for some amount of time as yet unknown. Have I got that right?"

"I did tell Ruth to forget I asked."

"Well," he went on, "it just happens that we're fairly well prepared. As you know, Ruth is in the process of getting a degree in psychology, though she isn't ready for patients. And my own skills are likely to come in handy in a situation like this."

"Are you saying you'll consider it?"

There was a pause, and I imagined them with hands over their phones, consulting with each other.

Nelson spoke again. "Is there any way you could come for a

day or two and bring him so we could meet each other? Middle of the week would be fine; I expect weekends are pretty busy for you."

"I think so. He's asleep now, but I can get back to you tomorrow. How soon?"

"The sooner the better. I'm sure you remember how crazy this town gets around Christmas."

CHAPTER 19

Over breakfast the next morning, I broached the subject of a visit to New York. His response was not enthusiastic.

"So this would be me on approval? To see if they like me?"

"You might not like them, you know. It goes both ways. I was thinking we'd go down early tomorrow, stay two nights, come home on Thursday." He stared into his coffee mug. "Besides, wouldn't it be fun to see the city all dressed up for Christmas?"

He seemed to be trying to smile. "Sure. Listen, I think I'll go home today. Been away too long. And those Assembly people can't do anything else to me."

I nodded. "I suppose you'll want to pack, too."

"Right."

"I've got a number of things I have to attend to today, especially if we'll be away. But shall we have dinner here?"

He let out a long breath. "You know, I think I've got to clean out my own fridge. Things are probably starting to be dangerous in there."

When he left to head home, Marshall hugged me for almost a full minute, and he gave me a kiss that was both sweet and sad.

My day was as busy as I'd expected. At home in the evening, I gave Marshall a call. Once again, I spoke to his machine.

"Hey. Just thought we should settle on a leaving time tomorrow. The drive will take six hours plus, so we should probably get as early a start as we can stand. Maybe seven? Let me know."

I had barely started to pack when I got a call from a parishioner.

"Reverend Spencer? Marion Talbot here. I'm sorry to call you so late. It's my sister's husband. We think he's on his way out." She paused to clear her throat. "Could be any minute now, really. Can you come?"

I'd known that Norman Temple had been on death's door for some time, in a bed that had been moved into the living room of the home he'd lived in all his adult life. Uncharitably, I hoped this pastoral visit wouldn't delay my trip to New York; after all, Marshall was important, too. But of course I went to the Temples'.

Norman was able to grasp my hand, his other between the hands of his wife Denise.

I smiled softly at the man, his seventy-eight years looking like more than that, given the amount of physical devastation cancer had caused.

"You are not alone," I told him. "We are all here with you, all in this river called life. Can you feel the gentle waters carrying you to the ocean?"

He gave me a soft blink as if to say "Yes."

"We are all drops, individual for a time, blending together eventually in the ocean that is God. There is nothing to fear. You will not be lost. You will become everything. You will know what those of us you leave behind can only guess at, can only hope for."

Denise seemed to be trying not to weep, but she was losing the battle. I was close to tears, myself.

"You will know pure joy. Pure beauty. Pure love. It's waiting for you, whenever you're ready."

There was nothing more I could say, and I wasn't entirely sure he could still hear me. Before long his grasp on my hand eased, then released, and his hand fell limp in mine. I laid his arm gently onto his chest. His eyes, empty of light, were mostly closed, and his jaw fell open. I touched his eyes to lower the lids.

He was gone. And yet he was everywhere.

Denise gave up any attempt to control her grief. I went to her and we stood, embracing, while we both dropped tears onto each other's shoulders.

This was my calling. *This* was why was there. I believed everything I had said to Norman Temple. No; not just believed. I *knew* it was true. Did I weep because someone had died? Or did I weep because I, too, wanted that joy? That sense of belonging, a sense so complete that there is no way to describe it? That peace that passes all understanding? That love for which there are no words?

I waited with Norman until the ambulance arrived to carry his remains away, and it was well past midnight before I got home. I sat for several minutes on my piano bench, the keyboard cover closed as I leaned my head on my arms and breathed, both celebrating that I was still alive and wondering when it would be my turn not to be.

When I stood to go back to my packing chore, my eyes fell on my answering machine. There was no message.

Marshall had not returned my call.

I didn't care how late it was; I called his number. The only answer was the machine, Marshall's recorded voice suggesting I leave my number.

Moving faster than I would have thought I could, I grabbed my coat and drove to the house I'd been in so seldom. I pulled into the spot where Marshall's little blue car should have been. It was missing.

No light came through the windows of his half of the house. I rang the bell for the other apartment, rang it and rang it. I pounded on Marshall's door until the upstairs neighbor appeared, a red plaid robe wrapped tightly around herself.

"What on earth...."

"I'm so sorry. But I can't find Marshall. He was supposed to be here."

"He left a few hours ago."

"Left? To where?" I could hear the panic in my voice.

"Look, I don't know. I have a key he gave me to water his plants. Do you want to go in?"

She disappeared to fetch the key, and once inside she leaned on the closed front door while I went around turning on lights and calling his name.

"I told you. He left."

I shook my head at her. "He can't have! Where would he go? We're supposed to go somewhere tomorrow. Together."

She shrugged. "All I can tell you is he went in and out several times. He was loading things into his car."

I stood in the middle of the room, a hand clutching frantically at my hair, turning in slow circles until my eyes fell on a white envelope propped by the phone. "Spencer" was hand-written on it. I tore it open. The note inside was also hand-written.

My love, my generous, tender-hearted man, I can't do what you want. I can't be in the place where you grew up. I can't stay with people who know you. I would see you everywhere, and when you weren't there I would despair every time.

Don't worry about me. I'll be fine. You'll know this is true because I've taken my vielle and much of my music. But if I must leave here, if I must leave you, I need it to be a true separation.

Maybe you'll hear from me again someday. Maybe you won't. But I'm sure you will not forget me just as I'm sure I will not forget you. Please know that you've made a huge difference in my life. Now I believe that there is love out there. Even for me.

Take care of Klondike. He will need you.

Love, always. M.

I fell to my knees and leaned on the floor, my head hanging and my tears dropping freely onto the carpet. At first the only word in my head was *No,* repeating over and over. And then, ridiculously, came a line from Joni Mitchell's song "Big Yellow Taxi:" *You don't know what you've got till it's gone.*

I'd forgotten about the woman standing at the door until she spoke. "Will you be okay?"

I sat back on my heels, head still hanging, not knowing what to say to her.

"He left something under my door," she told me. "I've just read it." I looked up at her. "Says he'll send for his stuff before the end of the month." She eyed me, concern on her face. "So it seems unlikely he'll be back, himself."

I nodded. "Thank you. I'll go now."

"You're that reverend, aren't you?"

"What?"

"At the UU church?"

"Oh. Yes."

"I guess you and Marshall were together. I always kind of thought he was... you know."

I looked right at her. "Gay. Yes. As am I."

"I'm sorry," she said. "He was a great guy."

"He *is* a great guy."

"Of course. Sorry."

"I need to leave now."

I heard her turn the lock as I stumbled toward my Jeep,

where I sat for another several minutes, arms on the steering wheel, head leaning on them. I think I said several things to Marshall. *Why? Why did you have to leave like this? Why couldn't you tell me what you were doing? Where have you gone? Why couldn't you tell me that? Why? Why? WHY?*

A crazy thought occurred, swiftly dismissed, to ask Ruth for the name of the private detective who'd located Donald when he was within the protective barricades of that cult. The next thing that occurred to me, only remotely related, was that I had never seen Marshall's handwriting before.

How odd.

My phone call to Ruth the next morning, after zero hours of sleep, was difficult. She knew me well enough to know that all was not well. I did my best to hold back tears as I told her what Marshall had done.

"Oh, Spencer, I'm so sorry. I know he meant a lot to you. It sounds like he did what he had to do, though. For himself, I mean. Isn't that a good sign in someone who's trying to get back on his feet?"

"I suppose." I wasn't convinced, but I didn't want to discuss it at that moment.

After several seconds of silence on both ends of the line, she said, "Spencer? Can I say something that might not... that you might not want to hear?"

I took a shuddering breath. "Go ahead."

"When you were with Donnie, he probably seemed like he had it all together. He's such a great actor, he could come across that way. But I knew he didn't. Selfishly, I did what I could to encourage the two of you to be together, because I could tell you were a stabilizing influence. Donnie was *not* all together. We know this because of how quickly he fell prey to that cult. And I think on some level, you knew that."

She paused, so I prompted, "What's your point?"

"Marshall doesn't have it all together, either. I hope soon you'll be able to ask yourself what it is about both of them that attracted you. I mean, whether you're mostly attracted to people who need help. *Your* help."

"Ah. The budding psychologist speaks."

More silence.

"Ruth, I'm sorry. That wasn't—"

"It's okay, Spencer. You're in pain. I'm not offended. And that's partly because I'm right, and I think you know it."

I'd had enough. "I need to let you go now. I want to start thinking about this flaw in my character right away."

"I know you're being sarcastic. But I hope you do just that. Bye for now."

I had cleared my calendar through Thursday afternoon, anticipating the trip to New York. Now, there was no need. But there was time. A lot of it.

Was Ruth right?

The most disturbing aspect of it, if she was right, was because of what it might mean. My calling, which was to help others find God or some semblance of it in all our lives, might be the same as this filter through which I chose romantic partners. In short, I was ministering not just to my congregants but also to my lovers. I found that possibility profoundly disturbing. And hadn't my attraction to Marshall increased when I realized he needed me?

Almost as though we were still on the phone, in my head I could hear Ruth's voice: *Time to turn that urge to minister inside. Help yourself.*

It's like she was telling me to examine my motives. What had Erik Stillman said? I think it was that I might be fooling myself. That my motives might not be entirely pure, and maybe I wouldn't even know it. The subject was different—an invitation to The Forest as opposed to selecting a romantic partner—but the problem was the same.

The only way I could think of to avoid wanting someone for the wrong reasons would be to avoid romance until I could see myself more clearly. Until I could be sure of being helped as much as I was helping.

And that made me weep all over again.

As if in protest to what Ruth thought I needed to do, I went into a whirlwind of helping. The first opportunity was when Jenny Pratt called me just after my conversation with Ruth.

"Spencer? I got the strangest phone message from Marshall. He said he won't be here to work with me on the teen group any more. Do you know what's going on?"

I told her as little as possible and assured her that I'd join her this afternoon and on Tuesday afternoons for the foreseeable future.

Next I visited parishioners I hadn't seen at church. I spent a couple of hours with Denise Temple, helping her with funeral arrangements for her husband. On Wednesday, in preparation for Duncan's next lesson, I dug up some music I thought he might like.

I (finally) arranged for the church piano to be tuned, and in a moment of insightful delegation I asked Violet if she could be there for the tuner. *See?* I told Ruth silently. *See? I can ask for help, too, not just give it.*

I walked Klondike between ministerial duties and chatted with Vanessa over tea and scones that I made for her.

And I worked feverishly on my sermon for the coming Sunday. Erik Stillman had said he would be there, and if I convinced him that I had learned enough about Yule, I would earn an invitation to their celebration that evening.

As I sat at my desk Thursday morning, working on that sermon, I had a brainstorm. I called Ben Marks.

"Ben, Spencer Hill. Listen, I don't want to ask you to move things along faster than you think wise, but—"

He interrupted me. "I was going to call you yesterday. Got distracted by a hit and run. Anyway, seems we've really started something, here. Reverend Foster didn't exactly say anything in detail, but it seems folks in church last week listened between the lines. I see a lot of people in my job, and some folks who aren't even in my church are asking me what I know about this. I guess they think once upon a time it was—or should have been—a police matter, and they figure I'd know something. Thank God no one mentioned my uncle, but they've cottoned onto the idea that maybe the right story didn't get told."

When he paused for breath I said, "Wow. Excellent. Because I was going to ask you what you thought about my saying something a little more specific in *my* church on Sunday—no details, but pointing in the direction of that event. Sounds like it might be time."

"Well…. We still don't have any evidence. Not sure we ever will."

"So all I would want to do is raise some doubt. You're right; we don't know absolutely, and maybe it isn't knowable. But here's the thing. I love that the folks in Assisi are beginning to question it. But I hadn't been able to come up with a way to introduce it to the Forest Dwellers. But I happen to know that one of them, at least, will be in my church on Sunday."

"Really? Well. That's… that's a little risky, don't you think?"

"Can you think of another way to plant a seed for them to mull over?"

After a long pause, I heard, "I can't. No."

"Then I think I'll risk it. As I said, no details. It's just a seed."

~

It was more than a seed, really. I had spent the last few sermons on topics related to questions like how we couldn't be sure of things we hadn't seen. I'd referred to the enmity between Assisi and Little Boundary as something we might want to turn our hearts to. Once I'd even referred, very obliquely, to The Forest.

I was barely ready for Duncan that afternoon, I got so caught up in my sermon planning. By Friday morning, I had a title and theme for Deena: Turning thought into action; working together to bring light to areas of darkness. And, best of all, I would use the celebration of Yule as a launching pad. Because that's what it was all about: the return of the light.

~

Sunday, at last. It had been five days, five days without Marshall in my life. I missed him more each day.

As the congregation gathered, I was delighted to see Vanessa in one of the front pews. The person I didn't see, the person who had promised to be here, was Erik Stillman. Looking around at the vibrant reds and greens, decorations I'd helped put up all around, I hoped that Erik hadn't peeked in and thought there was too much of Christianity here. He knew that these traditions were Pagan in origin, but he would be correct in thinking many here would not know that.

I had just stepped up to the pulpit, sending my best benevolent smile around the room, when I saw Erik come in. He wasn't alone. There was a woman with him, possibly his wife or sister.

And there was Adam. I looked directly at Erik and nodded a welcome. The three of them took seats in the last pew.

"Today," I intoned, gazing around, "is a very special day. For although it's the shortest day, the darkest day, the one day of the entire year when we might despair of light and warmth, we know it is also the last of these shortening days. Because beginning tomorrow, just the tiniest bit at first, the light will return. And with it, though it will take a little longer, the warmth.

"The earth has seemed dead. Or at least dormant. The air has grown cold. The trees appear to have given up on life. Or—not all the trees. The evergreens—the pines, the junipers, the hemlocks, the cedars—these trees refused to give up. Their boughs, ever green, symbolize the refusal of life to give up. They represent rebirth and renewal. They might even seem to have power over death.

"So the spark of life, kept safe in that green, is still there. The green reminds us not to give up. Not to despair. Not to fall silent and idle as though waiting for the darkness to win.

"And how do we do this? How do we demonstrate our trust in the light? How do we not give up on life, as so much around us seems to have done?" I paused here, wanting not only to make sure people were listening, but also to give them a moment to wonder, to speculate, perhaps to come up with their own ideas.

"Those who follow Christian beliefs might look to Jesus as an example of hope, of light, of love. But mankind killed Jesus. Does this say we deserve to lose the light? Or does it mean that we must call on the power within ourselves to find it again?

"And how do we do that?" Again I paused. Then, "Look around you."

I waited, but few people moved at all. "Really. Look around you. Look at each other. Look *to* each other. And then look outside this building. Look outside the boundaries of Assisi. For it is within ourselves and within each other that this light exists, this light that shines through the cracks of our own imperfections."

I stepped slightly away from the pulpit to make some space for what I was about to say.

"What if someone did something truly terrible? What if the blame for that deed fell on the wrong person? What if the truth came to light—there it is again, light—came to light eventually? Now, what if it had happened so long ago that when it was finally brought into the light, the person who did it was gone, dead, out of the picture? What do we do with the blame? Do we pass it on to someone else, or do we ourselves shine so brightly that the darkness of the deed is overcome and the blame disappears with it?"

All eyes were on me. If I could have read minds, I would have said many were wondering if I knew about the fire. And some of them would know there was now doubt about how it had started.

I bowed my head and drew a deep breath. When I looked up again, I smiled.

"Christmas. Hanukkah. Yule. To name just a few of the traditions that celebrate light and love." I chuckled softly. "I've heard that December is the time of year when all organized religions set aside their beliefs and celebrate Paganism."

My UU congregation came through. They chuckled with me. Also they were probably relieved that all that heavy sermonizing was over.

"For anyone who doesn't know, our favorite things about December holidays came to us from many centuries ago and had nothing to do with the carpenter from Nazareth. It was Pagans who first burned a Yule log and lit candles to encourage the return of light. Who celebrated the promise of returning life they saw in the evergreens. Who sang songs, and danced, and reveled in the love and goodwill that we have for each other.

"But the truth is it doesn't really matter who started it. What

matters is how we carry it on. What matters is that we believe in
the return of light and warmth, even when it's dark and cold.
That we trust that even when we see each other's flaws, when we
disagree with each other, we trust that beneath that there is light
and love."

I looked over at the piano, where Violet Verette waited for
my cue.

"In the spirit of this trust, I've asked Violet to play through a
few verses of a carol some of you might not have heard before. I
can't give you the text, but I can tell you that it barely mentions
Christmas at all, and it was probably not even originally a
Christmas carol. It speaks of the wonder of this time of the year
when light begins to return, shining on the poor as well as the
wealthy. It speaks of an end of sorrow and enmity, of singing and
dancing and renewal in body and spirit. And one line repeats at
the end of each verse, the reason for doing all these things: to
drive the cold winter away."

Violet had been practicing this piece since I'd suggested it to
her a few weeks ago, and when she began to play, the rollicking
nature of what was essentially a minor key seemed to capture
everyone's attention. We had agreed she would play quietly
while I spoke about the carol, repeating as needed. The third
time she played that last line, I spoke the words: "To drive the
cold winter away!"

The music ended. I raised my arms just below shoulder
height. "So to all I say, Merry Christmas. Happy Hanukkah. And
welcome, Yule!"

Several people in the congregation, including the Forest
Dwellers, responded in unison: "Welcome, Yule!"

As people were leaving, shaking my hand or not, speaking to me
or not, I sensed very different things from different people. There

were three major categories. One of these groups consisted of people who seemed to have no idea that I'd been referring to anything specific and who were either a little confused or who had liked the theme of light and love and had enjoyed the music. Another group of people seemed to know that much of what I'd said referred to that horrible fire, something they had scrupulously not spoken of for most of their lives, and they weren't entirely sure I should have broached it, however indirectly. And then there were the Forest Dwellers.

The MacPhersons had come to the service, choosing seats near the back, and they waited with Erik's group until all others had left before they approached me. Erik was clearly a leader, at least here.

He held out his hand, and I took it in both of mine.

"Reverend," he said, regarding my face intently, "we would be honored if you would join our Yule celebration tonight."

I had to close my eyes briefly as several emotions attempted to overwhelm me. For reasons I didn't understand, the honest, forthright invitation left me vulnerable to regretful feelings about Marshall, about what I might have done to precipitate his troubles, about the pain I still felt at his disappearance. When I opened my eyes, tears stood in them, unshed.

"Thank you. Thank you so much."

"Adam will stop by your house at nine o'clock tonight. Bring no one else. Adam will drive you. Dress warmly, and prepare to be with us until dawn."

The woman, to whom I had not been introduced, turned as she was about to follow Erik. "And Reverend? Don't eat dinner before you come." She smiled a knowing smile at me and winked.

CHAPTER 20

I was a nervous wreck long before Adam arrived to fetch me, though I couldn't have said why. Anxiety and I were not strangers, and I would have expected to feel anticipation, even excitement, at this invitation, but not this tension. The only reason for my nervousness that I could come up with was that so much was riding on Erik's response to my sermon. I was fairly sure he had approved of the connections I'd made to Paganism, the credit I'd given its history. What I was less sanguine about was how much he had understood regarding the fire. Had he heard enough subtext to know that I'd hinted at a misunderstanding about the perpetrators? And if so, how sure could I be that I was even right?

Waiting for Adam, I played piano to try and distract myself. Even so, through the Chopin and the Mozart and the Debussy, slipping between the notes were nerve-wracking doubts. Because even when I tallied up everything I'd heard—from the personal stories of Little Boundary folks to Ben's fearful suspicion, only recently lifted, that his own uncle had done the deed—all of it was essentially anecdotal, largely from different individuals' memories. As Ben Marks had said, there was no real evidence.

These doubts included doubts about myself. Who did I think I was, strolling into this remote town and upending a very old conviction held by two communities? By what right could I disrupt the status quo that was understood by many but spoken of by no one, thereby destroying a balance that had been carefully maintained by those who had been here so much longer than I had?

Who the fuck do you think you are? That was one voice in my head. But there was another.

It was my father's voice. First: *Adequate job on the Mozart, Spencer. I know you can do better.* But then: *Courage, son. If you're sure this is the right thing to do, don't be dissuaded by your doubts or anyone else's. Sometimes you must stand alone to lead others to truth. Be a fool for Christ, Spencer.*

Father had often used the expression of being a fool for Christ. Having been a Catholic priest before he left that life behind to marry my mother, he knew the New Testament well. He frequently quoted from the verses in First Corinthians about how God sees worldly wisdom as opposed to the wisdom of heaven. Father would stress that when we stand up for the message of Jesus in the face of the world's disdain, while appearing foolish to the world, we are wise before God.

It had never occurred to me, as a child, that he must have endured demonic doubts about leaving his calling. But he had done what he believed he had to do. Else, I would not exist. And in a way, I had followed in his footsteps, leaving the expectations of being an Episcopal priest behind to follow a different path, even though I now saw it was leading to the same destination.

Father and I had had our problems. I had seen him as aloof, having a strictness that fell short of Draconian but that felt harsh to me. But he must have had to endure the slings and arrows, as Shakespeare put it, of going against everything he had been expected to do. Everything he had expected himself to do.

I had never felt the warmth of love from him. I was beginning to see that not as a fault of his, but as a survival tactic. So here, in his example, was a cautionary tale: Stand alone if needs must when you believe in where you stand, but (and this is where, at least in part, I think he failed) don't assume a defensive carapace that will prevent not only arrows but also love from reaching you and from reaching out from you.

Layers. When Marshall had helped me with hiking gear, he'd told me layers were the best way to stay warm. "Just don't put on so many that you end up feeling like a sausage."

I had a difficult moment when it was time to put on my boots. Marshall had made me try on several pairs, even though I'd been ready to buy the second pair I'd tried.

He'd laughed at me. "You just like the color. Come over here to the slant step."

"The what?"

It was a short but very steep, free-standing, wooden incline.

"Walk up and down a few times. Pay attention to whether your heels slide up and down, and whether your toes touch the front of the boot on the descent."

He'd been right. I'd bought the fourth pair I tried. And as I fastened the laces to get ready for Yule, a deep sadness came over me. I could not have anticipated how very much I would miss my sweet man.

The ringing of the doorbell startled me.

Adam's hands were in the pockets of what appeared to be a down parka, but there was an outer shell, some dark fabric that was not synthetic. Wool? Some kind of blend? I couldn't tell. His long hair hung around his face, his expression maybe one of amusement, or it might have been patronizing. Again, I couldn't tell. Around his neck was a scarf of snowflake patterns in red, green, white, and golden yellow.

"Ready?"

"Just about. Would you like to come in?"

He hesitated and then shrugged. "I guess if we're inviting you to ours, I can come into yours." He stepped inside and immediately went to stand by the piano keyboard. "I heard you playing."

How long had he been out there before ringing the bell? "It seemed a good thing to do while I waited for you."

He reached one hand to the keyboard and poked at a few notes. Not looking at me, he asked, "Do you teach?"

"Piano? Not exactly. There is one boy whose interest I've sparked. He's enjoying the lessons, though I suspect he will turn to other instruments at some point."

Now Adam looked at me. "Why?"

"I've given him music from the classics to work on. He works on that. But he brings his own music sometimes, and it's of a more... let's say contemporary nature. Popular music."

"Does that annoy you?"

I barked out a laugh. "Of course not. I can show him my music, but he must find his own. He's doing that."

Both hands in pockets again, he regarded me, his head tilted. "You're an interesting person, Reverend Hill. Not what I expected."

I felt one side of my mouth lift in a wry smile. "Nor are you what I expected."

"It's good, this surprise. I like it. Shall we go?"

I grabbed my parka and a small satchel, and climbed into the green pickup truck beside Adam. The cab was warm, and the seat was comfortable.

"You know," I told Adam as he backed out onto the road, "I don't even know exactly where The Forest is."

"I'm glad to hear that. It means you haven't been snooping."

"I have not." I heard a certain testiness in my voice and did

230

my best to smooth it out. "As I told the MacPhersons and Mr. Stillman, I would not approach without an invitation."

"And now you have one. How does it make you feel?"

"Honored. Very honored. I understand why you guard your boundaries," a word I chose deliberately, "against people whose motives you can't be sure of."

"Indeed."

"Are you sure of mine, now?"

"Are *you?*"

"Who is?"

He laughed. "Touché. You are interesting, indeed."

We drove silently for about five minutes while I tried to track our direction. It was challenging, in the dark, on roads with few landmarks and many trees obscuring the distance. Soon we were on a surface more like gravel.

Adam had to raise his voice a little to be heard over the road noise. "In case you're wondering, I won't say anything about your sermon now. Erik will do that. After, I might have some things to say."

"I look forward to both opinions."

"Do you take criticism well?"

I gave a nervous laugh. "I hope so."

"As do I. I like you, Reverend Hill."

His words had a finality to them, as though not only was I not expected to reply, but also that I should not. So I didn't.

Soon there was a bright light ahead, but not from lamps. It must be a bonfire, I reasoned. It must be where the Forest Dwellers were gathering.

I was correct. Adam pulled the truck well away from the flames and I got out, transfixed by the sight of the biggest fire I'd ever seen.

Adam took my arm. "This way. Erik would have a word."

We walked away from the fire toward a cluster of rough-hewn buildings that appeared to be barns, with somewhat more refined houses beyond, all made of wood, all no doubt constructed by the Forest Dwellers.

We approached one of the larger homes, light evident behind curtained windows. The smell of wood smoke permeated the air all around. We left our boots in a large bin near the door, and when Adam led me into a large, open room, I was not surprised to see a massive wood-burning stove against the outside wall. Erik stood beside it.

"Welcome," he said, his hand out. "Thank you. Thank you very much." I held the satchel out to him. "Please accept this gift in gratitude for your hospitality."

He tilted his head as though surprised and opened the satchel. He held aloft the bottle of a relatively expensive Châteauneuf-du-Pape I'd brought from my parents' home.

"French," he said, gazing at the label. "I haven't been in Provence in years. Thank you."

It was an effort to hide my surprise that he'd ever been to Provence. Clearly I knew nothing about these people.

He gestured toward one of two chairs positioned near the stove. They were wooden, shaped like captain's chairs, with soft seat cushions in a colorful pattern. "Give Adam your coat and anything else you'd like to shed while you're inside."

Adam seemed deferential toward Erik. He took my winter layers as instructed and left the room.

"You did as I asked," Erik told me. "I wasn't sure you'd be able to."

"Really? Did the colors in my aura lead you to think I couldn't?" Immediately his face took on a guarded expression. "Please, don't think I meant that as anything but curiosity. I'm completely ignorant of the perception and the meaning of auras.

And I know that just because I don't see them doesn't mean they don't exist."

Erik nodded. "Very well. Yes, they did give me pause." He sat back and regarded me. "For what it's worth, the white is less muddy today. Not quite clear, but clearer."

"Have you seen clear white on others?"

He paused. Then, "There's something else I want to talk to you about. During your sermon you employed the use of a hypothetical situation to demonstrate the return of light that dispels darkness. And neutralizes blame."

"I did. Yes."

"I have a feeling that hypothetical example was culled from reality. Tell me what the reality is."

I inhaled deeply. Here was my chance, and I must not ruin it.

"I haven't been in Assisi long, as you must know. Until very recently, I'd heard nothing about the tragic event that I now believe caused the Forest Dwellers to pull back from Assisi."

"We pulled back from Little Boundary as well."

"Thanks for telling me." I nodded. "The reactions I was getting whenever I spoke with a Forest Dweller troubled me. Now that I know about your disconnection from Little Boundary as well, I'm even more sure of the picture I've been forming."

"And that is?"

"Quite by accident, when I was visiting a church in Little Boundary, I heard about the fire in which some Forest Dwellers died. The person who told me about it seemed convinced that the culprits had been from Little Boundary. This horrified me, but I didn't yet know that Assisi had been blamed, because no one there had said anything to me about it at all."

"Little Boundary. They were from Little Boundary?" I tried to interpret his tone and failed. Surprised, yes; but also angry? Incredulous? Confused?

"I heard the same thing from other Little Boundary residents, and when I enlisted the help of two colleagues from Assisi, they spoke to their counterparts in Little Boundary and heard the same thing. Then, by talking to several people in Assisi who, I might add, were loath to discuss what had happened, I discovered the suspicion—or the belief—that a man from Assisi had set the fire, or had set the event in motion, because someone here recognized him. But the more people I spoke to, from both towns, the more I came to believe that the recognition of that man had been in error. If the stories from Little Boundary are correct, there was a particular family there who instigated it. And the people I spoke with there think it's unlikely someone from Assisi would have joined with them in anything, after the strife caused by the legal battle over the gold that was discovered."

"It was more than strife. I don't know of anyone who was killed, but there were some physical encounters that were violent."

I nodded. "And that's one more piece of the puzzle I've been trying to put together."

"Your sermon pointed a finger at an unsuspected culprit."

"I hope it also stressed that blame at this point would not be productive. Certainly, it would not be in the spirit of Yule, or Christmas, or any similar approach to moving forward together with goodwill."

I wasn't sure I liked the way he was looking at me. "So you'd have us lift our condemnation off of Assisi without placing it on Little Boundary?"

"Yes." Simple. Direct.

He drew a deep breath, seeming to grow larger with it. "Without playing my own beliefs against me, tell me how I am to do this."

I guessed he didn't like my bringing Yule into this equation. "Your beliefs are not very different from mine. I don't think any of my UU parishioners felt slighted by the emphasis I placed on Paganism this morning. Both your people and mine believe in love, light, and goodwill. And I fully expect that Paganism sees forgiveness much as Christianity and Judaism and other religions see it; that is, it's something that benefits the one who forgives. The very process of forgiving insists that the forgiven has committed a wrong. If the forgiven person perceives no benefit, that does not reduce the benefit to the forgiving one. It does nothing to deny the accountability."

"Surely you do not expect us to tell whoever did this that we forgive them."

"Whom would you tell?"

It was a simple question, and yet it seemed to stymie Erik, because he didn't respond for several seconds. "Well... who was responsible?"

"All I have are anecdotes. And while I think they are convincing enough to relieve Assisi of responsibility, I can't provide you with any evidence. And anyway, I'm not going to point a finger at someone who is either dead or dying. And unless their progeny commit a similar atrocity, I don't think blame should fall on them."

We regarded each other—stared at each other—for another span of time. At first I thought it was one of those situations where he who speaks first loses. But I wasn't afraid of losing. Regardless of who spoke next, if there would be loss here, it would be Erik's. It would the Forest Dwellers'.

I said, "I'm not suggesting that a change in how you see your neighbors would be easy or quick. Rather, given the enormity of the event, it seems likely the process will be slow and perhaps even somewhat painful. But consider what's on the other side." I paused, waiting to see what he'd say, if anything.

"And that is?"

"Love."

Now the staring was a scowl. "My mother died in that fire."

I bowed my head briefly in respect, but it didn't change anything. "I very much want you to feel joy once again. Joy for the connection you had with her. The connection you still have. Wouldn't you?"

"How?"

"That's your work to do. What I can tell you is that as long as you hold hatred in your heart, it won't happen."

He stood and faced the stove, his back to me. I waited.

He wheeled toward me. "You bring news of exoneration of Assisi, if your anecdotes are correct. Yet you allow us nowhere else to turn our anger?"

"Not me. Time has done that. If you had found the culprits immediately and punished them, that would not have brought your mother back to you. If you now find the descendants of those culprits, how much less effective would that punishment be? How much less satisfaction would it give you? I tell you, it would merely be another barrier to joy."

I was beginning to worry that I wasn't going to be able to prevent an upsurge of conflict, this time between The Forest and Little Boundary. This was not at all what I wanted to happen.

"You're forsaking your own scripture? Your own Bible? An eye for an eye?"

I stifled a sigh. "Well, first, Christianity worships a god of love. But as I've said, I would not call myself Christian. Nor is the Bible my scripture. I can tell you this, though: That expression—an eye for an eye, a tooth for a tooth—is not Jewish or Christian in origin. It comes from the nomadic tribes of people who lived all through the Middle East for millennia. But it is not a guarantee of justice. It's a ceiling of retribution."

Erick look confused. "But...."

"A nomadic tribe cannot function, and in particular cannot get up and move, without the members being able to perform the hard work of a nomad's life. Men and women. But men tend to fight. If, say, Ahmed and Hari fight, and Ahmed puts out Hari's eye, the tribe now has one half-blind man. And if Ahmed suffers no consequences, then Hari and his family will attack Ahmed and his family, and there will be escalation that could destroy the entire tribe. So the sheik, or whoever the leader is says, 'Ahmed, you have put out Hari's eye. Hari, you may put out one of Ahmed's eyes. But no more!' That way, there is balance. There is closure."

Erik made a scoffing sound. "So who is to be our sheik?"

"If we lived in a society like that of nomadic tribes, you'd need a sheik's intervention. But we don't. You don't. You need a different kind of leader. One with their eye on the future, not on the past."

I knew I was on thin ice, now. By all appearances, Erik had at least some kind of leadership role here. And I had just implied that he might be stuck in the past and not doing a good job of leading his people.

Once again, we were staring at each other. I tried to keep my expression as open and hopeful as possible against the darkness of his internal burning anger. Then, without my knowing how it happened, there was someone else in the room. It was a woman.

She was older than Erik, with long silver hair, wearing a sort of kimono or formal robe of sky blue. This was not the woman who had come to my church. Erik stood, and I saw his posture change to one of apparent submission, so I stood also.

She wasn't tall, her face was wrinkled and a little shrunken, and her frame was not slender. In many ways she looked like an old woman. In others, she was almost a vision. Around her neck, hanging to mid-chest, was a silver chain. On it hung a silver circle, and within that a pentagram.

"Reverend Spencer Hill, I am Elaine Gault." She held out a hand, palm down. It made no sense to do anything other than bow to her and kiss the back of her hand. Then I moved aside so she could take my chair.

"I have listened carefully," she told me, "to what you've said. I see the wisdom in what you would have us do." I opened my mouth to speak, but she held up a hand and I remained silent.

"You are a newcomer to our area. You can't know the depth of feeling that has festered within our community for a long time. While I would not say you are misguided, or that what you ask is unreasonable, it will be extremely difficult. It will take time. At this point, I see no good coming from your continued discussion with Erik. He is wise and protective of our people, and he has suffered greatly from this affliction. He knows how much others have suffered as well. So I think it is time for this talk to end. We will carry it forward within our circle. You have made your case well."

All I could say was, "As you wish."

She smiled, though it wasn't clear to me why. "And now," she waved her fingers at someone standing in the doorway through which she must have come, "Adam will take you outside." *How many people had been standing just outside the room, listening?* "We are about to begin our revelry. You, Reverend Spencer Hill, are henceforth deemed the ambassador from Assisi, if you will accept that mantle."

Responding to Elaine, I felt almost as though I were addressing royalty in some time long past, and she had just tapped my shoulders with the flat side of a broadsword. I did my best to recover from shock at what she had just said.

"I must tell you I am officially the leader for only one spiritual community there. Not all residents attend any services, let alone mine. But I do have connections with other spiritual leaders, and I will do my best to do as you ask."

"We ask that you do only what you can. I believe you will do so with a good heart and generous intention. Now, Adam? Please take charge of our guest."

≈

Outside, the mood could not have been much more different from either the tension of my conversation with Erik or the nearly royal atmosphere created by Elaine. There was snow on the ground, but it had been trampled by enough boots that walking was not difficult. Around the bonfire were so many people that the crowd must have been made up of everyone else in the community. A number of them held hands and moved in a circle around the fire. Behind them were tables overflowing with food. Adam led me to one of the tables in the food area, where a large caldron sat over a grate. Coals under the grate kept the caldron warm but not hot. A large woman, large in every respect and dressed in colorful garb, ladled liquid into two ceramic mugs and handed them to Adam. He gave one to me and, holding my eyes with his, he lifted his mug to mine.

"To the future," he said.

"To the future."

The drink was potent, and I nearly coughed as I swallowed a mouthful. Adam laughed.

"Wassail," he said, "spiked with fermented juniper berries. The word wassail derives from the Old English words waes hael, meaning be well. Essentially, to your health. The official response is drinc hael, or drink to health."

"Try it again," I said, and this time I didn't cough, and my response was traditional.

We wandered around the food tables, picking up what appealed. There was so much food, some cold and some kept warm over small flames. Whether it was my lightened mood or mild inebriation, it was all delicious. We ate as we stood, watching the crowd.

Adam asked, "Shall I show you around the village?"

"I would love that."

He pointed out common buildings such as the grammar school. The meeting hall, he said, served prosaic as well as spiritual needs. On the houses, I noticed evergreen wreaths. I asked Adam the significance of them in Paganism.

"Wreaths represent the wheel of the year, with Solstice

marking the completion of another cycle. You already know the meaning of the evergreen boughs. We decorate them with cones and berries, things found in nature, to add texture and color. One of my favorite things about them is that they're sometimes given as gifts. Then they represent goodwill, friendship, and joy from the returning light."

Suddenly there was an uproar and cheering from people at the bonfire.

"Come!" Adam turned and trotted toward the fire, and I followed.

A very large tripod was now erected over the remains of the bonfire, which had burned down quite a bit since I'd arrived. From the tripod, hanging on a thick rope, was a massive log, as thick as a horse's midriff and maybe five feet long. Some young people, teenage boys mostly, laughed and jumped at the log, slapping at it to make it spin. It was too heavy for their efforts to have much effect, but they kept trying.

Adam took my mug. "Wait here." When he returned, both our mugs were once again full of wassail. I started to drink, but he said, "Not yet. Watch."

Slowly, the log lowered toward the remains of the bonfire. No doubt there was a winch someplace, but I couldn't see through the crowd, and I was partially blinded by the glowing embers and remaining flames of the fire.

The crowed fell silent as the log continued its slow journey toward the fire. When it was maybe a foot above the coals, there was a *thwack*. Someone must have cut the rope with a hatchet, and the log and a length of rope landed on the coals with a dull thud. Sparks flew high into the air. Someone picked up the straggling end of the rope, curled it, and flung it onto the log. Everyone waited silently, watching the log. I noticed Erik and Elaine, both now in warm outer clothes, across the circle, also watching the log.

I was beginning to wonder how long we would all stand here,

when suddenly flames shot up from beneath the log, curling around the sides in great orange-yellow spikes with blue roots. A loud cheer went up and then grew quiet. Everyone looked toward Elaine.

Her voice was clear and strong. "Tonight we celebrate the festival of the winter solstice, the rebirth of the sun, and the return of light to Earth. As the wheel of the year turns once more, we honor the eternal cycle of birth, life, death and rebirth. Listen to the wisdom of those who have come before you, and yet be wise enough to make your own way. Never forget that each year feeds into the next, and the next. And each time the sun seems to fade, we know it will return."

She beamed a smile that was almost like the sun itself, raised her mug, and cried, "Welcome, Yule!"

In unison, everyone else echoed her with "Welcome, Yule!" as they raised their own mugs. I joined them, loving the sense of connection I was feeling with people whose names I didn't even know. Of course, some of that warmth likely came from the spiked wassail. But I didn't care.

Someone handed me a long candle. Everyone seemed to have one. We all leaned close enough to the fire to light our candles.

This was as good as I'd felt since Marshall had left.

Hours passed, and yet time seemed to stand still. Revelry was, indeed, the best description of what was happening all around me. Couples were dancing. Groups of three or more people, arms on shoulders or around waists, did the same. Musicians played so many different kinds of instruments I'm not sure I saw them all. There were fiddles, recorders, tin whistles, guitars, banjos, even an accordion.

At one point Adam disappeared again, returning very soon with a grin on his beautiful face.

"What?" I asked. "What is it?"

He just grinned at me. "Wait for it. You'll know."

The music came to the end of a tune and another began. I laughed out loud. Around me, people began to sing words to the tune. It was the carol from today's service. I didn't know the words to the verses well enough to join in, but I always managed to bellow at the final line of the chorus each time: "To drive the cold winter away!"

When no one could remember any more verses, the instrumentalists played one more verse through. Everyone sang the last line and the song ended. Raucous laughter came from all around me. My own laughter was equally loud and uninhibited.

Raising his voice so I could hear him, Adam told me, "Erik noticed all the references you made during your sermon. But I think the thing that clinched it was that you chose that carol."

"It was one of my favorites as a child."

"Really? Your parents...."

"Very Christian, actually."

"Yet you protest that you are not."

"True."

"Come." Still holding a lit candle, he led the way to one of several other smaller fires burning nearby. A long log rested on the ground near it, and we sat there. I admit that the amount of wassail I'd consumed meant I had to focus on not falling off the thing.

"So you are not Christian," Adam picked up where he'd left off. "But your parents are?"

"Were." I gave him a thumbnail sketch of my early life. My father, the erstwhile Catholic priest. My mother, the nearly-nun. Their move to the Episcopal church, and my youthful conviction that I would find my calling there.

"What changed your mind?"

"The Episcopal church itself." I paused to take another swallow of wassail, and he waited. "You might already know that I'm gay. The Church hasn't yet figured out what it wants to do with people like me. I could be ordained, even given a ministry. But I would get into serious trouble if my… we'll call it my behavior gave anyone any reason to doubt my dedication."

"Loving a man sheds doubt on your dedication? How is that?"

"You might well ask. And they could give no answer that didn't rankle. It meant I was studying to become a priest among other candidates who would be not just allowed but probably encouraged to live full lives. Spouses. Children. Families in homes that should shine as examples of love and togetherness. And I would be excluded from that."

"That's bullshit."

I laughed a little too freely. "I agree. And I had a bit of a falling out with them over it. Then a friend introduced me to the Unitarian Universalist tradition." I took another swallow. "It didn't take me long to realize that's where I belonged."

"I could never be a minister. No patience."

I chuckled. "That's what my most recent boyfriend said."

"Marshall."

I half-turned on the log, nearly falling off. "What…. How did you know?"

Adam turned only his face toward me, a knowing smile on it. "We here know much about what goes on in Assisi."

"Seriously? But how would you know about Marshall and me?"

"I also know what happened with him."

"Do you know where he's gone?"

"No."

"Stop nickel-and-diming me. What do you know, and how do you know it?"

"I know he was fired from his teaching job for being gay. I know this because he had attracted my attention."

I shook my head. "What does that even mean?"

"You knew him better than I did. Didn't you find he had an honesty, an openness we don't see in most people? He had a clear heart, but his was a troubled soul."

"But why were you intrigued by him, particularly?"

He smiled that smile again.

"Adam, are you gay?"

"No."

"Then—"

"I guess pansexual might be the most accurate."

Pansexual. A term I'd heard, certainly, but I didn't really understand it. We sat quietly for a few minutes, occasionally sipping our wassail. My third mug. Unless it was my fourth. And then I had a question for him.

"I understand that when I saw you in the woods last September, you knew I was watching."

He laughed. "I did. Yes. I'd seen you walking along the trail. But I didn't put on a show for you. I did what I'd gone there to do. I just didn't let your presence interfere."

"Interesting, if I believe you. But I got the distinct impression, after that, that you thought very little of me."

"I thought you were just some do-gooder, some holier-than-thou religious type. I was wrong." He stood and offered me a hand. "Shall we rejoin the revelers?"

I let him help me rise. But he held onto my hand as he started to walk. Startled, confused, I pulled away.

He shrugged. "Have it your way. Come along. I'll introduce you to a few people who might not remember you later because of how much wassail they've had."

Adam kept me moving. We entered a few buildings from time to time to warm up. He didn't leave my side. As the sky began to lighten, everyone gathered around the bonfire again. Our candles were gone, consumed by fire, and no longer needed. They'd done their part. The Yule log was visible only by the outline of its ashes.

Adam and I stood near Elaine as everyone joined hands, and once again Adam held mine, but because it was part of the ceremony I didn't pull away. There was silence for a moment, and then a chant began. I couldn't make out the words. I'm not sure they were English. The chanting grew louder as it became evident the sun was about to rise, and then there was silence again. All hands, still joined, were in the air over our heads as we waited for I knew not what. And then the first rays of the sun shone through the trees.

"The Yule log has done its job!" Elaine called. "Welcome, sun!"

Everyone echoed, "Welcome, sun!" There was much cheering, and people released their joined hands so they could clap. Several people embraced. And that included Adam, embracing me. Smiling, he pulled a little away, hands on my shoulders.

"I hope you've enjoyed your first Yule celebration," he told me. "Let's give our regards to Erik and to Elaine, and then I'll drive you home."

Adam said nothing on the drive to my house, and neither did I. Parked there, with the engine still running, we looked at each other. Still he was silent.

So I asked, "Was I your job for the festival?"

"What do you mean?"

"Were you told never to leave me alone?"

He threw back his head and laughed. "Do you think we're afraid of you? No. I was asked to fetch you and bring you home. I was asked to usher you in to Erik's house. You saw Elaine bring me in and ask me to introduce you to the festivities. That's all."

"And yet you stayed with me the whole time."

He smiled in a way that gave his face an expression somewhere between sultry and demonic. "I did."

"Why?"

He watched my face for a few seconds, and then before I knew what was happening (or so I tell myself) his tongue was deep inside my mouth. Something told me to push him away. Something else told me to respond to his kiss with my own. I did the latter.

"I will never love you, Spencer Hill. And you would be foolish to love me. Wanting is something else entirely." He handed me a piece of paper with a number on it. "Erik's phone." Then he leaned across me and released the door handle. "Good morning."

CHAPTER 21

To say my emotions were mixed would be a monumental understatement.

Elaine had named me an ambassador. But I was an ambassador from Assisi, and typically the location where the ambassador is from makes the designation. So what Elaine had said, essentially, is that I am someone they would accept. And I'd heard subtext that implied an ambassador was needed, because there would never be any real mixing between Assisi and The Forest.

The implication did not trouble me; I had never wanted or expected a blending of the two communities. But the title would be something only Forest Dwellers would know. Certainly, I would never tell anyone here in town that I'd been given this role. I didn't even know what it meant. Had I wanted some kind of connection? Yes. Had I then stuck my proverbial neck out to correct a decades-old misunderstanding? Yes. Had I succeeded? I had no idea.

And then there was Adam. What the fuck....

I was still reeling from how it had felt. By this point in my life, I'd kissed several people, most of them men. I knew passion. I knew sweetness and tenderness, and I knew the rough insistence of purely masculine aggression. Adam's kiss had seemed to combine all that and then add one more characteristic: mystery.

My answering machine was blinking at me. I ignored it. I needed a lot of water and a hefty dose of aspirin, and then I needed sleep. I knew that if I listened to my messages, I would feel obliged to respond to them. What I needed was a day off.

I slept the sleep of the dead until mid-afternoon.

After a shower, I sat down to a peanut butter sandwich and a glass of milk. I allowed myself these small luxuries before I played the messages that waited for me. As I ate, it hit me that Adam had never answered my question about how he'd known anything about Marshall. I drained my glass, set it down, and the dull thud focused my mind on a question: Had Adam and Marshall ever been together?

Surely, Marshall would have told me.

Right?

I set my napkin on the table and got up.

The answering machine held just a couple of calls. There was a request for use of the church function hall and another asking me to perform a wedding ceremony ("Small. Just family and a few friends"). It would be the day after Christmas, and the bride was a young woman who, I was fairly sure, had found herself in the family way and wanted to seal the deal sooner than later.

Before I had time to return the calls, my phone rang. It was Loraine. I barely recognized her voice because of the emotion in it.

"They've taken Vanessa to the hospital," she said, diving right in without preamble.

"Why? What's going on?"

She paused, and then, "Did you know she'd refused a third round of treatment?"

My chest tightened. "No. I don't even know what kind of cancer she has."

"Breast cancer. She'd had a single mastectomy after the first diagnosis, and the other breast was removed the second time. Last spring, they said it had spread to her lymph nodes. She was given maybe a year without treatment, but she refused to go through it again."

As though they were getting into the habit, my eyes began to fill with tears. "Where is she?"

I heard silence, and then Loraine began to cry. I could barely understand what she said. "Newport."

"My God. I was just with her! She seemed tired, maybe even weak, but she was conversational and alert. And she attended services yesterday."

"Yeah. She was great at hiding her pain. She usually took meds only at night."

"How long ago did she leave?"

"They just left. I had gone over to get Klondike for a walk. I have a key so I could do that if she wasn't home. But I heard Klondike barking frantically, which he never does, and when I went in, Vanessa was on the couch, nearly unconscious."

"Did anyone go with her?"

"They wouldn't let me in the ambulance."

"Okay. Do you want to drive, or shall I?"

"Could you? I don't trust myself right now. Just give me a few minutes to walk Klondike."

I made a few calls to let people know what had happened and that I wouldn't be available for the rest of the day, and then I drove to Vanessa's. Loraine was waiting outside, a box of tissues in her hand.

It would be about a forty-five minute drive, I figured. Loraine knew the route. Once we were on a major road, she fell silent, except for the occasional sniffle. After another ten minutes or so, she said, "I don't know what to do about Klondike.

Marshall was supposed to take him. I can't; I have two cats, and he nearly killed one of them when I tried to introduce them."

"I imagine there would be many people willing to take him. Certainly, I could take him at least for now, and then we'll see."

"Thank you."

Loraine did not seem like herself. I tried asking her a few distracting questions, but I got not much more than monosyllables. As we got close to Newport, though, Loraine grew noticeably agitated.

"Before we see her," she said, "there's something I need to tell you."

I couldn't say why it came to me suddenly, but I nodded. "About you and Vanessa?"

"How did you know?"

"I didn't. Something in your voice just now, I guess. You didn't want anyone to know?"

"Vanessa didn't. I wanted to be open, but I respected her preference."

"How bad do you think this episode is?"

Loraine blew her nose. "Honestly, I'm afraid the next step is hospice care. So whoever takes Klondike—" She gave in to a moment of weeping. "Whoever takes him, takes him for good."

"Hospice care. As in institutionalized?"

Loraine let out a long, shaky breath. "I don't know how else it could happen. She can't afford in-home care, and neither can I. And with my job, I can't be there enough. Without my job, I have no money."

Silently, I vowed Vanessa would go home if I had to pay for her care, myself.

~

She was heavily medicated, awake but not very alert, when Loraine and I got to her room. She saw us and tried to smile.

Loraine pulled a chair to the bed and took one of Vanessa's hands in both of her own.

"Spencer knows," she said. "No more hiding."

I could barely hear Vanessa say, "No more hiding."

I nodded to Vanessa and went to find the cafeteria to give them some time alone. Maybe half an hour later, when I returned, the mood in the room was lighter. It seems Vanessa's collapse was not directly related to her cancer. It was more a case of exhaustion and dehydration, brought on by her attempt to complete an ambitious amount of house cleaning. However, she'd been told she was not to live alone, so that problem was still unresolved.

Vanessa would stay in the hospital overnight, and Loraine would drive back tomorrow to bring her home. On the drive back to Assisi that evening, I was contemplating how to let Loraine know that I was prepared to pay for in-home care for Vanessa when she scooped me.

"Spencer, I have a favor to ask."

"Name it."

"If you can take Klondike right away, my cats and I can move in with Vanessa. That way she won't be living alone. Together we might be able to pay for someone to come in and clean and cook a few days a week."

"Of course. I've already said I could take Klondike, at least for now." And though the prospect felt daunting, I added, "Maybe permanently. He'll be going back to where he used to live. Now, as for someone to come in, I would very much like to help with finances for that."

"How can you do that? I happen to know what your salary is."

I laughed. "Loraine, I came here from New York City. My parents, both deceased, owned a very nice single-family town-house in an exclusive area. I sold it. So please, let me help with this expense. I will feel so much better about Vanessa's prospects

if I can do that."
    "She might not like it."
    "I'll talk to her."

∽

Later, as I was about to fall asleep, I remembered the meal Loraine and I had shared in the diner, my first week in Assisi. She had proposed a program she felt would move forward her goal of acceptance for gay people. Now that I knew more about her relationship with Vanessa, I saw that program as her idea for a path toward going public. I chuckled; no wonder she'd been slow to see the more general goal I'd described.

∽

Wednesday morning, after Vanessa had been home for a day, I spoke to her about arrangements. Loraine had brought some of her things over but not her cats yet, so I brought Klondike over for a visit.

    "Loraine told me about your offer," Vanessa said. "I can't accept."

    "Don't do it for yourself. Do it for Loraine. She needs to be able to work at her job knowing that although she can't be with you all day, you're not on your own. Think how distracted she'd be, and how guilty she'd feel otherwise. And it would be a shame to drain both your bank accounts for something that's easy for me to do."

    She closed her eyes briefly. "I'll need to think about it."

∽

When I got home there was a message from Jenny. "Spencer? Um, I know you've been distracted lately, what with Vanessa and

252

all. But, um, do you think you'll be able to continue with Teens for Truth? It's just that I was on my own last night, and Marshall used to do the lion's share of leading."

Shit. I'd completely forgotten about the teen meeting. I had told Jenny I'd be there. I called back and got her voicemail. I apologized and promised to be there the following Tuesday.

So much was happening all at once: Yule, Vanessa, the teen group, and Friday was Christmas! Not leading a truly Christian church, I didn't have to do any of the typical things I would have had to do as an Episcopal priest, but UU tradition calls for a big celebration on Christmas eve. There would be readings and carols and a sermon that was more like a story. I already knew that this congregation would expect a ritual where everyone holds an unlit candle, then the church lights dim, and I would start a flame that gets passed from person to person. After all, a lit chalice is the symbol of Unitarian Universalism.

At the piano, Violet would softly play snatches of standard carols while I would speak to the ways we weave UU principles into our daily lives and especially into our holiday celebrations. Then there would be a festival of song where people sang along with various carols, as they saw fit, and there would be a reception in the function hall.

The function hall! Christ! I had to talk to someone about decorations and punch and food....

And then there was the wedding on Sunday for the young couple about to be in the family way.

I was just about ready to pull my hair out when my phone rang. I almost didn't answer it.

"Spencer Hill, here," I said, sounding exhausted to my own ears.

"Well, you sound like shit." Adam. I think I'd know his voice anywhere.

"Makes sense. I feel like I've been digested and excreted, and some dog is about to come and—"

"Never mind! I got it. But maybe I can take one thing off your plate."

"Please. Which one?"

"The kids who come in for that teen group say Jenny was alone, with Marshall gone."

"I was supposed to be there. But Vanessa––"

"I heard."

"Of course you did."

He laughed. "How would it be if one of our grammar school teachers came in with the Forest kids and did the thing with Jenny?"

I sat down hard on my desk chair. "I can't tell you how much that would help."

"Good. So Myra Langtree will be there next Tuesday. Can you let Jenny know Myra will be calling her this week?"

"Yes. Certainly. And thank you."

I gave him Jenny's number and we hung up, and it was only afterward that I appreciated what had just happened. Maybe Assisi couldn't go to The Forest, but The Forest would come to Assisi. In a sense, Myra would be their ambassador to us.

It was working. It was *working!*

I heaved a huge, grateful sigh and turned my attention back to my list of chores.

Fortunately, Vanessa had run a very organized church volunteer group, and preparations were already well underway for Christmas festivities. I made a note to myself to purchase gift cards for everyone who helped out with the tasks I would not have to do, just oversee. I made a silent pledge to follow her example during my ministry.

At noon I met with Janice and Bert, the young couple, to be sure all was ready for Saturday. We would use the church, but it would be a small gathering, and her sisters were taking charge of everything.

By evening I felt almost relaxed as I walked Klondike, who seemed to understand that even though he visited with Vanessa every day (at least, until the cats moved in), he was more or less my dog now. This felt more real to me after Vanessa handed over her records for his vet visits and vaccinations.

I had a dog. I'd never had a pet at all, and now this beautiful, friendly, wonderful creature and I belonged to each other. It was the best part of the week. Until that night.

Klondike and I were on our way home when I saw a green pickup truck parked in front of the house. Adam rolled down his window as I approached.

"Got dinner plans?" he asked.

"Leftovers, actually."

"Alone?"

"Just me and Klondike."

"And me."

Without my inviting him in, he followed behind Klondike and me, holding a couple of shopping bags that turned out to be full of food. There was a small beef roast and mashed potatoes, already cooked and just needing reheating; there were fresh carrots and pearl onions; and in a bag on its own was a small apple pie.

I watched, dumbfounded, as Adam lifted each dish from the bags and set them on the counter. Then he looked at me, a big smile on his face.

"Look good?"

I grinned, but I had to ask, "What's going on? Why are you doing this?"

"I wanted to see you again." I wracked my brain to land on something that would help me make sense of that and failed. All he said after that was, "I presume you have wine."

"How does a 1981 Saint-Emilion sound?"

"That's a special kind of wine? Erik knows about wines. I just drink them."

Adam took over getting everything ready, finding pans and utensils without asking me where anything was. I put on some light jazz, opened and decanted the wine, set the table, and gave Klondike a healthy-sized dinner of his own. When Adam and I sat across from each other at the table, I asked for more of an explanation.

"What's this all about, anyway?"

"We heard about Vanessa, and then we heard about the teen group needing help, and we figured you were also trying to get ready for Christmas." He held up a hand. "I know, I know, you aren't Christian. Even so...."

"You're right, actually. There is a lot to do. People in the congregation are doing much of the work, but I'll be busy."

"So I figured you could use a good meal and a little company, someone unrelated to all the stuff you have to do, all the people you have to worry about."

I raised my glass, as did he, and we clinked them together. "This is a very welcome distraction. Thank you."

"And," he said after a sip of wine, "as I said, I wanted to see you again." It was a moment when he might have held my gaze to communicate some kind of intention, but instead he glanced down at his plate and began to cut a bite-sized piece of the beef.

Why? It was on the tip of my tongue. *Why me? Why now?* Did he feel sorry for me, bereft of my lover? Was I some kind of sociology project? I decided to go on the offensive.

"I know little to nothing about The Forest. And almost as little about you. For example, what do you do for work?"

"I sculpt. One of my favorite things to do is to work on the trunk of a tree that has fallen, and out of that I create something beautiful, or meaningful, or intriguing."

"Is there any money in that?"

"More than you might think. I've never worked in Assisi, but

—believe it or not—I have worked on trees in Little Boundary, among other places. Sometimes I must travel and stay on-site someplace that's too far to travel as a commute. I've done tree trunks in people's yards. I've done stone and wood sculptures for museum grounds, and I've done works that are on display on the grounds of large businesses. I also carve small pieces and sell them on consignment in gift stores. There's a lot of business in ski lodges."

For some reason, this fascinated me. "But never in Assis? Is that because...."

"Of the fire. Yes. And the misunderstanding about its origin." He sat back in his chair, his fork of potatoes half-way to his face. "I wonder if you have any idea what you've done."

"Done?"

"The fire."

"Oh. Well, I don't think it's clear yet. I know what I *wanted* to do."

We ate quietly for a few minutes, and as Adam regarded me intently I began to feel uncomfortable. Then he said, "So you had plans to be an Episcopal priest."

I shrugged and nodded. "Once upon a time."

"What do you miss most?"

This time it was my fork that froze in mid-air. It was not a question anyone else had asked. It was not a question I had asked myself. I glanced sideways, and Adam let me think.

"What I miss most—and I miss these things a lot—is a combination of things that are usually present only in large Episcopal cathedrals. And in New York City, there is no shortage of cathedrals."

"And you miss... what?"

"The music." I closed my eyes. "The chants. The tropes. The professional choirs and the exquisite music they sing." I opened my eyes. "I miss the trappings. The robes and the colors and the theatre of it. I even miss the smoke from the incense. But most of all," I took a deep breath, "I miss the mystery that all these things together made me feel."

"There's no mystery in UU?"

I waved a hand. "Oh, sure, there absolutely is. There's mystery in everything. A tree. A dog. A pot of boiling water. But high mass in a cathedral seemed to concentrate it and present to me. All I had to do was be there, and it would wash over me and send an ineffable warmth all through me."

I picked up a stick of carrot and pointed it at Adam. "Mind you," I said, "that mystery, that warmth is something I strive for in my own ministry. And sometimes it comes. And when it's at its most powerful, it goes deeper and stays with me much longer than any high mass."

"Doesn't it also spread?"

"Pardon?"

"When you felt that in a cathedral, that was just you. When you create it, you share it with others."

I couldn't have said why, but Adam's words made my eyes water. "Yes. Those are the times when I am most sure that this is my calling."

He nodded, seeming to take what I'd said as somehow obvious. We ate in silence for a time, and when his plate was empty he sat back. "You know what I'd love?"

I swallowed the last of my potato and just looked at him, feeling apprehensive for no particular reason.

"Before we have dessert, would you play something for me? On your piano? Perhaps your favorite piece, if you have one?"

~

I played my favorite piece. I played the Chopin Barcarolle in F sharp major.

There was something about Adam that allowed me to forget he was there, and I allowed myself to become one with the music. I felt my body sway as I played, and at times I closed my eyes. The opening section has a sweetness tinged with something almost like melancholy before nearly jumping into more energetic phrases that give way to joy, subtle at first and occasionally allowing some of the melancholy back in before the final joyful explosions and the long, liquid runs that lead to the final cadence.

When I lifted my hands from the keys I realized I had tears on my face. Then I remembered that I wasn't alone. I looked up at Adam and saw something I hadn't seen since the first time I'd played that piece for Donald. That is, Adam's eyes held tears as well.

He approached the piano and held a hand toward me. I took it, and without a word we went upstairs together.

I can't recall how we undressed, how we got into my bed. I barely recall any of those specifics. What I remember is the slight scent of Adam, a mixture of wood smoke, something musky, and something fruity at the same time, the way one might detect notes in a fine wine.

I don't think there was an inch of me that didn't receive Adam's attention: my ears, my neck, my shoulders and arms and fingers and the palms of my hands; my nipples and my navel. He took his time, giving each sensation its own space. And he found that place on my body that has always been especially erotic, the divot just above the crack of my ass. He found that, and he knew it was special. He licked and massaged that spot until I was breathless, and only then did I hear the soft tear of a condom wrapper.

I clenched the pillow beneath my head and panted deeply, knowing what was to come, wanting the anticipation to last and also wanting to feel his penis deep inside me at the same time. When he entered me, I heard my own gasp of sweet pain and Adam's harsh exhale before he began to undulate, reaching slowly and inexorably inside me, pulling tantalizingly just far enough away to allow for another gentle, insistent thrust. Over and over he pushed and pulled. It should have felt the same each time. It didn't.

I came first, in what felt like a warm waterfall that began high above the earth and descended in an ecstatic rush. I think I screamed. I know I heard Adam make a sound somewhere between a pant and a laugh, and then he thrust deep inside me and gripped my shoulders hard as he came. I remember wishing there had been no condom. I remember wishing I had taken his essence into myself, where I could hold it forever.

We held our bodies still as his penis seemed to shudder several times before it fell away from me, sated and exhausted. He fell onto the bed beside me, on his back, one arm bent over his face as he seemed to grab the air with his lungs for several breaths. And then he laughed.

He laughed quietly, deeply, in a way that seemed profoundly like him and no one else. I turned on my side to watch him, and he turned his head to look at me.

"That," he said softly between breaths, "was the hallelujah."

Was he referring to our conversation earlier? Was he picking up on my description of cathedral services? "I think I need a little more."

He laughed again and reached a hand toward my face, letting one finger stroke my cheek. "Do you know the song? By Leonard Cohen?"

I shook my head no.

"The hallelujah is that state of being where the physical and spiritual are one. There is no separation. His point is that this state can be reached through sex, when the people involved lose sight of the things that divide them, the things that keep them separate, when they become one together. Though it seldom happens that way. We keep trying, but too often we're concerned with the details of what we're doing, how we're feeling, how we're making someone else feel. That is, we tend to approach the sacred through intellectual intent rather than just allowing it to be."

"This is a song I need to hear."

"I don't know all the words. I think Cohen wrote a prodigious number of verses, adding them over time. But the most poignant, I think, goes like this: 'Remember when I moved in you, and the holy dove was moving too, and every breath we drew was hallelujah?' He's mourning the loss of it. But I think we just found it."

He sat up and crossed his ankles in front of him. "We might never find it again, you and I. Or we might. It's not something you aim for."

"Like epiphany."

"How so?"

"You can't seek epiphany. It finds you."

"Then, yes. Like that."

~

After Adam left, as I turned away from my closed front door, my eyes fell on something on the piano. I picked it up.

It was made of wood. The lower part was of a deep purple color, and the color grew lighter toward the top. It was small enough that I could almost wrap the fingers of one hand around it.

There was a flat base, apparently a neck, and the outlines of a clerical collar were carved into it. But instead of a head above that collar there was a sun. Its face was benevolent, and the rays around the outside edge were not sharp. Instead they fell in graceful curves in various directions. The eyes of the face were closed as if dreaming sweet dreams. The mouth smiled a smile that was somehow both knowing and humble, unassuming.

I knew that, for Adam, this was me.

I didn't know if he and I would ever be together again as we had been tonight. I hoped so. But if not, then—well, then not. He was right about the difference between loving and wanting. He was also right that we would never be romantic partners. Even so, tonight had removed one more brick in the wall between his community and mine.

CHAPTER 22

Christmas Eve. Everyone had done their part to be ready for it, and I was beyond grateful. And before I headed over to the church to oversee the final preparations, I paid a visit to Vanessa.

Loraine was pretty much settled in by this point, though as soon as she opened the door she began assuring me of improvements she intended to make. I hugged her and wished her a Merry Christmas.

This living room, like mine, had been pressed into double duty. In my case, it was my piano. Here, there was a hospital-style bed and all the accessories associated with such a piece of furniture. Vanessa didn't spend all her time there, but it was available as needed. And she was sure to need it more and more as time went on.

The three of us sat around the kitchen table as one of Loraine's cats wound itself around my ankles. The kitchen overflowed with offerings from parishioners who had brought food for Vanessa and Loraine, and I was sure that if I had opened the refrigerator, I would have seen that it was packed full.

I told them, "I can't tell you how delightful it is to see the two of you here together like this."

I think Vanessa might have blushed, which is not something I would thought could happen. Loraine beamed.

"Thanks. It does feel right at last." Loraine turned to Vanessa. "Shall we tell him?"

"Oh, I think we'd better. He's going to be involved."

Loraine turned an absolutely shining face to me. "We want you to marry us. New Year's Day."

I must have looked shocked, or dubious, or both. Vanessa actually laughed.

She said, "Spencer, surely you realize that UU ministers have been performing marriages for same-sex couples for quite some time. These unions aren't recognized legally, of course, but they still provide couples and their families with a sense of the solidity and recognition that a marriage can provide."

The grin on my face was so broad it almost hurt. "I can't tell you how honored I would feel to celebrate your union."

We spent the rest of the visit talking about the wedding. Vanessa was hoping to feel well enough to hold the ceremony in the church, and Loraine assured her of that even if a wheelchair was necessary to get her there.

"And," Vanessa told me, "I want Klondike to be the ring bearer. We can attach a small bag with the rings in it to his collar."

I laughed. "He seems well enough behaved for that. I'll be sure he's thoroughly walked in advance."

That night, the church was resplendent, from the colorful altar cloth to the garlands along the aisles to the many poinsettia plants scattered throughout the space. Even the piano was festooned with strings of paper circles in red, white, and green, made by school children and shared among the community's churches.

As the members of my parish began to come through the doors, I looked at each one of them and allowed different feelings, like colored glass panes, to move across my mind's eye, according to what I knew of each individual. The mood was as festive as their clothing.

A big part of a typical UU Christmas Eve service is singing. Lots of singing. Hymns, sure, but also the Christmas carols so many of us grew up singing. But in a UU service, if you listen you'll hear that some people are singing slightly different lyrics from those that most of us learned as children. They've changed some words to reflect their own beliefs. If there's one thing a UU doesn't tolerate, it's being told what to believe.

I remember almost no specifics of the service itself, which seems appropriate. For it wasn't about details. It was about light, and love, and hope. And that was enough. That was perfect.

~

When I got home on Saturday after sending Janice and Bert off into the world as a married couple, there was a voicemail waiting for me. I saw the blinking light, and suddenly my heart was in my throat. Had Marshall called? There was no reason to think he had, and certainly I had messages on that machine every day. That blinking light could mean anything. Or nothing. I decided to take Klondike on a short walk before listening.

The message was not from Marshall. It was from Adam.

"Hey, Reverend Hill. I was wondering if maybe you're allowed a day off. I know you have a service tomorrow, but school's out next week, and Myra and I want to invite you to lunch at our house Monday, to be followed by a walk in the woods if you're up for it. The weather's supposed to be pretty nice for December." He left a number, which I wrote down.

Our house. He and Myra Langtree lived together? It hadn't occurred to me until now that when I'd been in The

Forest for Yule, Adam had never shown me where he lived. I shook my head as though to rid itself of something my brain couldn't hold onto. Adam had said he was pansexual. Was he married? Was Myra a girlfriend? A roommate? Half-sister?

Adam had offered to come pick me up for our Monday outing, but I didn't want that.

"I have a Jeep. The road shouldn't present too much of a problem. Besides, you know where *I* live."

He'd laughed. "Fair enough."

"Can I bring my dog?"

There was a pause. "You have a dog?"

"I do now. He's large, and white. A Great Pyrenees. You saw him at my house."

"Klondike is yours now?"

Was there anything about Assisi these Forest Dwellers didn't know? But maybe there was.

"Ha!" I said in triumph. "You know whose dog he *was*, but you don't know that the person taking care of Vanessa now has two cats. So I've inherited my first-ever pet."

"Interesting. I hope you'll tell me more. Meanwhile, yeah. Bring Klondike."

So around eleven on that bracing, sunny Monday morning, after I'd confirmed arrangements with a woman who would visit Vanessa a few times a week for housecleaning and cooking, Klondike and I headed out. Adam's directions were precise, but there were several places where one could take a wrong turn. I think I took three, one that turned out to be someone's long driveway and another that was very challenging to get back out of.

Adam's house was a refined log structure with a large field-stone fireplace, the chimney for which was visible from the outside. It appeared to be large enough for more than two people. It was Myra who opened the door, accompanied by a black, mixed breed dog about half Klondike's size. They sniffed each other's butts affably and dashed off together down a hallway. I couldn't help wondering if they'd met before.

Myra looked to be about thirty, very slight, with long reddish hair pulled back not unlike the way Adam often wore his. Her face put me in mind of pixies. She wore pants and a bulky wool sweater the color of spring green shot through with creamy white, knitted in a cabled pattern.

"Spencer! Welcome. I'd been hoping to meet you."

"Thank you. Yes. I can't tell you how grateful I am that you'll be working with Jenny and the teens." I unlaced my boots and left them beside others I saw on a mat beside the door.

She laughed lightly. "Jenny and I had a long phone chat. She seems great."

"She is. We rely on her quite a bit."

The floor plan for the common areas was very open, leaving lots of room for people to move about. As I gazed around, Adam came through an open doorway from what I guessed would be the kitchen, wiping his hands on a towel. He smiled, and without a word walked up to me and wrapped his arms around me.

"Welcome to my abode." He backed away a little, hands on my shoulders. "We've been cooking all morning. Come."

In the kitchen was a long wooden table, several chairs around it and pushed under neatly, out of the way. Three of these, one at one end and one on either side of it, were laid with placemats and flatware.

"Smells wonderful!" I said as I side-stepped to avoid the rambunctious dogs.

"Dopey!" Myra called in a voice I wouldn't have expected from her. It commanded authority and demanded immediate attention, which the dog gave her. "Sit!" Myra pointed to a corner where there were a couple of woolen mats on the floor. Klondike followed Dopey, and they both plopped themselves onto the mats. Myra gave each of them a large bone to chew on.

Lunch was a hearty soup along the lines of a minestrone, accompanied by freshly baked bread Adam said he had made, with lots of different grains and seeds in it, and a large slab of cool butter on a separate plate. I was beginning to see why people would want to live out here; it seemed to want for nothing, and the environment was inspiring.

"There are quite a few chairs here," I said, slathering butter on a large chunk of bread. "Do you entertain a lot?"

They both laughed. Myra said, "We do seem to be kind of a central place. Adam and I live here, separately," and here she gave me an arch look, "along with three other people. I don't think you'll see them today."

"This butter is amazing."

"Our own cows," Adam told me.

We enjoyed our meal in silence for a minute, and then Myra picked up the conversation.

"Adam tells me your parents were both in Catholic careers before they married."

"Vocations. Yes. Well, my mother was a novice; she left the convent before taking her final vows."

"And you were going to follow in your father's footsteps?"

My mouth full of buttered bread, I shook my head. Adam responded for me. "He was going to be an Episcopal priest, not a Catholic one."

"Even so," Myra went on, "he must have been very proud of you, taking up the priest's collar he'd set aside, even if it was for a different church."

"I'll never know."

She gave me an odd look and then asked a different question. "I admit that I don't understand much about the difference between the Catholic and Episcopal churches. They both have priests?"

I nodded "Without going into too much detail, the Episcopal Church came into being after the Church of England had taken root. King Henry VIII had something to do with it, but by the time he severed ties with the Pope, England already had its own church. The Episcopal Church, as an integral member of the Anglican Communion of Churches, is part of the one, holy, catholic, and apostolic Church of Jesus Christ. To them, the Pope is the Bishop of Rome. Anglican and Episcopal priests are not only allowed but are encouraged to marry and have families."

"Well, it seems to me that the UU Church is a better place for a gay man. And, like your father, you gave up something you'd been sure you wanted for something that was more true to you." I was still taking that in when she added, "I've heard it said that you don't consider yourself Christian. Doesn't the UU Church include people with various belief systems?"

"It does."

"So why can't you still be Christian?"

"I could. But I decided that the best way for me to cut a new path for myself, as it were, would be a clean separation from everything I had taken for granted."

"Does the UU Church have a doctrine?"

"We have seven leading principles, which you could say comprise our doctrine. A short list would include things like the inherent worth and dignity of everyone, spiritual growth, the search for truth, genuine inclusion and compassion, and working for a peaceful and just world community. And, quoting here, 'respect for the interdependent web of all existence of which we are a part.'"

Myra nodded and then chuckled. "That sounds admirable. Almost like Paganism." Then she shifted the topic. "I really like what you're doing with Teens for Truth."

"I can't take much credit. It's true that I wanted to do something to involve younger people, with the admitted agenda of hoping to draw Assisi kids to services. But most of the work was done by Marshall Savage and Jenny Pratt." I heard my voice crack just a tad when I said Marshall's name. Despite Adam's attentions, I missed Marshall's mischievous nature, his musical talents, his intelligence, his generous heart, his warmth... so many things.

Myra said, "Jenny tells me the kids from Assisi and from The Forest are getting to know each other much better than they ever did in school."

"I'm so glad."

"She also repeated to me something I hope will please you." She waited until I glanced at her. "Duncan Beale thinks the world of you. Of course, that's not how he put it. I believe Jenny said his words were 'The Rev's a pretty cool guy.'"

I sat back in my chair, surprised and yet not surprised, and then I laughed. "You should have witnessed our first meeting. Things then seemed extremely unlikely to go in a good direction."

"So you've accomplished something wonderful there. And then...." She paused.

Adam looked at me as though he knew what Myra was going to say.

"And then, what?" I asked.

"Spencer, I don't know whether you're aware of how much you've influenced things between us and Assisi. Erik isn't quite ready to throw open the floodgates of camaraderie and brotherhood, but I'm sure he'll get there. And he hasn't made any effort to discourage others."

I swallowed hard a couple of times and then said, "That means so very much. Thank you for telling me."

All our bowls and plates were pretty much empty by now. Myra stood. "Adam will help clear. Let's go for that walk now, yes? And when we get back we'll have some mulled wine."

It was everything I could do not to declare that I hoped to be a frequent visitor here. It was rustic, warm, and had an energy of loving friendship.

We headed out into the cold, which wasn't so cold as to be uncomfortable, outfitted as we were. Myra left Dopey at home. "His coat isn't warm enough for spending very much time out in this weather." Klondike, meanwhile, bounded through snow banks and into woods on either side of the trail the humans followed. I was glad I'd remembered to bring his whistle, and I used it a couple of times.

We'd been walking a fairly well-worn path for perhaps fifteen minutes, when the thick forest around us seemed to thin somewhat, and the trail veered off to the right. Myra and Adam were about to follow it when Klondike came to a sudden stop, obviously at full attention.

I asked, "Are there bears in these woods?" Adam assured me they'd be hibernating. To Klondike, I said, "What is it, boy?"

The dog was frozen in place, his nose in the air actively seeking something. Then he began to bark, and he bounded ahead, away from the trail, clearly on a mission.

Adam said, "Something's wrong. Let's go."

We followed the dog as well as we could, and within a couple of minutes we came in sight of cleared land, with a large house and an even larger barn. From the barn we could see— and, now, smell—smoke.

Klondike stood outside the barn's closed door, barking for all he was worth, pawing at the wood.

Adam reached him first. "Stand back," he said to us. "The fire could come outside suddenly." I took hold of Klondike's collar as Adam grabbed a wrought iron handle in his gloved right hand and pulled, but the door resisted.

I took the opportunity to fasten one end of Klondike's lead to his collar and tie the other around a tree far enough away from the barn to be out of danger. When I turned back to the barn, Adam had one foot beside the door and was wrenching on the handle. As the door opened, smoke billowed out, and we could hear human cries and the sounds of horses in distress.

Batting at the air in front of us in an effort to see, all three of us went in as Klondike barked in frustration behind us. Flames were apparent in only one area, in a back corner, and two young children huddled as far from it as possible. Myra lifted the little girl and I lifted the boy, and we ran. I didn't see what Adam was doing.

When we were well clear of the barn, Myra and I set the children down. Adam was still in the barn. I said, "I'm going back in." She nodded.

The fire was bigger now. Through the smoke, I saw Adam's form by the horse stalls. He had one stall open and was trying to get a harness onto a panicked animal.

Between coughs, I shouted, "How can I help?"

"Do you know anything about horses?"

"No."

"Then get out of here. Go to the house. Call for help."

Unsure what to do, I turned and saw Myra there. "I'll help Adam. The kids have run to the house. They're okay. Go get help."

Feeling helpless and useless, I did as I was told. I ran fast enough to get to the house right behind the children. As they threw the door open, I saw a woman approaching. She appeared to be some sort of maid, or a cook, or something.

"The barn's on fire!" I shouted at her. "Is there a fire department you can call?" I knew many small towns were limited to volunteer fire departments, and I wasn't quite sure where we were.

The woman nodded and disappeared. I rushed back to the barn.

Outside the barn, Myra was holding the harness of one horse, a gorgeous white animal, a piece of blanket or something like that over its eyes. She shouted, "Can you just hold onto him? There are two more horses."

There was no time for fear, despite the fact that I was about to do something I'd never done in my life. I nodded and grabbed the straps as she released them. The horse whinnied and skittered so much the cloth fell to the ground. The animal's eyes were wide enough to show the whites, and its ears lay flat back against its skull. I think I was nearly as afraid as the horse. At least it didn't appear to be burned. Slowly it began to calm, snorting through its nostrils as though trying to rid them of smoke.

Almost immediately, both Adam and Myra were nearby, each with a white horse they were attempting to control. Adam, some leather straps in one hand, led the way toward the house. I remember thinking, *Why on earth are they all white?*

"We need a place to tie them," Adam said, coughing as he stroked the long nose of his animal. Myra, also coughing, pointed to an iron fence along the side of a garden and tested it for stability. Adam declared it "good enough."

With the horses calmer now, and well secured, I headed back to the house. I wanted to make sure the kids were all right.

The back door stood open, and we all went inside, shutting it behind us. The maid reappeared.

"I've called the fire department and the Jermins."

"Jermins?" I echoed. "As in Alan Jermin?"

Adam asked, "Do you know him?"

All white horses. "I've met him." I turned to the maid. "Are the children all right?"

Hands on her hips, she turned toward what I think was the dining room, where they huddled. "More all right than they have any reason to be." To me, she said, "It seems Norman had decided to try smoking his daddy's pipe."

I peered into the room and saw Norman slap his sister. "Tattle-tale."

I dashed toward him and grabbed his arm as the little girl ran to the maid for comfort. "Stop that this minute!" I released the boy. "Is it true?"

Norman was obviously not inclined to be contrite. He sat on the floor, knees up, arms around them, and pouted.

It was not my job to discipline him. I wondered what his father would have to say.

Two vehicles arrived more or less simultaneously outside. One was a fire engine, which went directly toward the barn. The other was a dark red Volvo sedan, and Alan Jermin got out from behind the wheel as a woman, probably his wife, exited the passenger side. He ran to the horses. She ran to the house.

The woman, understandably, ignored us and fussed over the children. I decided it was time to leave. To Adam and Myra I said, "I think we've done all we can here, and I doubt the man of the house would be glad to see us." I headed for the door.

Behind me, Adam said, "I can't wait to hear more about this."

We had just stepped outside when Alan Jermin, looking like an angel of wrath, approached the house. From his safe distance, Klondike growled. Alan glared at me. "Did you do this?"

"Are you mad?" I said. "Your own son did this."

He glared next at Adam. "You're one of *them!*"

I stepped between them. "These people saved your children,

and they saved your horses. You owe them a debt of gratitude you can never repay."

I thought he might explode. "Get off my land!"

Myra stepped slowly toward him, smiling sweetly, and placed a hand on his shoulder. "You're welcome." We left him standing there, sputtering in impotent rage. I reclaimed Klondike and together we disappeared into the woods whence we had come.

CHAPTER 23

After less than a minute, Adam said, "Spencer? Spill."

I stopped walking and stood still, stroking Klondike's thick white coat. "Do you know anything about the Assembly of God Church?" They both said No. So I told them.

I described their belief in literalism, in miracles, in the physical resurrection of Jesus and his eventual return. "They're highly focused on sin and its eradication." I stopped short of mentioning Marshall's history with them. "Alan Jermin is the pastor at that church in Little Boundary. I've encountered him twice before. Once he called me a sodomizer. Both times he refused to shake hands. I think he might be extreme even for his church, and maybe that's why all his horses are white."

Adam laughed. "You know, I didn't notice that until we were leaving."

Myra said, "That man has very bad energy."

"Energy?" I asked. "Can you read auras, too?"

"Too?"

"Like Erik."

She shook her head. "No, but I do sense people's energy. I could probably find Adam in a crowd."

"Anyway," Adam decided, "that guy sounds like someone we want to avoid."

"And yet," I said, "it was in my second meeting with him that I found out about the nineteen-oh-four fire. So in a way, I have him to thank for setting me on a mission to find out more."

Myra held her arms out, face to the sky. "It's like the solstice."

I shook my head, confused. "Why?"

"There will always be darkness. But there will also always be light. From the darkness of that man's hard heart came a seed that sent you to find truth." She lowered her gaze to me and smiled.

Back at the house, Myra was as good as her word and served us warm, mulled wine with thin lemon slices floating on the surface in each mug.

Adam told her, "You make the best mulled wine in the community. You've adjusted really well. Especially considering where you came from."

I asked her, "You're not from here?"

She shook her head. "I'm from Sedona. It works out better if not everyone who was born into a community like this one stays there, and if new blood comes in. Genetic diversity, and all that."

"Wow. You sure chose a different climate."

"And I did choose it, quite deliberately, three years ago. I decided I wanted to get to know snow, and I wanted to see more green around me."

Adam said, "There aren't very many communities like The Forest. Most people who are Pagan live in cities and towns all over, just like people of most religious traditions. Sometimes they feel kind of alone. I mean, we aren't organized like UU, so it can be hard to find other Pagans."

"And how do you find each other?"

Myra said, "There are Pagan festivals at different times of the year, and word gets around, often through newsletters like *Harvest*. I met Adam and few others from The Forest at a festival in Sedona."

Adam nodded. "That's probably the best way to make connections."

I looked at Myra. "Do you expect to stay here?"

She and Adam exchanged a glance. Adam said, "We're considering marrying."

I hoped my face didn't show the depth of my surprise, but it must have revealed something.

Myra laughed. "Spencer, it's all right. I know you and Adam have been together. And you probably will again. If we do marry, Adam and I will come to some agreement about fidelity and what that would look like for us. It might be that we don't marry. But we're thinking about it."

What came to my mind was the aspect of Perfectionism in which everyone shared everything, even each other. "So… is this open attitude common here in The Forest?"

Adam laughed. "No. We're free to define our unions however we want. As far as I know, it's more common for marriages here to be monogamous." He shrugged. "And maybe, if I marry, my marriage will be, too."

I was pretty sure Myra was at least six or seven years older than Adam, not that the age difference should matter. But what I knew of Adam—which was, admittedly, not a lot—made me suspect it would be a while before he committed to anyone.

My drive home, in the gathering dusk, through snow-shrouded woods for a large part of the journey, felt very mellow. Klondike slept in the back seat, tuckered out from the walk and the joyful welcome from Dopey upon his return to the house. I drifted home feeling softened by the warm wine, the welcoming house, the combination of adventure and relaxation, and what I hoped would be lasting friendships.

Fortunately there were no messages at home that I couldn't put off until tomorrow. I was almost too tired for dinner, so it was nothing more elaborate than grilled cheese and soup, and after that a good book in a soft chair, a glass of Scotch beside me. Klondike settled onto his bed, and I gazed at him from time to time, aware that my affection for the white beast was growing every day.

After a short while the pages blurred, and in my mind I recalled different scenes from the day. One thing Myra had said kept echoing around my brain. She'd said my father must have been proud of me for taking up the collar he'd set aside. I hadn't enlightened her. I hadn't told her that Father would never know that I'd set my own collar aside, at least the one Father had expected to see on me. So would he have been proud of me? Would he approve of the path I'd chosen instead of the one he'd expected me to take, the one I'd expected to take, myself? I wasn't so sure.

But Myra had said something else, too. *Like your father, you gave up something you'd been sure you wanted for something that was more true to you.* Like my father. It was true he'd left Catholicism for the Episcopal Church. And I'd left the Episcopal Church for a life in the UU tradition. I'd reconciled myself to this change, this desertion as some might see it, as a life that was, in fact, more true to myself. Could the same have been said for Father? I had to believe it could. I knew that he had adored Mother, despite the stilted ways I'd seen that love displayed.

And then something I'd never thought of hit me hard. Perhaps that stilted demeanor, if not softened by the love he felt for Mother and the love she felt for him, would have prevented him from being the kind of priest he thought he should be.

Perhaps he would have been one of those stern, stiff men who seem to have a stick up their ass, men who can't flex and bend as needed to minister to the imperfect members of their congregations. Certainly he had expected at least some level of perfection from me, a perfection I'd never been able to give him. I might have stood in for those imperfect parishioners, a pascal victim offered up to suffer for their sins.

I set my book aside and rubbed my eyes. What was it Ruth had told me? I think she'd said I gravitated toward the needy, toward people like Donald and Marshall, people who had some emotional lack I could fill. Or, that I thought I could fill. And I'd failed both times. Donald had left me by falling under the influence of that cult, essentially right after I'd realized I wasn't destined to be a priest, when it would have been reasonable to say I had unmet needs Donald couldn't fill, just as I clearly couldn't fill his. Marshall left me because I couldn't salve his wounds, and when I couldn't do that, I'd tried to control his life.

Father had done what he needed to do for himself. I seemed to be making myself into a house for other people's demons.

The ringing telephone made me jump, and that made Klondike lift his head and look at me. I took a few deep breaths before answering.

"Spencer?"

Oh. My. God. "Donald."

"I, uh, I've called a few times to wish you Merry Christmas, but you've been out a lot."

"It goes with the territory. But I didn't get a message from you."

"No. I didn't leave one."

Okay.... "Well, a Merry Christmas to you as well. Or perhaps I should say Happy New Year at this point."

"Happy Gregorian New Year to you, too."

"Pardon?"

Donald chuckled. "I've been wanting to apologize to you for Bruce showing up with guns blazing, challenging you to a duel."

"I had a lot of support here. He was dispatched without injury to anyone. But what's that got to do with—"

"I've also wanted to tell you that I'm seeing a really nice guy now. He's Jewish, at least by heritage. Hence the Gregorian modifier."

I felt my heart lurch. "Ah. Got it. His new year was in September."

"Jonathan. I think you'd like him. He kind of looks like you."

My breath stopped, just for a few seconds. I did my best to keep things light. "Oh, that's unlikely. No one looks like me but me."

Donald chuckled. "I suppose that's true. You always were a handsome fellow." There was an awkward pause, and then he asked, "So is there a beautiful man warming your bed for you these days?"

I don't know what possessed me. Wait; that's not true. I do. It was a sickly green color, and huge, and nasty. Its name was Jealousy. "A very beautiful man, as it happens. A sculptor."

"My, my. And I guess up there where it's so cold and snowy, warm beauty comes in handy. Would I like him, do you think?"

"I suspect you might not know what to make of him."

"Is he anything like me?"

I paused. "Do you want him to be?"

He paused. "Well, we're in an awkward place."

I had to bring this to an end before either of us—or both of us —said something we wished we hadn't. "It was good to hear from you, Donald. I'm glad you're with someone who's good for you."

"Spencer?"

"Yes?"

"Do you remember that performance of *A Midsummer Night's Dream*?"

"The one where you sprinkled the audience with the magic dust you were supposed to throw over Lysander? That one?"

"That one. Do you still think of me like that at all?"

Another pause. "I do. Good night, Puck." I hung up.

Klondike was still watching me. I sat on the floor beside him, took one of his gold-tipped ears in my hand, and leaned my face into his fur.

Over the next few days I spent an inordinate amount of time preparing my remarks for Vanessa's and Loraine's wedding. They would, of course, write their own vows, but what I said would pertain to both of them and, if done right, to the witnesses who would gather. This would be only the second wedding ceremony where I would officiate, but it would possibly be the most memorable.

The Episcopal Church had refused to welcome me as it welcomed heterosexual people. Unitarian Universalism welcomed everyone equally. Myra had been right; this was more true to me. And it was overwhelmingly magnificent that, so early in my vocation here, I would marry two women who loved each other every bit as deeply, who were as committed to each other, as any mixed couple could be.

News about the ceremony had spread fast throughout our community, and already it seemed people were nearly competing to contribute time and food, for decoration and for the reception. Everyone seemed to think they were automatically invited, and I suppose they were.

That Friday, New Year's Day, my church was so crowded for the ceremony that it was nearly full. I felt overwhelmed at the joyful response I saw to what would be a marriage between two women. If I had doubted my congregation's acceptance, I would have been so wrong. I couldn't help wondering how many of them knew about Vanessa and Loraine long before I did, long before they proclaimed their love openly. It didn't seem to matter.

The sight of Vanessa in her wheelchair, Loraine at her side, both dressed in powder blue and holding white roses, moved me so much I was concerned I might not be able to speak. It was easier to rest my eyes on Klondike, who sat quietly at the other side of Vanessa's chair. He made a very impressive ring-bearer.

Fortunately I had decided to include enough hymns about love to keep everyone engaged, and to keep my speech quite short. And I couldn't think of a better starting and ending point than chapter thirteen, verse thirteen from Paul's first letter to the Corinthians. He wrote that of all the wisdom we might accrue, the three most important things in life are faith, hope, and love. And the greatest of these is love.

As the two women stated their vows and exchanged rings, I was nearly overwhelmed with joy. I could barely get out these words loudly enough for all to hear: "For as much as you have committed yourselves to one another, exchanging vows before the witnesses here gathered, by the authority vested in me as minister of this Unitarian Universalist congregation, I declare that you are now wives unto each other and partners in a union as sacred as it is magnificent. Go forth in love."

The reception, in the church function hall, was a true celebration. Vanessa and Loraine were certainly the center of the festivities, but it seemed to me that everyone was taking pleasure in the joy of this wedding.

At one point I moved into a corner where I could just watch, and smile, and wipe the occasional happy tear away. I couldn't have said why, but something about today—or maybe it was something about the past four months—had finally made me feel free of the expectations for my life that I'd left behind. There wasn't even a shred of apprehension about whether Father would have approved. I was sure he would, even if he had lacked the words to say so. After all, I really was following in his footsteps. Both of us had left behind a life that was almost but not quite suited to us. And in doing so, my father had shown me how to live. He had also—indirectly, but still—taught me that I must learn to love myself, whether or not I felt love from others. And in making me doubt his love for me, he had shown me what it was like to love deeply without knowing how to express it. I will not make the same mistake.

Thank you, Father.

ACKNOWLEDGEMENT

As with many of my books, in writing *For Love Of Self* I had the benefit of help from people who know more about some of the plot subjects than I do. For this book, I was grateful for the help of two experts: Jane Wicker and Christopher Croucher. Their expertise and generosity have helped make this story as good as it can be.

JANE WICKER

A person of remarkable empathy and caring, Jane Wicker is a lay minister in the Unitarian Universalist (UU) church to which she belongs. The typical UU parish is fairly liberal, welcoming into their communities people who are Christian, Jewish, Buddhist, Muslim, Pagan, Bahai, Hmong, Zoroastrian, agnostic, atheistic, or really from any (or no) religious or spiritual background. Most congregations are also completely accepting of people whose identities are not necessarily heterosexual or cisgender. Despite knowing this much, when I decided my protagonist would become a UU minister, I needed guidance from someone who knew more about it than I did. That person is Jane Wicker.

ACKNOWLEDGEMENT

Jane's experience as a UU lay minister was invaluable to me, but what made working with her a joy was her warm heart, her careful and pertinent research, and her delightful sense of humor, which is one thing I've learned is necessary for any UU community member.

In my experience, I've found that people with the most lively sense of humor are those who can laugh at themselves. UU members not only do this, but they also create jokes about themselves and laugh heartily at the quirks of their own religious practices. At the same time, they display profound empathy and concern for the feelings and rights of others. Just don't try to tell them what they should believe, and they'll welcome you warmly. Jane exemplifies UU's marvelous spiritual approach beautifully and in the most thoughtful and heart-felt way imaginable.

CHRISTOPHER CROUCHER

I think of Christopher Croucher as a professional Pagan. But that's not how he refers to himself. On his website (https://www.ccroucherarts.com), Chris tells us he's an artist, a performer, a dancer, and a healer, and all of this work stems from his nature-based spiritual practice. That's where the Paganism comes in.

In *For Love Of Self*, readers will meet members of a fictional community of Pagans who refer to themselves as Forest Dwellers. My knowledge about Paganism is not nothing, but it is limited. One thing I know is that it is so far from institutionalized that one Pagan's practice and another's might bear only a passing resemblance to each other. Chris helped ensure that the Forest Dwellers, their practices, and their attitudes are rendered in the story in a respectful way that is at least not out of line with his extensive knowledge and experience. When I asked questions to which he had no immediate answer, he scoured various resources to tell me what I needed to know.

It was a joy to work with Chris. I thank him not only for his help with my story, but also for deepening my own understanding of the world of Paganism. I look forward to working with him again for the third and final book in my *Blessed Be* series, *For Love*.

FOR LOVE OF SELF

(Blessed Be Series, Book 2)

Robin Reardon

About This Guide

The suggested questions are included to enhance your group's reading of Robin Reardon's novel, FOR LOVE OF SELF, Book 2 of the BLESSED BE series.

DISCUSSION QUESTIONS

Note: The questions in this guide contain spoiler information. It is recommended that you finish the book before reading the questions.

1. What experience, if any, do you have of religious cults? What do you think it would mean for a religion to be a cult?
2. When Vanessa asked Spencer if he had "sussed" Marshall out, Spencer didn't know what she meant. Did you?
3. How clearly do you understand Spencer's view of God? Is it anything like yours? Why, or why not?
4. Spencer's first impression upon seeing Adam Cooper naked and dancing in the woods was of uninhibited, natural grace. What were your first impressions of Adam? How did they change as you learned more about him?
5. Does what you read in this story change any ideas you might have had about Paganism? How would you describe this spiritual practice after reading this

book? What do you see as sacred to Pagans? Did it surprise you that Spencer seemed to be meeting with resistance as he tried to get to know the Forest Dwellers?

6. What do you think it was about Donald that made him give Bruce Cobb so much control? Have you seen similar relationships among people you know?

7. How much do you know about conversion therapy? Do you know anyone who was subjected to it?

8. At one point, Spencer says this about his feelings for Marshall: "I had felt desired, wanted, even to some extent loved. But this, with Marshall, was different. With him, I felt needed." Can you understand how compelling this would be? Do you think love between two people is enhanced or diminished when there is also need? Do you think Spencer needed Marshall?

9. Did it surprise you when Marshall wanted Spencer to choke him during sex? What do you think your reaction would have been if you were in Spencer's place?

10. After the Assembly of God proselytizers visit Marshall, he tells Spencer that the incident at the conversion camp was not the only time he had tried to commit suicide. The second had been after someone he loved had died. Spencer sees that the only connection between the two attempts is Marshall, himself. What does this tell you about Marshall? Spencer's feelings "bounced wildly between wanting to protect him and keep him safe," and knowing "I would always be terrified of failure." If you've know someone who attempted suicide, do Spencer's feelings echo yours?

11. In his attempt to correct history and remove the blame of the 1904 fire from Assisi, Spencer stirs up a

couple of hornets' nests. He worries that his repeated attempts to speak with Paster Jermin inspired the Assembly of God congregation to proselytize in Assisi, which eventually resulted in Marshall being fired. Do you see these results as Spencer's fault? Was he pushing too hard for a change because of a personal agenda? In hindsight, were his efforts worth the results, or do you think he should have left things alone?

12. Did it surprise you that Loraine and Vanessa were lovers? The story takes place in 1987. How seriously do you think the people of Assisi, outside of their congregation, would take this marriage? How seriously do you think you would have taken it at that time?

13. What do you think Marshall's chances are for learning to love himself? What about Spencer? What might hold each of them back?

14. How do you think Spencer's father would feel about his son's chosen vocation?

AUTHOR'S NOTE

In Chapter Seven of *For Love Of Self*, the main character (Spencer Hill) researches the history of the area in northern Vermont where he has been assigned as a minister in the Unitarian Universalist Church in Assis, a fictional town.

Although most of what Spencer describes about the Mormon and Perfectionist traditions is factual, there was no nineteenth century offshoot of the Perfectionists who took up residence in the far north. Also, to my knowledge there was no migration north in the eighteenth century of accused witches who found their way to the same area. The genesis of the Pagan community in the book, The Forest, is completely fictional, as is the community itself.

If you enjoyed this book, please consider posting a review on the online sites of your choice. This is the best way to ensure that more titles by this author will become available.

If you would like to be notified with news about this author's work, including when new titles are released, you can sign up for Robin's mailing list at robinreardon.com/contact.

ABOUT THE AUTHOR

Robin Reardon is an inveterate observer of human nature, and her primary writing goal is to create stories about all kinds of people whose destinies should not be determined solely by their sexual orientation or gender identity. Her secondary writing goal is to introduce readers to concepts and information they might not know very much about.

Robin's motto is this: The only thing wrong with being queer is how some people treat you when they find out.

Interests outside of writing include singing, nature photography, and the study of comparative religions. Robin writes in a butter yellow study with a view of the Boston, Massachusetts skyline.

Robin blogs (And now, this) about various subjects that influence her writing, as well as about the writing process itself, on her website.

Other Works by Robin Reardon

Novels
FOR LOVE OF GOD (Book 1 of the *Blessed Be* series)
ON CHOCORUA (Book 1 of the *Trailblazer* series)
ON THE KALALAU TRAIL (Book 2 of the *Trailblazer* series)
ON THE PRECIPICE (Book 3 of the *Trailblazer* series)
AND IF I FALL
WAITING FOR WALKER
THROWING STONES
(Published by **IAM Books**)
EDUCATING SIMON
THE EVOLUTION OF ETHAN POE
A QUESTION OF MANHOOD
THINKING STRAIGHT
A SECRET EDGE
(Published by Kensington Publishing Corp.)

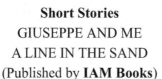

Short Stories
GIUSEPPE AND ME
A LINE IN THE SAND
(Published by **IAM Books**)

Essay
THE CASE FOR ACCEPTANCE: AN OPEN LETTER TO
HUMANITY
(Published by **IAM Books**)

Printed in Great Britain
by Amazon